BAD COPS

A Henry Christie thriller

Nick Oldham

This first world edition published 2017
in Great Britain and the USA by
SEVERN HOUSE PUBLISHERS LTD of
Eardley House, 4 Uxbridge Street, London W8 7SY
Trade paperback edition first published
in Great Britain and the USA 2018 by
SEVERN HOUSE PUBLISHERS LTD

British Library Cataloguing in Publication Data
A CIP catalogue record for this title is available from the British Library.

ISBN-13: 978-0-7278-8767-2 (cased)
ISBN-13: 978-1-84751-882-8 (trade paper)
ISBN-13: 978-1-78010-944-2 (e-book)

All Severn House titles are printed on acid-free paper.

Severn House Publishers support the Forest Stewardship Council™ [FSC™],
the leading international forest certification organisation.
All our titles that are printed on FSC certified paper carry the FSC logo.

Typeset by Palimpsest Book Production Ltd.,
Falkirk, Stirlingshire, Scotland.
Printed and bound in Great Britain by
TJ International, Padstow, Cornwall.

For Belinda

ONE

The woman had to travel a long way to pick up the killer.

Not that driving across the breadth of northern England and Wales, then back again, coast to coast, was a problem as such. It was motorway and dual carriageway for the most part, though circumnavigating Manchester was slow and painful, but the journey was an inconvenience, if a necessary one, she could well have done without, particularly as the distance and timing of the pick-up meant an overnight stop had to be factored in. Having to meet the overnight ferry into Holyhead from Cork ensured she spent a lonely but thoughtful night at the Premier Inn just outside Bangor in North Wales, before driving over Britannia Bridge, which spans the glorious but deadly Menai Straits, then across Anglesey on the A55 to meet the ferry.

It was a beautiful dawn, the sun flashing gold and platinum across an unusually flat, calm Irish Sea, but the breathtaking vista was all but lost on the woman. Her mind churned with more important matters.

Her face blank, she watched the ponderous arrival of the ferry as it nudged into the port, the ramps and gangways clattering down, car and foot passengers descending like beetles and ants and exiting through the arrival gates.

She brought her hawk-like eyes into focus and tried to pick out the killer among the crowd, her only clue being the knowledge that he would be travelling solo. But there were many men disembarking and she failed to spot him or even hazard a guess as to which one he was. His forte was melting into backgrounds.

Maybe it was for the best, never to look him in the eye.

With a shrug, she made her way back to the Citroën Picasso in the car park, got in, sat and waited.

He would come to her.

He had been contracted, and paid good money to carry out a grim task at which, supposedly, he was very good at indeed.

The foot passengers began to filter through the customs building, neither challenged nor even document-checked by the tired staff, who lazily waved everyone through with irritable gestures to hurry up. They met waiting loved ones, maybe business associates or friends, made their way to their own vehicles or simply walked into Holyhead itself.

The woman did not turn to look when the door opened, but was aware of a rucksack being lobbed across the back seat directly behind her and the dip of the suspension as the man slid on to the rear nearside seat and gently closed the door.

'Going east?' he inquired.

'All the way,' she responded, concluding the short, slightly awkward but previously agreed exchange of words to confirm they were both the right people and everything was OK.

Then, despite trying not to, she glanced quickly into the rear-view mirror and, just for the most fleeting of moments, her eyes met his in reflection in the instant before he slid on a pair of Aviator-style sunglasses, pulled his hood down over his forehead and effectively obscured his features in shadow.

She tore her gaze away.

'Best we see as little of each other as possible,' he drawled. An American accent. She supposed it would be New York because she assumed that was the point of origin of his journey, though did not know for certain. 'It won't be easy, but we should try.'

'I know. I get it, but you can see me.'

'Yep,' he said. That was how he liked it. Psychological advantage.

She sensed him making himself comfortable.

'Got it?' he asked.

'Under the seat in front of you.'

He reached forwards between his legs and picked up the large, padded, quite bulky and heavy envelope.

She started the engine. The car began to roll.

Once clear of Holyhead, back on the A55 – the road that effectively sliced Anglesey in half – the man put on a pair of latex gloves from his pocket and opened the envelope, sliding the contents on to his lap. One automatic pistol, one spare magazine, full.

'That's the gun you'll have to use,' the woman said unnecessarily, glimpsing into the mirror again but still not seeing his face.

He inspected the weapon, keeping it under the line of the windowsill, out of sight.

It was a nine-millimetre Makarov that had seen better days. The serial number had been filed off, though the man knew this was generally a fairly useless undertaking, as for years ballistic scientists had been able to read such numbers because of the way gunmetal was indented during manufacture. But there wasn't a problem in this case; it wouldn't matter if the number could ever be read.

He slid out the magazine, thumb-flipped each bullet on to the envelope resting on his lap and did the same with the spare mag, then, after checking each round, he reloaded them. Next, he dismantled and reassembled the gun expertly, checking the springs and the action – still nice and smooth despite the wear and tear; it was satisfactory and would not let him down, adequate for the task ahead. He slotted one of the mags back into the gun.

'Does it have provenance?' he asked.

'It has whatever provenance we need, I'll see to that,' she assured him. Then added, 'But I'm sure it won't come to that.'

'You think you'll be able to control this?'

'I'm certain.' She glanced in the mirror again.

A moment later, the woman felt a hard jab in her ribcage. The man leaned forwards between the front seats, his mouth close to her ear, and she felt his hot breath on her cheek.

Inside, she curdled, but continued to drive.

'Do not try to look at me,' he whispered. 'Ever.'

'Got it,' she said through gritted teeth.

'Good.' He breathed out, and she could smell his breath. He needed to clean his teeth. He sat back, put the gun back into the envelope and placed it down in the footwell between his feet. After removing the latex gloves, he settled into the seat and wriggled himself comfortable. His chin dipped to his chest and he fell instantly asleep. It had already been a long journey.

There were many things at play in Tom Salter's mind, but the recurring nightmare was the one about the eyes.

Almost all the violence he could endure, live with.

But the eyes had got to him, just one pair.

As the shaft of fluorescent light had cut diagonally across the girl's face, he had seen the fear.

More than fear, actually.

Sheer terror.

That was the moment he knew he could not go on.

Yes, he had seen many, but his head had been in the sand, he had been in denial, and it was just that one single moment, lasting maybe three seconds at most, that had changed everything within him.

The girl had started on what she had believed would be the journey of a lifetime, all her hopes and dreams about to come true. Some wealth, maybe; a better life for definite. Some money to send home. Although she had not known it at the time, these were all promises that would never be kept, and she only realized how terribly she had been lied to once the journey had begun, her passport had been ripped from her thin fingers and her travelling money taken from her, by which time it was all too late. She had been sucked into the system.

She was in the pipeline. And like oil in a pipeline, she would not escape until the very end.

Tom Salter jerked awake from sleep. His own eyes flashed open and he sat up quickly, sweat dripping from his close-cropped hair. Then, slowly, he lay back, the eyes burning him still, swirling around his brain.

The woman next to him stirred and woke up.

'You all right?'

'No, not really.'

'You're all jittery again and clammy.' She touched his back. Her name was Miriam.

'I know.' He swallowed something thick and horrible in his throat.

Miriam edged closer to him, shuffling up tightly, crushing her soft breasts against his ribs. She kissed his shoulder and her right hand slithered across his hairy chest, brushing a nipple before slowly traversing his body.

Salter was trying to control his breathing and heart rate, all to no avail.

Miriam's fingers took hold of him and, in spite of the situation, he began to react – fairly sluggishly – to her gentle but firm manipulation, more, he guessed, due to the Viagra still sluicing around his bloodstream than from a real desire to fuck again.

For a few moments, he enjoyed the sensation. She excelled at this.

But then he took hold of her hand, unpeeled her fingers and stopped the movement.

'No, babe, no,' he said softly. 'I can't concentrate on it.'

'Which is exactly why you need it,' she insisted.

'No, please,' he said. They had made love an hour earlier, a fumbling, too-quick function on his part, leaving her puzzled and dissatisfied and a little tearful. This was unusual for Tom. Normally he was a good lover, often gentle, sometimes brutal and exciting, so for once she could live with this.

'I know it's a big night,' she said.

'Fucking right it is,' he blurted as his erection waned. 'It's not every day you try to extract yourself from a business deal with the New York underworld, but enough is enough.'

Miriam propped herself up on one elbow. 'I know,' she said gently.

'If I can pull this off . . .' he said, not finishing the sentence. He blew out his cheeks. 'There's gonna be some angry people out there. Shit.' He closed his eyes tightly.

'I'll be with you all the way,' she promised.

'I know . . . Then we have another issue to contend with,' he said pointedly.

He sat up on the edge of the bed. 'I need to go. Got to kick this thing in motion, set it all up, just in case it goes pear-shaped, and get my head together before this meeting.'

'Look, seriously, let me do this thing for you,' Miriam insisted. 'It will chill you, calm you down, help you focus . . . honest . . . I know these things.'

Tenderly, she drew him back down, then began kissing him from the neck down, until she had him in her mouth and he submitted to the inevitable.

TWO

Six months later

Henry Christie's scream of agony reverberated around the empty house, then died away.

He swore a little – a lot, actually – as he peeled the dressing away from the gunshot wound in his right shoulder. Though the injury seemed to be healing well some three months after taking the bullet, it still had a tendency to seep somewhat after any exertion, then dry up, and it was the removal of the dressing from the caked blood that made him emit what even he admitted was a pathetic scream.

He had allowed himself to do it because, like a tree falling in a forest, there was no one else around to hear him and roll their eyes at what a wimp he, a detective superintendent in Lancashire Constabulary's Force Major Investigation Team (FMIT), was.

He stepped on the foot pedal of the waste bin in the bathroom and dropped the blood-speckled dressing into it. Then, from his sitting position on the edge of the bath, he stood up and surveyed his sorry reflection in the large, circular mirror on the wall. If he contorted his head he could just about see the wound, but it was easier to inspect using the mirror.

Firstly, though, he looked at his face.

Without doubt, he had lost a lot of weight since the incident.

He shook his head. What a hell of a way to shed the pounds.

When he'd joined the police all those years before – almost too many to contemplate – it had been drilled into him that as a cop you can never predict what lies around the corner, and he had found that to be true, pretty much. He might have imagined it, but he thought that somewhere in his subconscious this little nugget, which had stuck with him throughout his less-than-glorious career, surfaced when – unexpectedly around that very corner – he'd been ushered at gunpoint into a storeroom at

Blackburn Royal Infirmary and then been shot by a very angry, nay, livid and deranged young lady who he had quite liked up to the point when he had discovered her nasty little schemes. She had been brandishing a snub-nosed six-shot revolver of indeterminate manufacture. Fortunately for Henry, as he lunged wildly in an attempt to disarm her, only the first bullet fired. The remaining five (she had tried to fire a full load into him, so had clearly meant to kill him) had all failed to discharge. Long live homemade ammunition, Henry had toasted at a later date.

Or, as the young woman had said, 'Shitty fucking ammo.'

She had escaped, gone on the run, only to be cornered some days later by French Gendarmerie in Marseille where, in a bloody but short siege, she had met a gory end in a hail of bullets. Henry had seen the crime-scene photographs much later and watched bodycam footage of heavily armed cops bursting through the door of a squalid bedsit (or was it a pied-à-terre? Henry speculated). She had been almost sliced in half by a stream of bullets from machine pistols.

Henry had survived and, in recovery, his weight had cascaded from him, leaving him grey-haired and gaunt. His eyes were set deep and dark in cave-like recesses, giving him a hunted look.

When he'd dived at the woman in the vain attempt to disarm her, he had been around the fifteen-stone-plus mark. Now, without trying, the scales just about tipped thirteen.

One of the most effective and quickest ways of losing weight: get shot, shed the pounds.

Henry thought he could maybe make money from a DVD of it, although it would be a fairly dull watch after the blood-soaked opening.

However, now that he had regained his appetite, he was eating like a horse again, and realized the weight, if unchecked, would soon pile back on.

Hence this morning's attempt at jogging for a while.

He had done three laid-back, loping miles around Blackpool – flat terrain but still tough going, especially when he reached the invisible brick wall after the first mile and almost called it a day.

He stared back at his eyes, then glanced at the wound.

After the bullet had been removed, it had been cleaned up,

disinfected and repaired, and now it looked like a pair of puckered lips, slightly deformed and not kissable. Fortunately, the bullet had only caused mainly muscle damage, though it had just clipped his right clavicle – that strut of horizontal bone between the shoulder blade and sternum. But he had lost a lot of blood; the whole area remained stiff and tender, and he had to continually and gently roll the shoulder to stop it from seizing up.

He exhaled, a steam-like hissing noise through clenched teeth.

'You look like I feel – shit,' he complimented his reflection.

He slid out of his running shorts and stood naked for a moment before grabbing the bath towel hanging over the radiator and wrapping it around his middle as he walked out on to the landing. He was going to take a shower in the en suite next to the main bedroom, and had stopped off in the family bathroom because there was more space for self-inspection and introspection – and the mirror on the wall was bigger.

At the top of the stairs, he glanced down into the front hall. A shadow crossed the welcome mat. Someone was at the front door.

He stopped, expecting post pushed through the letter box. He wasn't expecting anyone or anything else.

Alison Marsh, his fiancée, was busy working at The Tawny Owl, the pub and country hotel she owned way out in the wilds of north-east Lancashire; his daughter, Leanne, who still lived here, was away, and he did not expect anyone from work to be contacting him. He was signed off sick with no plans to return any day soon. For once, he was going to milk the system.

He waited for the clatter of the letter-box flap.

No post landed on the mat.

But there was an urgent knock on the door, followed by the letter box rattling and an insistent ringing of the doorbell. Then someone called through it.

'Henry? You fucking in?'

Henry winced, then sighed stoically. He'd been found. For a fleeting and serious moment, he considered diving for cover and bluffing this out, like his mum used to do when the man from the Prudential called for payment, but the fact that his car was on the drive and his keys were dangling in the door were just a bit of a giveaway.

'Henry,' the voice called again. 'Open up. This is your chief constable calling . . . and I heard you screaming like a wuss, so I know you're in there.'

After letting him in – and finding he was accompanied by another man Henry did not know, though vaguely recognized – Henry made the chief constable wait.

He took a long shower – hot – then dabbed his wound carefully to dry it and redressed it just as carefully before pulling on a pair of jeans and an old Rolling Stones T-shirt and joining the two men who he had ushered into the conservatory at the back of the house, which overlooked the garden and farmland beyond.

Both visitors had a mug of coffee in their hands and were chatting in a subdued manner when Henry appeared fresh and clean, bearing his own brew of coffee.

The chief constable was called Robert Fanshaw-Bayley, known as 'FB' to friends and foe alike. Henry had known him for almost the entire length of his own police service. They had first encountered each other in the Rossendale Valley in the early eighties when Henry had been a young uniformed constable with an attitude to control and aspirations to become a detective. FB was the detective inspector in charge of CID operations in the valley, reigning with a rod of iron and not a smidgen of self-awareness or modesty. He had been the stereotypical DI of the times, interested only in ruling the roost and clear-up rates.

His and Henry's paths had crossed frequently since then, not necessarily in happy ways. FB had gone on to become chief constable while Henry had clambered unspectacularly to the rank of detective superintendent, more by luck than by cunning, and much to the vexation of other, possibly more deserving officers.

The two visitors had made themselves comfortable on the cane-backed chairs. Henry sat opposite, a glass-topped coffee table between them, and glanced from one to the other, his eyes narrowing in a slightly apprehensive way. He felt queasy, but it was nothing to do with having been shot. He knew FB well – too well, probably – and could only speculate negatively as to his intentions.

Hence the queasiness.

FB always had an agenda. It was one of his characteristics.

Henry eyed the other man, trying to work out why he was faintly familiar, unable to quite pin it down.

'How's the shoulder?' FB asked. Before Henry could even open his mouth to respond, FB butted in. 'Is it going to keep you off work much longer?'

Henry almost spluttered into his coffee. 'Doctor says another month, just to be on the safe side. Then I can have a phased return on light duties.'

'Really?' FB sneered, unimpressed.

'Well, it did kind of hurt and I very nearly lost a full body of blood,' he pointed out with no exaggeration. 'Thank goodness I got shot in a hospital – got plugged straight into the blood banks.' He smiled. In reality, he was making light of it, but if he hadn't been found by a hospital porter who'd noticed blood glugging from under the storeroom door, he would have bled out. 'So I'm full of other people's blood and, just at the moment, I'm dealing with heavy psychological issues . . . my personality is split several ways now.'

'So you're back to normal, then?' FB said, deadpan.

'Yeah, yeah,' Henry retreated dully, not having the energy to continue with banter. He could do without these men here. All he wanted to do was lock up the house and head to The Tawny Owl to be pampered by Alison. She was a former military nurse who combined medical expertise with TLC. He smiled thinly at FB, his eyes fleetingly taking in the other man, who was looking increasingly familiar. 'But I am off for a couple more weeks at least.'

'Pah!' FB blurted, and exchanged a quick glance with his companion. He said to Henry, 'How do you feel about coming back earlier than that?'

Henry sipped his coffee, then pursed his lips. 'Depends, I suppose. I'd hate to go against medical advice . . . health and safety and insurance, and all that.'

'You could sign an indemnity,' FB suggested.

Henry wasn't sure if he was kidding or not. He screwed up his face. 'Maybe you'd better explain why you want me to come back, then we can talk,' he suggested in response.

FB nodded and gestured to the man with him. 'Let me introduce you to John Burnham . . .'

The name clinched it. However, he continued to feign ignorance and let FB carry on with the introduction.

'John is the chief constable of Central Yorkshire Police.'

Burnham leaned forward and reached across the coffee table to shake hands with Henry, who mirrored the gesture but rather more gingerly; already his right shoulder was starting to stiffen up again.

'Pleased to meet you,' Burnham said.

'Likewise.'

Henry tried not to second-guess this, but two chief constables turning up on the doorstep, he thought – second-guessing just to himself – meant something big in the offing.

'I actually do know you, vaguely,' Henry said, fitting the little pieces together. 'We were at Bruche together.' Bruche was the police training centre just outside Warrington. 'Initial training, ten weeks, same class. Got the class photo somewhere. I look like someone stood on my foot, if I recall rightly.'

Burnham squinted at Henry through his chunky, black-framed glasses.

They hadn't been great mates, had not got to know each other very well by any means. Henry recalled Burnham being part of the serious, bookish clique, the ones who vied for top marks in the weekly multiple-choice exams they all had to endure in those days of classroom-based instruction. Henry's only goal had been to pass with a mark high enough to avoid having to attend the embarrassing remedial classes. Most of the rest of the time he spent drinking and pursuing the very limited number of probationer lady cops on the courses, female officers being few and far between in those days. Notwithstanding the lack of numbers, he did have some notable successes in that department, while he seemed to recall Burnham winning the class prize and getting the highest overall mark in the whole intake.

'You were in the West Yorkshire Police,' Henry said. Burnham was one of the few unfortunate ones sent across the Pennines for initial training. Most Yorkshire recruits went to the regional training centre at Dishforth, but some were hived off over the hills into enemy territory.

Henry had thoroughly enjoyed his time at Bruche, which, like all the other regional police training centres, had now closed forever to become a housing estate.

'Yeah, that's right,' Burnham said. 'I transferred later to Northumbria, where I got on the Special Course, as it was, then eventually ended up in Central Yorks.'

Henry nodded, thought for a moment, then said, 'Special Course . . . 'course you did.' The Special Course meant accelerated promotion for officers with potential to become chief officers. It was another thing that had passed Henry by, though again, like the disappeared police training centres, the Special Course no longer existed.

'As its chief constable?' Henry asked.

'Only after I left on promotion, then came back again five years later,' he said, reminding Henry of the mystery of how chief officers flitted around the country from force to force like butterflies chasing promotion, although Henry usually substituted the word butterfly with something less pretty. 'To save it,' Burnham added bleakly.

Henry nodded. As a superintendent, he was reasonably aware of what was going on in the bigger world of policing, and he knew that Central Yorkshire (CY), as it was commonly known, was under considerable pressure financially and operationally, compounded by a damning inspection report from the HMIC, the body responsible for independently assessing police forces across the country. There was talk about carving up CY, but Henry didn't really know the full details. Every force in the country was under the cosh, hit with cutbacks and microscopic scrutiny, including his own, Lancashire, which was just about staying afloat.

'How's that going?' he asked Burnham, who winced a little. 'So-so.'

Henry shrugged. 'How can I help?'

Burnham glanced at FB, then back at Henry. 'Your chief speaks very highly of you,' he said. Henry tried desperately to keep a cynical mouth-twist off his face, managing to raise his eyebrows modestly instead.

'That's kind of him.'

'It's pretty much a make-or-break time for the force and my task, basically, is to drag it out of the last century, where it still lounges – a lack of capital investment and investment in training and development being the primary causes. I've been in charge for about six months now and a few things are starting to happen for the good. Anyway, a big part of my strategy is to ensure that, when my officers interface with the general public, it is spot on. That, to me, is where it all begins and ends.'

Henry could not disagree.

'I want us to be efficient and effective in everything we do; do it right first time, every time,' he said earnestly.

Henry blinked at the management speak and could see that Burnham would be good in interviews for jobs. But he did know that if the public was looked after properly and that 'bit' was working, everything else behind could be addressed in good time. He knew it wasn't that simple, but it was a starting point. However, he wasn't sure where he came into this until Burnham started speaking his language.

'And that applies from domestic disputes to murder investigations.'

Henry nodded with a touch more enthusiasm. He was a senior investigating officer (SIO) in FMIT. He investigated murders. He saw it as his job, his lot in life, maybe even the thing he was put on this earth to do. Hunt down and bring killers to justice. Fight for the dead.

He acknowledged it to be a pretty lofty aspiration, but at least it was an honest one. Plus, there was nothing more thrilling in life than charging someone with that terrible offence, looking into their eyes and knowing they had done it.

Henry refrained from saying, 'So I presume that's where I come in,' even if that was what he was thinking. He just waited and thought through what little knowledge he had of Central Yorkshire Police. In some respects, it was a mini-version of Lancashire, but the main city on the east coast had proper docks that still worked, unlike Preston, which had given up the maritime ghost many years before. He tried to rake his brain for the name of that city, but could not dredge it up. It was not an area he knew well, nor had any reason to frequent.

Perhaps he would soon learn more.

'OK,' he said.

'When I took over the force, the SIO team was already

depleted. One detective super had retired on ill health and the remaining one, Jack Culver, was bearing the load. There were, what, six murder investigations up and running and he was flitting between them all like a headless chicken – and doing a pretty good job, I hasten to add. Four were solved but there are now, still, two running, and I want to get a result on those.'

'OK,' Henry said again, his voice dubious. He already did not like the possibility of putting another super's nose out of joint by sticking his own into their business, which is the conclusion he immediately jumped to.

'So what I would like,' Burnham said, bracing himself, 'is for you to go over and review those two murder enquiries . . . fresh perspective and all that. I've had a long discussion with Bob, here,' he nodded at FB, 'and he thinks you're just the man. Therefore, so do I. And it seems you're between jobs at the moment.'

'What does Superintendent Culver think about it? There might be some very good reasons why the investigations are dragging on. Sometimes it happens.' Henry shrugged without enthusiasm.

'I know. I was an SIO myself at one point.'

Henry thought fast. 'If I did go,' he said, 'which I haven't said I would, because I do want a proper medical sign-off for everyone's sake, then I would want Mr Culver to be happy about what's happening.'

Burnham and FB exchanged a curious glance that unsettled Henry, who frowned and said, 'What?'

'Superintendent Culver doesn't run investigations now,' Burnham said.

Henry was about to say, 'Well, that makes it OK, then,' but didn't get the chance.

Burnham said, 'He was killed in a road traffic accident last week. His car collided with a stolen car which tipped him off the road. He was missing for two days before we found him.'

THREE

'Who's the guy?'

'I don't know.'

'In that case, you need to find out and then do what you have to do.'

'What the hell does that mean?'

'You fucking know – sort it, sort him, sort them . . . I don't have time for this shit just now.'

Detective Chief Inspector Jane Runcie ended the call on her iPhone with an angry stab of her thumb and hissed the word, 'Tosser.' She slid the device back into her trouser pocket, wiped the grimy sweat from her forehead, caught her breath and then gathered her ponytail at the back of her head, slid off the elastic band, bunched her hair and fitted the band again.

She had wanted to take the call from Silverthwaite, but it had come in at an inopportune moment to say the least. With her nostrils flaring wide, she looked down at the unmoving form of the man at her feet lying splayed out, face down on the painted concrete floor of cell number six in wing two. It was her favourite cell because, despite its low number, it was situated furthest away from the custody office.

A pool of blood was spreading wide from the man's crushed face on the non-porous surface.

Runcie swore and squatted down on her haunches, reaching out with the index and middle fingers of her right hand to check for a pulse in the soft flesh just under the man's chin in the carotid artery.

It was still there. Weak, but there.

'Is he still alive?'

Runcie rose stiffly to her full height, her knees popping. She was a tall, rangy woman, just under six feet tall without heels, so she usually wore flats to work. She eyed the man standing opposite her on the other side of the prostrate guy, noticing his suit, like hers, was splattered with flecks of blood.

''Course he fucking is,' she said.

'What do we do now?' The man, older than Runcie, wiped his face, which was also blood-spattered, stretching his tired features.

Runcie's face twitched. Under her calm exterior, her mind was racing, working out the angles, the possibilities, thinking about what she had in place for eventualities like this – a man beaten half to death in a police cell.

She put her hands on her hips.

'Let's think.' She invited the man – his name was John Saul and he was a detective constable – to consider. 'We have a man lying on the floor in front of us, who we strongly believe of being the man who abducted and raped four children and murdered them, burying their bodies in the woods . . .'

'Yet he denies it,' Saul pointed out insipidly.

'Oh, he did it, he fucking did it,' Runcie stated with exacting certainty. 'So I think this: he's been in police custody, been released without charge after interview, decided he can take no more and, in a fit of despairing remorse, he tops himself . . . What do you reckon to that scenario?'

A smile quivered on Saul's lips. 'All fits,' he agreed. 'Just a bit of a problem.' Saul looked down at the man's body, which shuddered slightly as a moan escaped from his mouth.

Still very much alive.

Runcie nodded. 'You got your two p's?' she asked. Saul nodded. 'How many prisoners are along this corridor as we speak?'

'Four, I think.'

'OK, you sort out the CCTV while I speak to the custody officer.'

The two detectives backed out of the cell, closing the heavy, steel-clad door with a gentle clunk. They walked quietly down the cell corridor, Runcie pausing at each cell that was occupied, easily identifiable as all empty cells were left with the doors wide open. She put her eye to each circular, toughened glass peephole just above the inspection hatches and peered into each cell.

Saul had been correct. Four prisoners in total. Two were laid out on their benches, sleeping soundly. The other two were awake, both sitting on the benches, their legs drawn up. As Runcie's eyes appeared at the holes, each man looked up at her. One stayed seated; the other rose and crossed to the door, but Runcie did not stay to talk.

She and Saul entered the custody office where the single sergeant on duty was making entries into custody records, keeping them up to date. Her name was PS Anna Calder and she eyed the detectives warily as they split.

Runcie approached the sergeant while Saul went to a small office behind the custody desk.

The young sergeant looked strained as Runcie leaned on the desk.

'The cameras are going off for five minutes,' the DCI said. 'That pesky intermittent fault.'

The sergeant's throat rose and fell visibly as she seemed to swallow something approaching the size of half a house brick. 'Why?' she whispered huskily.

'We're taking him out . . . so he needs to be booked out, released with no charge,' Runcie explained.

'OK,' Calder said weakly. It was now clear that her mouth had dried up as she swallowed and licked her lips.

Runcie reached across and gripped the woman's shoulder, grasping her epaulette, which displayed the shiny sergeant's stripes. 'Don't worry, lass . . . it's all under control.' She arched her eyebrows and nodded reassuringly. 'Get his property out and his custody record and get it signed out to him.'

'I'll need his signature.'

'Just mark it, "refused to sign".'

DC Saul appeared from the back office and gave Runcie a quick thumbs up: the CCTV cameras covering the custody suite had been dealt with.

The sergeant unlocked and opened the prisoners' property cupboard and removed a large, sealed polythene ziplocked bag with the name *Sowerbutts* on the label. She broke the seal, tipped the few contents on to the desk and made the entry in the record as instructed.

Runcie watched her calculatingly. 'On the custody record itself, put an entry to the effect that the prisoner has been interviewed, denies all offences and, until further evidence is uncovered – or otherwise – has been released without charge. You know the wording.'

The sergeant nodded and complied with a shaking pen.

Runcie looked at Saul. 'Two-pence pieces?'

Saul shuffled a handful of the copper-coloured coins out on to his palm, four of them and a small ball of Blu-Tack. Runcie smiled conspiratorially. 'You know what to do with them.'

He disappeared into the cell corridor.

Runcie followed a few moments later, then both entered the cell of the injured man. Saul hoofed him over on to his back and recoiled slightly at the vision of the man's smashed and flattened face, damaged beyond recognition.

'Shit. He's a mess.' He blew out his cheeks.

'And a rapist, a child molester and murderer,' Runcie reminded him.

'Yeah, yeah,' he conceded.

'You take his shoulders, I'll do the legs.'

Saul was a very long-in-the-tooth detective, just short of the fifty mark, but was still a big, handy man with good strength across his chest and shoulders. He slid his hands under the prisoner's armpits and heaved him up while Runcie grabbed his ankles. They began to manoeuvre him out of the cell and down the corridor, carrying him between them like a roll of carpet, leaving a smear of blood the full length of the passageway.

As Runcie shuffled along, she checked each occupied cell and saw that Saul's two-pence pieces were still in place, effectively blocking each peephole in which the coins were a perfect fit, held in place by the Blu-Tack.

Best, she thought, to have no hostile witnesses.

Detective Sergeant Eric Silverthwaite looked accusingly at his iPhone, which had gone dead in his hand when Jane Runcie had abruptly ended the call.

'Bitch. Boss bitch, but bitch nevertheless.'

He slithered down low in the driving seat of his Vauxhall Insignia and glanced at the man sitting alongside him.

His name was Hawkswood, a black man from the deep reaches of Leeds, who Silverthwaite had pretty much loathed for a long time until Hawkswood proved that he was just as crooked and corrupt as the rest of them on Runcie's team.

'What?' Hawkswood asked.

'Sort it, sort them, she said,' Silverthwaite told him.

Hawkswood slithered low and deep into his seat too, and swore.

'So we need to find out who he's visiting and why,' Silverthwaite said.

'We pretty much know the why,' Hawkswood said, 'so it doesn't really matter who, does it?'

'Suppose not, but let's do it anyway.'

They settled into their seats, their eyes on the detached house some one hundred yards along the avenue with the 'For Sale' sign erected in the front garden. Silverthwaite raised his phone, focused the in-built camera on the sign and took a photograph, which he enlarged with his thumb and forefinger so he could read the number of the estate agent. 'Could give these a ring, maybe,' he suggested.

Hawkswood had his own phone out and was punching a number into it, holding the phone to his ear while looking sideways at Silverthwaite, who he continued to despise even though both were equally as corrupt as the other. 'Or this,' he said as the call connected and he spoke. 'Hi, DC Hawkswood here, Portsea Serious Crime Team . . . Yeah, yeah . . . I'm currently doing some work in Blackpool, part of an ongoing investigation . . . Yeah, I know,' he chuckled and rolled his eyes, 'all the good places. Just wondering, could you go online and do a check on the electoral register for me for an address out here? You can? Great.' Hawkswood gave the address, then waited. 'Yeah . . . still here . . . go on.' He jammed the slim phone between his shoulder and ear and, using a pen from his jacket, wrote on the palm of his left hand. 'OK, thanks so much . . . got it . . . yeah . . . It's Andrea, isn't it? Thought so. Yeah, seen you about too . . . Yep, gotta go, thanks so much.'

He ended the call and turned triumphantly to Silverthwaite. 'One simple call reveals all.'

'And leaves a trail,' the other detective said warningly.

'Doubt it.'

'Anyway, what've you got?'

Hawkswood read his palm. 'A family, it would seem. Could be mum, dad and daughter, I'm guessing.'

'Name?' Silverthwaite said with impatience.

'Two females, Katherine and Leanne, and one male, who is probably the one we're interested in. Name: Henry James Christie.'

At the revelation of Detective Superintendent Culver's death, Henry James Christie thought, *Shit*. However, to Burnham, he said, 'Do you have any reason to think that is connected to either of these outstanding murder enquiries?'

'I'd like to believe not,' Burnham said warily, then seemed to reach a conclusion. 'No . . . unlikely . . . just a wrong place at the wrong time scenario, although neither the stolen car, nor its driver have been found as yet . . . sadly, it's just one of those things, I hope. A coincidence.'

'OK,' Henry drawled, the word 'coincidence' not being one he particularly liked, especially in relation to serious crime.

'So where do we stand, Henry?' FB interjected, having glanced at his chunky Rolex. 'You up for this or not? A few days of your time, that's all that's being asked.' FB was perched on the edge of his chair and now apparently in a hurry to get going.

Burnham had come in bearing a fairly heavy-looking briefcase, which had been at his feet. He raised it on to his lap, flipped the catches and opened it. Henry noticed Burnham's initials – JB – in gold leaf in the leather. He delved into it and extracted two thick, ring-bound files.

'I copied the murder books without anyone else's knowledge. Thought you might like to peruse them out of interest anyway. Even if you decided not to physically go over to Central Yorkshire, I'd be interested in your thoughts . . . if you don't mind?' He placed them on the glass-topped coffee table.

Henry regarded them with his mouth askew.

Murder books were the documents that senior investigating officers were required to keep and record all decisions made – and just about anything else of interest during a murder investigation. They very much related the story and progress of an enquiry, and could either be very boring or make good bedtime reading – as good as any thriller, depending on the literacy level of the SIO.

Henry eyed both men over the bait.

'Why come to Lancashire?' he asked Burnham.

'Your reputation as a force. Bob and I go way back. And you come highly recommended,' he explained succinctly.

Henry nodded. 'I'll have to convince my fiancée and then my doctor,' he said, noting FB's roll of his eyeballs. 'And in that order – and if I can do that, I'll let you know first thing tomorrow. I'm not playing hard to get, but someone did shoot me. I'm healing well, but I don't want to overdo anything.'

'Wimp,' FB coughed.

Henry just grinned at him.

'I can assure you, it'll be non-physical. Just have a look at how they're going on and, if you think all is OK, that all that needs doing is being done, then fine,' Burnham said. 'We'll even put you up in a decent hotel for the duration.'

'OK,' Henry said again.

'Thank you,' Burnham said.

'I told him you were a soft touch where murder is concerned.' FB grinned.

'I'll let the lead investigator know you're coming once you give me the nod,' Burnham said. 'Just as a courtesy, and I'll get my secretary to book a room at a hotel.'

Although there was a feeling of being railroaded, Henry was warming to the job now. A few nights in a half-decent hotel appealed to him, and also seeing part of the country he wasn't familiar with. Inside, though, he knew the hurdle he would have to jump wouldn't be the doctor . . . it would be Alison.

FB and Burnham rose to their feet. Burnham shook Henry's hand.

'Are you off back now?' Henry asked as he walked the men through to the front door.

'Some further business with Bob here, just chatting about efficiencies and effectiveness, neighbourhood policing . . . then I think we're out for a meal. I'm staying overnight at a relative's house, then back first thing tomorrow.'

At the front door, Burnham shook Henry's hand again. Henry saw a look of relief on the man's stressed-out face. 'Glad to have you on board, Henry. I won't pat you on the shoulder.'

Henry opened the door, thinking that Burnham might be jumping the gun a bit.

Burnham filed out, followed by FB who, when he came face-to-face with Henry on the threshold, stopped momentarily and said, 'Thanks, mate.'

He did slap Henry on the shoulder.

Rubbing and rolling his arm and joint, Henry glared at FB's back as the two men got into FB's Jaguar. He watched them drive away with a grimace on his face and swear words spoken behind his gritted teeth.

As he stood watching it disappear, he did notice the car parked further down the road and thought he could make out two shapes sitting inside it, but nothing about the vehicle made him suspicious.

He sighed and walked down the driveway where the 'For Sale' sign was implanted in the front flower bed. Even though Henry's house was two miles inland from Blackpool promenade, the wind from the Irish Sea had whipped through the cuts and ginnels of the resort and knocked the sign sideways. Henry pulled it upright and looked at it.

For Sale: the notice that truly meant he was moving on with his life now – practically at least. Emotionally, he was still in a bit of turmoil. He was only staying here, at the house he had shared with his now-deceased wife, Kate, in order to show a couple of potential buyers around and sign some papers at the solicitor's.

He swallowed. He knew he had met someone very special in Alison Marsh, the landlady of The Tawny Owl, someone he wanted to spend the rest of his life with, but that did not make the transition easy. He sighed, gave his moist eyes a rub, stamped on the soil in which the sign was planted to firm it up and walked back to the front door, noticing the car again, which he thought could have been a Vauxhall, but attached no significance to.

Just a car. Two people on board. That was all. Lots of cars parked around here.

'You got him?' Silverthwaite glanced at Hawkswood.

'Certainly did.' Hawkswood looked at the photographs he'd taken with his phone of the three men emerging from the house, then two of the men driving away in the fancy Jag, leaving the other man – presumably the householder – watching the car go, then that man looking directly at him and Silverthwaite in the car while Hawkswood clicked away. They watched him realign the 'For Sale' sign, then go back indoors with just another glance in their direction. 'Got some good ones,' he said, gleefully expanding one of them with his fingertips. 'Old guy. Think it's this Henry Christie character?'

'Not going to make any assumptions, but I'd guess so,' Silverthwaite said, leaning over to see the image on the screen. 'Send her one of them,' he said.

FOUR

'He's dead. I'm fucking certain,' DC Saul said desperately.

DCI Runcie shrugged as she looked into the boot of the stolen car at the unmoving body of the prisoner they had managed to sneak out of the custody suite into the back of her car and then, still unseen, transfer into the back of a stolen car which Saul had then driven out to Salterforth Cliffs, a very rugged section of coastline, difficult to access either by car or on foot. The high cliffs overlooked jagged rocks below and beyond lay the harsh North Sea. Several miles out, two large container vessels ploughed through the water, one heading north, the other south.

Once more, Runcie felt for a pulse in the man's neck, pressing her fingers into his soft flesh.

This time, there was nothing.

She rose up and looked at Saul. His face was ashen as she confirmed, 'Yep, he's dead.'

She glanced down into the boot again. While still alive, the man's body had been folded untidily to fit into the space, which was fairly generous, but he'd been left face up rather than in any sort of recovery position.

'Looks like he drowned in his own blood,' she said.

'What do we do?'

'What we planned to do in the first place. Drive this car to the edge of the cliff, put him behind the steering wheel and push him over. The suicide of a deranged child killer wracked by remorse . . . we'll make it fit.' She smiled grimly. 'It's what we do.'

Saul nodded.

Her car was pulled up behind the stolen one, having followed Saul to this isolated spot.

They drove both vehicles across the field to the cliff and parked them side by side.

Runcie walked to the cliff edge to check the almost perpendicular drop of nearly 200 feet down on to sharp, jagged and dangerous rocks. Satisfied this was the best place, she returned to the vehicles and, together with Saul, they heaved the dead man out of the boot and manhandled him into the driver's seat of the stolen car. The body slumped sideways, but Runcie dragged him upright and balanced him carefully. She closely inspected his facial injuries, having been caused by slamming his face repeatedly into the floor of the cell, flattening his features. Not really consistent with the accident he was about to have.

She grabbed his hair at the back of his head and looked thoughtfully at the damaged face for a few moments, her brow furrowed. 'This won't do.' She looked around at Saul, who was hovering nervously behind her. 'So . . . just in case.'

She stood back slightly, tightened her grip on the man's hair, braced herself and then pounded his face into the rim of the steering wheel, adding further to the dead man's already catastrophic injuries. Then she forced his head between the spokes of the steering wheel and wedged it there sideways. He seemed to be looking through one half-open eye at her, the other one being clamped tightly shut.

Runcie winked back at him. 'This is what you call comeuppance, Mr Sowerbutts.'

She threaded her arm through the folded 'V' shape formed between the dead man's chest and his thighs and released the handbrake. Backing off, she closed the driver's door and she and Saul together pushed the car towards the edge of the cliff, through a broken section of fencing through which another vehicle had once careened, killing two drunken teenagers on a joyride.

The two detectives got some momentum, particularly as the last fifteen metres or so sloped towards the edge.

The dead man's head, jammed into the steering wheel, kept the car going straight on.

Five metres short of the cliff edge, the detectives gave one final heave and watched the van hurtle over the cliff, out of sight. They heard it crash down with a tearing, rending of metal, and they just made it to the edge to witness it smash into the rocks below. By the time it reached that point it was a wreck anyway.

Runcie rubbed her hands together. 'Sorted,' she said. 'Agreed?'

Saul said, 'Agreed.' They high-fived each other.

That was the moment at which her phone vibrated as a message landed. She fished the device out as she and Saul went back to her car.

She opened the message and saw that a photograph had landed, together with some text. It was from Hawkswood, sending one of the photos he had taken of the man that Burnham and FB had been visiting. The text read, *We think the guy is called Henry Christie. Mean anything to you?*

Runcie shaded the screen with her hand, then angled it for Saul to see. 'Guy called Henry Christie. You know him?'

Runcie saw Saul's expression change as he recognized the man and muttered, 'Oh, sweet Jesus.'

Having bagged a few things into a holdall, Henry locked up the house, then, a few minutes later, having taken one last glance as ever in his rear-view mirror as he drove away, he was powering east along the M55 away from Blackpool. Less than ten minutes after that, he had joined the northbound M6 and relaxed slightly, steering the Audi with just a fingertip while glancing repeatedly and longingly at the two murder books lying tantalizingly on the passenger seat.

He could not deny it. They were exercising an almost mesmeric pull on him.

He knew he would weaken.

It was in his DNA.

Yet he did know someone who would be less than enamoured with the prospect of him going across the country to review two stalled murder investigations.

His speed remained around the seventy mph mark until, less than ten minutes later, he was slowing down to exit the motorway at junction thirty-four, Lancaster north. He did not head towards the city but turned right on the A683, through the village of Caton, which straddled that main road, then shortly after took a right and plunged into the network of narrow, winding country roads until he picked up the signpost for Kendleton, one of those small, picturesque, hidden-gem Lancashire villages nestling in a small valley through which a tributary of the River Lune trickled – and which few people knew existed.

If he was honest, he was not really looking forward to facing up to the tender wrath of Alison Marsh.

As he negotiated the last bend before Kendleton, a huge Red Deer stag suddenly appeared from the bushes on his right-hand side and skittered to an ungainly halt on the road surface, the hooves of the magnificent beast not really designed for tarmac. Henry slammed on the brakes and almost collided with the animal, and would have done had its muscles not quickly tensed around powerful haunches and back quarters and it powered itself off the road, over the low bushes on the left, disappearing like a spectre into the woods.

Henry's car fishtailed, almost tipping into the roadside ditch but stopping as he wrestled with the wheel, yanking and jarring the muscles in his right shoulder, sending a flame of agony through his upper chest and neck.

'Fucking stupid animal!' he shouted, then gasped at the pain while holding on to the wheel. 'Fucking accident waiting to happen.'

A minute later, he drove sedately into the car park at the front of The Tawny Owl, still creased up in agony. He climbed out of the car and tried manfully to give the impression he was in no pain whatsoever – no wincing, no bending double – just in case Alison was watching him.

'He nearly wasn't a problem in any way, shape or form,' Silverthwaite told Runcie. 'He almost stuffed his car into a frickin' huge deer.'

Silverthwaite was speaking on his mobile phone. He and Hawkswood had tailed Henry from Blackpool all the way to Kendleton, certain they hadn't been clocked by him, even on the quiet back roads beyond the motorway. They had been close enough behind to witness the deer leaping out in front of him, but far enough back not to get noticed themselves. As Henry had driven into the car park of what appeared to be the only pub in the one-horse village that was Kendleton, Silverthwaite and Hawkswood had driven past the opening and stopped further down the road. Looking back in their mirrors, they had seen Henry hobble stiffly from his car into the pub.

They had tried to get a phone signal, which had proved to be a problem out in the sticks, and eventually managed to get a few unreliable bars, which is when Silverthwaite called Runcie.

'You say he's a detective?' Silverthwaite asked with a touch of disbelief.

At the other end of the line, Runcie was back in her office at divisional HQ, her door firmly closed, with Saul pacing the space on the opposite side of her desk while she watched him coldly.

'Yes,' she said. 'Saul recognized him from the photo you sent.'

Hearing his name, Saul stopped mid-pace, folded his arms and looked at his boss.

'Remembers him coming to give a talk a few years back on one of his detective courses. I've done a bit of digging, too. The guy's an SIO with Lancashire, a detective super. He can't be a million miles off retirement.'

'Well, he walks like an old man,' Silverthwaite commented cruelly.

'Question is why has our chief constable been to see him?' Runcie asked.

'You no wiser?' Silverthwaite said.

'I'm working on it.'

'Thought you had a snout in Burnham's office?'

'I do, and that's what I'm waiting for.'

'OK.'

'You know, the word is that Burnham's not one hundred per cent with us,' Runcie said.

'Tell me something I don't know,' Silverthwaite snarled.

'If Jack Culver got to him, we could be backs against the wall.'

'So what d'you want us to do, boss?' Silverthwaite asked.

'Where is Christie right now?'

'Driven to a pub in the middle of nowhere. Looks like he could be here for the duration – took a holdall in with him.'

'Look, got a call coming in,' Runcie said. 'This could be what I'm after. Just hang fire and I'll get back to you.' She ended that call and took the new one indicated on her mobile. 'Elise,' she cooed, 'you got something for me, honey?'

Henry pushed his way through the front doors of The Tawny Owl, not allowing himself to cringe as his right arm brushed the door frame. He immediately caught sight of Alison leaving the kitchen at the rear of the pub, bearing two plates of steaming hot food for a couple of customers sitting in the main bar area. She was actually reversing out through the swing doors and did not see Henry straight away.

But he saw her.

With her lioness-coloured hair scraped back tightly into a businesslike ponytail, wearing an unflattering blouse and skirt covered by a Tawny Owl apron, and flat shoes, she should not have looked stunning – especially balancing two big dinner plates and with a tea towel slung over her shoulder – but she did and, as ever, took Henry's breath away.

He had only a fleeting moment to take her in before she caught him in his appraisal. For a second, her face had been a tense mask of concentration but, when she spotted him, the veneer dropped and her eyes widened slightly. She half-smiled and stuck out the tip of her tongue briefly. Then everything returned to full concentration and she entered the bar after subtly blowing him a kiss.

Henry realized he was still breathless. He inhaled with a judder, then made his way through the door leading to the spacious ground-floor owner's accommodation right at the back of the pub.

He was now feeling slightly guilty.

Not many weeks before, he had promised Alison in no uncertain terms that he would retire from the cops in the 'near future', once he had cleared his desk. And that he would go down on one knee and propose to her somewhere tropical, as opposed to the location he had actually popped the question.

His guilt was that here he was, still off sick, and actually knowing he would be taking on extra work in the guise of visiting another force to review a couple of murders, and returning to work just for that purpose.

She would not be impressed. Not one little bit. And he couldn't blame her.

'Henry!' she blasted.

He recoiled just a smidgen.

'I cannot believe my ears. You're still in recovery. You were shot. You almost bled dry. And you're still getting over your mum's death – don't say you aren't,' Alison warned him. Henry's mother had died in hospital at much the same time as Henry had been bleeding out in another hospital. Her death had quietly devastated him, but he had kept his feelings – publicly, at least – under control, only allowing himself to 'lose it' when alone with Alison, who had been brilliant throughout.

Now he felt like he was betraying her.

They were in the living room. Henry had just made himself a mug of tea and was just about to make his way to the front of The Tawny Owl, where he intended to settle down and start on the murder books. He'd mentioned his intent to Alison, catching her in passing as she carried out two more meals from the kitchen. He'd hoped, in his man-like, cowardly way, that her brain might be too overloaded to take in what he'd said and she would just accept it as a given. Once more, he'd underestimated her. When she burst through to the living room, he knew he was in deep.

'You are not fit to go back,' she remonstrated with him. 'You're still as weak as a kitten.'

'B-but . . .' he stammered.

'B-but what?' she mimicked him.

'It's just a case review job, that's all. Not real live murders.'

'Murders?' she demanded. 'You said murder, not murders plural.'

'Slip of the tongue,' he lied. 'It seems I'm the best man for the job, chosen from hundreds of other hopefuls.' He gave her a twisted grin. 'Like the *X Factor*.'

'You're a complete fricking idiot,' she informed him. And despite the insult, it was just at that moment he thought he might be OK here. One of the things he'd come to accept about Alison

– love, even – was that when she became irate, she started to use very base language indeed. The fact she hadn't called him a 'fucking idiot' gave him cause for hope.

She rolled her eyes, uttered a guttural 'Ugh!' of scorn, spun and left him standing with the two murder books under his arm.

He exhaled, took a sip of his tea, waited until he was certain she'd gone, then crept cautiously out to the front of the pub with his brew and reading material.

Runcie listened carefully to what the woman called Elise had to say.

Elise Makerfield worked as an administrative assistant in the chief constable's team, holding the lowest position within that team, the most ignored yet put-upon person there, although the new chief, Burnham, always found time to have a little chat with her and she found him unusually pleasant, even though he was also all business. Burnham had inherited the admin team when he took up his position, always intending to slowly re-staff and restructure it to suit his needs. So far, he hadn't had time to do that. Taking the reins of a failing police force meant he had to concentrate on more urgent matters than a team reshuffle. Though they seemed to be good and dedicated, the key was that he had 'inherited' them.

And that meant Elise Makerfield.

She had previously been in several positions within the force during her less-than-illustrious career, and before she had moved on to the chief's team she had been an admin assistant on CID, where she had first encountered DCI Jane Runcie. Runcie had discovered her weaknesses, exploited them and finally found a useful home for Elise in the chief's office, where there was always the chance of proving herself useful. Eyes and ears in that location were always good things to have.

Runcie referred to Elise as a 'rat duster', even to her face.

'It's not all that easy,' Elise whispered over the phone. She had sneaked out of the office that housed the chief's team and gone outside the old headquarters building to a smoking shelter, which at the moment was unoccupied. 'The new boss isn't as careless as the old one . . . he puts stuff away.'

'Look, Elise, I'll tell you what's easy and what isn't,' Runcie said harshly. 'Fucking up your dear son good and proper, that's easy. You owe me, you little bitch, so don't start whining when I ask for favours.'

'I know, I know,' Elise groaned, feeling queasy. She'd come under the control and manipulation of this nasty woman to firstly get her son off a minor drugs trafficking charge – he'd been buying from a dealer, then selling it on – only then to find that Runcie wanted her to get a job on the chief's entourage and feed back interesting information to her.

'Come on, then,' Runcie urged her. 'What've you found out?'

Elise told her things which only really confirmed what Runcie already knew. It was the last piece of the jigsaw.

She hung up, and called Silverthwaite again.

Spring had just about got into gear. The days were gradually growing longer, the light lasting all that much more, but there was still a distinct chill in the air, which was why Henry wrapped himself in a fleece while sitting out at the front of the pub. There were a couple of picnic benches on an uneven terrace which was going to be replaced by some fairly extensive and expensive decking in the near future as part of Alison's ongoing plans for the pub, which she'd bought a few years earlier when it was neglected, unloved and very close to being shut down forever. She and her stepdaughter Ginny had resurrected the place and reversed its fortunes, bringing back local and passing trade a-plenty.

For the time being, though, Henry made do with sitting carefully on a rickety old picnic bench, and opened the first murder book.

Mark James Wright, born January 21, 1973. He would have been forty years old this year, but had been murdered in October 2012, so he never actually made that milestone, a fact that automatically made Henry slightly sad. Forty was a big event in any person's life, and Mark James Wright would never celebrate it. This was one of the myriad reasons that tended to drive Henry on while investigating murder. He hated the thought of people not having the chance to live their lives until their natural end because some other bastard took it away from them.

Henry liked such people to be punished. Sometimes, though, they weren't. Henry had occasionally known murderers walk free from court against the most compelling evidence, but he had learned to accept the foibles of a flawed justice system and, as galling as it was, he lived with such decisions because his job was to find the killer and bring him/her/them to court and present as watertight a case as possible. Beyond that, it was up to the courts.

That is what he was good at. Mostly and despite everything, he did feel a little smug that FB had chosen him for this job (even though it had been FB choosing him to investigate three unsolved murders at the end of last year that led him to getting shot); on the other hand, he rarely trusted FB's thought processes. There was usually an agenda behind them.

Henry opened Mark James Wright's murder book but, before he could get anywhere with it, he glanced up and watched a Vauxhall Insignia pull up on the car park and stop alongside his Audi. He raised his face and narrowed his eyes at the arrival. Two men got out and walked towards the pub. From the way they were focused, he was fairly sure they hadn't actually seen him at the bench, even though he wasn't hidden from view.

Cops, he thought, then looked at their car again, frowning slightly.

They were chatting to each other, which was probably why they hadn't seen him and, as they came up the steps, Henry called amicably, 'Hi, guys, how you doing?'

Their reaction showed he was right – they hadn't seen him. They turned and looked at him as if they'd been caught stealing from the biscuit tin.

One was a tall, lanky man, his brown suit hanging loosely from his thin frame, the trousers baggy at the knees. The other was younger, smarter, more compact, and his body filled out his suit which, as opposed to the other man, was tight, particularly around the shoulders and biceps. Henry could tell this one worked out, while the taller man looked as though he abused his body with cigarettes and alcohol.

Their reaction came under smooth control.

'Hey, didn't see you there, mate.' The lanky man gave him a friendly wave.

Henry grinned. 'I'm good at hiding in plain sight,' he replied affably.

Lanky Man – as Henry had named him – jerked his head at the other man and Henry realized that this one, the older man, was probably the one with a bit of rank behind him, maybe a DS.

Tight Fit (also named by Henry) nodded and followed him towards Henry, who closed the murder book and laid his hands over the title in order to cover it, though he was aware that the words Central Yorkshire Police and the force crest were still visible in the header section.

'We're just passing through,' Lanky Man said. 'Reps, you know,' he added unconvincingly.

Henry blinked at the blatant untruth. 'Really? Selling what?'

The men exchanged a quick, nervous glance, before Lanky Man answered, 'Agricultural machinery.'

'Oh, OK.' Henry sat back slightly, keeping his hands over the front of the murder book. 'What sort?'

'Uh, tractors. John Deere,' Lanky Man said feebly.

'Come to the right area, then.' Henry smiled. 'Nowt but tractors round here.'

'Yeah, uh, we just thought we'd grab a bite before we hit the road back. That's if this place serves it,' Tight Fit cut in firmly, trying to end the lie before they got tied in knots. 'Can you recommend it?'

'Yeah, I'd say so,' Henry said.

Lanky Man gave him a lazy thank-you salute and the two guys went through the door, leaving Henry wondering about them and also if he was just being suspicious for no reason. Maybe they were agricultural reps, but he doubted it.

He gathered up the murder books and his newly drained mug and retreated inside, checking the bar before going into the owner's accommodation to dump the books. He was back a few minutes later and went into the bar. The two visitors had got themselves a drink and were at a table in the bay window, perusing menus. Henry knew they were watching him over the tops of the menus like old-fashioned spies. He gave them an amicable nod and went to sit at the bar, which was propping up one of the regulars, an old farmer called Don Singleton, who, had there been a competition for the most stereotypical farmer, would have won hands down. He was ruddy-faced, sun-blasted (although his bulbous, veined nose was more a result of alcohol than the weather), and always sported a battered tweed flat cap, an open-neck check shirt, loose trousers held up by a twine belt and cut-off Wellington boots.

'Afternoon, Don,' Henry said, sliding alongside the customer.

'Henry,' he acknowledged, drained his second pint of real ale and slammed the empty glass on the bar.

Alison came from the kitchen with her pen and pad, about to take the order from the two reps.

Henry smiled wickedly to himself and, with a jerk of his head in the direction of the visitors, asked Don, 'Those two guys been to see you today?'

Don's big head turned and looked. 'No. Why?'

'They sell farm machinery.'

'Never seen 'em before.' Don's hand still encircled his beer glass and he rolled it cheekily on the counter, the meaning very apparent. He was angling for a pint on the house.

'Do you know most of the reps who cover this neck of the woods?'

'All of 'em. Like flies on a carcass, always trying to get me money.' He tapped the glass on the bar. Henry glanced at the young lady behind the bar and said, 'One on me, please. And don't give him a fresh glass.' Henry knew that Don insisted on using the same glass throughout a drinking session because he thought it was unlucky to keep getting a clean one. 'And they aren't any of them,' Don said.

Henry considered this, then asked Don, 'What sort of tractor you got these days?'

'Got four, all for different things.'

'Any John Deeres?'

'Nah, shite . . . I'm a Massey Ferguson nut.'

'Know anything about John Deeres?'

The refilled pint – a Lancaster Bomber – arrived in front of him. He sucked off the foam. 'I know everything about any tractor . . . tractor mags are my porn.' His eyes glazed over at the thought of page after page of tractor ads.

Henry knew he had to act quickly, before the alcohol in Don's system made him insensible. 'Will you do me a favour?' he said quietly into Don's large, cauliflower ear.

Lanky Man was ordering the steak-and-ale pie. As he did so, his eyes roved up and down Alison's body as she wrote down the order. She noticed the appraisal and squirmed inside but tried to ignore it. Sometimes it was what customers did. However, Lanky Man looked guiltily at Henry when he came up behind her with Don Singleton in tow. Lanky Man's lustful thoughts towards Alison were instantly shelved by caution.

'Lasagne for me,' Tight Fit said. 'With salad. No chips.'

'OK, thanks for that, gents.' Alison collected the menus, then turned to Henry, who she hadn't noticed creeping up behind her.

'Hi, sweetie,' he said, sidestepping to allow her past.

The two visitors eyed him shiftily.

Henry said, 'Apologies for this, I know this is just a pit stop and you're on your way back to wherever "back" is, but I just mentioned to Don here' – he indicated the farmer now alongside him – 'who's a farmer, incidentally, that you were John Deere reps. I know he's interested in that make. Just wondered if you could have a chat with him, maybe talk through some options.' Henry leaned forward conspiratorially and whispered, 'He's loaded, by the way.'

'I don't think so,' Lanky Man said stonily.

'But . . .'

'Work's done for the day. We haven't really got time to chat. We need to eat and go. Got a bit of a journey ahead.' He tried to sound apologetic.

'What about all that commission?'

'We don't work on commission. We're salaried,' Tight Fit said.

'Oh, OK,' Henry said. He was trying to sound taken aback. 'That's a shame. However, could you leave Don your card? He really is interested. And maybe when you're next in the area . . .' He arched his eyebrows.

'Run out of business cards,' Lanky Man said firmly. 'And to be fair, we're not really interested.'

'You must be the only reps in the world not interested in making a sale,' Henry remarked.

Lanky Man shrugged. Tight Fit looked at Henry coldly.

'Whatever.' He shrugged and drew Don back to the bar.

'Shit,' Hawkswood said through the side of his mouth. 'Bad fuckin' idea, this.'

Silverthwaite's mobile rang. It had a weak signal by virtue of him being in the bay window.

He answered.

'Where are you now?' Runcie demanded.

'Just about to eat,' he said, keeping it vague.

'Where's Henry Christie?'

'Er . . . we know where he is . . . not a million miles from where we are.'

'What's that supposed to mean?'

'That we know exactly where he is, OK?' His voice was tetchy now.

'You haven't made contact with him, have you?' she asked.

'Kind of,' he admitted sheepishly.

He heard Runcie emit an exasperated grunt at the other end of the line. 'So he knows who you are?'

'No, no, we spun him a yarn.'

'And you think he swallowed it?'

It was a doubtful, 'Yes,' although Runcie's forthright response wasn't doubtful at all as she castigated him.

'Sorry, boss.'

'I told you to hang fire.' Silverthwaite could tell she was seething between gritted teeth, and he could imagine the ferocious look on her face.

'What's the problem, though?'

'The problem is that our chief constable has asked Lancashire's chief constable, Fanshaw-Bayley, to send someone over and review our two unsolved murder cases – that someone being Henry Christie – and you two, by not fucking listening, have revealed your identities . . .'

'No, we haven't,' he protested.

'You might as well've done, you imbeciles!'

'He thinks we're sales reps.'

'And you think he's a gullible idiot. Let me tell you something – he isn't.'

A few moments of strained silence descended on the line, broken by Runcie. 'We'll just have to keep you two out of the way if he does actually get across here, I suppose.'

'What does that mean?'

'It means you might have to put him out of action. But first things first – our gung-ho chief constable needs sorting.'

'You want us to do that?' It was both a question and an offer.

'I'm just thinking out loud here,' Runcie said. 'A review might just disappear, or at least get put on the back burner if the chief somehow doesn't make it back across the Pennines and if Henry Christie . . . I dunno . . . breaks a leg, say?'

'Or two.'

'Or two,' Runcie confirmed.

'Where is Burnham now?' Silverthwaite asked. 'I thought he'd be back in the force.'

'No, no, he isn't, but I know more or less where he is.'

Alison brought out the meals for the two travelling salesmen, then went to the bar where Henry was propped up, chatting to Don Singleton, who had been joined by his usual drinking companion, the local general practitioner, Dr Lott. Between the two of them, they consumed a considerable amount of beer and spirits, and it was rumoured the profits from sales to them were solely responsible for saving The Tawny Owl from bankruptcy. This wasn't true, just a product of the village rumour mill.

'They seem nice guys,' Alison said to Henry. 'One's a bit leery, though . . . Still, that's blokes for you.'

'They're liars,' Henry said.

'What?'

'Oh, nothing. Tell you later. Need me to do anything?' Although technically against police regulations for Henry, as a serving officer, to either live or work in licensed premises, this did not deter him from helping out. His ultimate aim was to become co-owner when he retired anyway, so the powers that be didn't look too closely at his involvement. 'But I am still on light duties,' he reminded her.

She tutted and rolled her eyes so far back, Henry thought they would do a full three-sixty in their sockets.

'Mm, let me think . . . How about checking the back door of the cellar? The drayman whinged it was sticking again. Maybe it just needs some WD40 or something. A man's job,' she teased him. 'Can you handle it?'

'I'll have a look,' Henry said. She patted his shoulder – gently – and disappeared back into the kitchen.

It took a while before he prised himself away from the bar – noticing the two reps had left – and walked out of the pub into the increasing darkness and chill of the early evening. It had become quite cold quite quickly, and Henry shivered as a little nip of breeze caught him as he stepped out through the front door. Spring might well have been on its way, but winter was keeping a grip.

Henry actually said, 'Brr.'

From the doorway, he turned left and walked along the front of the pub, then turned left again at the gable end to the back corner, where there was a turning circle for brewery wagons to deliver crates and kegs filled with all types of liquids that Henry liked to imbibe. The vehicles preferred to reverse up to the circle and park next to the gentle slope leading down to the wide double doors of the cellar, which stretched right under the whole of the pub – a vast, dank warren of interconnecting rooms.

Next to the slope was a set of steps. Henry paused at the top one. There were fourteen, he knew, having been up and down them countless times.

He frowned, sensing something amiss.

A movement – a blur behind him.

Then he felt the push in the middle of his back, between his shoulder blades. He reached to grab the handrail, missed, then spiralled down the concrete steps, everything blurred, his injured shoulder glancing on a step, his head grazing the wall as he whirled down as though caught in a vortex, coming to a crashing stop at the foot of them, glimpsing a figure at the top of the steps, who was there, then gone.

FIVE

'Would you like me to give you a hand to get out of there?'

Henry Christie opened his eyes – he'd almost fallen asleep in the hot bath – and looked down the length of his body, seeing it reflected uncomfortably in the chrome plug turner on the end of the bath, just underneath the taps. He looked up at Alison and gave her a crooked, lazy grin.

She was standing by the bath holding a huge bath sheet spread between her hands.

'I was concerned. Thought you'd drowned.'

'I'm OK,' he said, groaning as he pushed himself up into a sitting position, the water and suds sluicing off him. He looked down at his left arm and left leg, the limbs that had taken the brunt of his tumble. Both displayed a series of bruises like a zebra, plus a swelling on his left elbow.

'And I ask again – what were you thinking?'

He cricked his neck painfully. 'I remind myself of that old joke.'

'Which is?' Alison asked reluctantly. His jokes were rarely laugh out loud, mostly cringeworthy in the extreme.

'Who discovered Victoria Falls?'

'I don't know – who discovered Victoria Falls?' Alison went gamely along with the gag.

'The person who pushed her.' Henry gave the weak punchline. 'Bu-bum!'

At least Alison didn't roll her eyes at that one, though her lips twisted disdainfully. 'You're saying you were pushed down the steps?'

He raised his eyebrows painfully. Even they were hurting. 'If I'm honest, I'm not sure now. I thought so at first; now it's a bit of a haze.'

'More likely you should have taken a torch with you and watched out for the green mould on the top step. You slipped and went A over T, simple.'

'I think I was pushed,' he insisted.

'OK, you were pushed. But by whom, and why? Makes no sense.'

'Tell me about it.' He heaved himself up and gingerly stepped out of the bath into the waiting folds of the fluffy sheet that Alison wrapped around his middle.

'I'm assuming there will be no chance of any . . . y'know?' she said, glancing down at his genitals before they went out of sight behind the sheet.

Henry said, 'There's no chance of me even thinking about it.' Then he had second thoughts about the matter. 'Unless, of course, you are very, very gentle with me.'

'I'm never gentle – you know that.'

'I could hardly hang around to see if he was OK or not, could I?' Hawkswood said. He was on the mobile to Runcie. 'I saw a chance and took it. He didn't see me – no one did. Just snuck up behind him and gave him a good push.'

'You don't know how he is?'

'I couldn't nip down and check his pulse. Might've given the game away,' he whined, frustrated at Runcie's questions. 'Even if he's dead, or uninjured or unhurt, there's nothing lost, I promise you. And if he is unhurt, then I'll just go back and do some real damage as and when necessary.'

'OK, OK,' she relented.

'He *was* reading the murder books, though. At least, I'm pretty sure that's what he had in front of him.'

'The murder books?'

'That's what they looked like. He put his hand over the cover, but I could see our force name and crest.'

'That means Burnham got them somehow and passed them on to him.'

Hawkswood did not comment, but waited for Runcie to continue.

'I now know the exact address where Burnham's staying tonight,' she said.

Suitably drugged up with analgesics, Henry poured himself a more-than-generous shot of Macallan Fine Oak twelve-year-old whisky – just to help the over-the-counter drugs to ease his aches and pains more effectively – and settled himself at the desk in one corner of the living room, placed the two murder books down, one on top of the other, and connected his laptop to the internet.

He logged on to the website of the Central Yorkshire Police, just to get a better idea, geographically, of where it was and where he was going to have to go to see the town in which the murders had taken place.

Looking at the map of the force, Henry was amazed it hadn't been amalgamated, divvied up into the other two big forces surrounding it. It was thin and elongated, with its own stretch of coastline, and reminded Henry of the Gambia, the tiny West African country he'd once visited for a holiday with Kate many years before. That, too, was surrounded by its neighbours, except for a stretch of Atlantic coastline. Like the Gambia, Central Yorkshire was essentially situated on either side of a river, in this case the River Wilton which ran from its source in North Yorkshire and poured through Central Yorkshire, spewing out into the North Sea at Portsea, the largest city in the county. It straddled the estuary of the river and was a busy working port which had been in existence since Roman times.

Unlike the Gambia, it was not tropical.

Henry had a further look at Portsea on Wikipedia. It was the name of the port he couldn't quite remember when he'd been talking to the two chief constables. He saw that it was actually a city now, having only recently achieved that status.

But the important thing for him was to get some kind of grip on the location where the murders took place. An old, thriving, east coast port. The question already lurking in his mind – just one of the many an SIO should have at the back of his or her mind – was is this location in any way connected with these deaths? And will this help me to make sense of them better? Any SIO worth their salt would be immediately asking that in order to start to build up a picture and ensure that logic would drive the investigative process, even if the mind of the offender might be less than logical. That said, Henry knew only too well that even apparently bizarre actions by offenders may well be rooted in deep-seated motivations and consistent with them.

The problem Henry had was that he was coming in cold to review two murders that were months old, and getting the 'feel' of them would be hard. Nor did it help that the SIO was no longer available – he was dead. Jack Culver's thought processes would have been useful to mine but Henry wasn't going to get them – unless there was something in the murder books other than just a blow-by-blow account of the investigations. Henry would also have to rely on the cooperation and support of the officer who had inherited the investigations.

That, too, Henry knew, could be delicate. Probing questions could easily upset them, and they could feel that they were being sidelined if he didn't tread carefully.

Looking at the cover sheets of the murder books, he saw that the lead investigator in each was the same person, DCI J. Runcie, who ran Portsea's Serious Crime Team.

That would at least simplify some aspects of his enquiries. One single point of contact for both who, he hoped, would play ball with him and not make him feel he was having his nose shoved out of joint.

He would be gentle with the guy.

Henry reopened the murder book relating to Mark James Wright, which chronologically recorded the progress of the investigation from the notification of the crime. He jotted down some notes on a pad as he read through under the headings of 'Location', 'Victim', 'Offender', 'Scene Forensics', 'Post-Mortem', 'Method of Investigation' and 'Fast-Track Options'.

It was all fairly basic stuff for an experienced detective, let alone an SIO. The key was never to take anything for granted, not to get tunnel vision.

'So, Mark James Wright,' Henry said to himself, 'what got *you* murdered?'

An almost forty-year-old man had, seemingly, been dragged out of his vehicle on a lonely country road and stabbed to death in a brutal, frenzied attack. He'd had thirty-eight puncture wounds in him, the fatal ones being six to his heart. A horrible, painful death.

Wright was a single, divorced man from further up the coast in Sunderland. He ran a small business hiring out diggers and screeners and all sorts of other heavy machinery associated with the excavation and reclamation of stone and rubble back into hard core, usually from buildings that were being demolished. It was the sort of trade Henry knew little about, one of those businesses that was very much under the radar for the general public, but lucrative nonetheless.

Wright had been found on a country road, lying in a field close to a lay-by in which his car was parked, engine still running. It appeared he'd been forcibly taken from the car and killed, his body then dumped over a low hedge. The road was a minor one which led north from the docks at Portsea, next stop Sunderland.

There were no witnesses, no CCTV cameras, and no sign of Wright's mobile phone, although Henry guessed he would have had one. He was in the kind of business where one would be an invaluable tool of his trade.

Wright's movements prior to the discovery of his body were unknown.

No actual motive for the murder had been uncovered either.

Yet while Henry already appreciated the difficulties inherent in the location of this murder, he knew that no one gets dragged out of a car in the middle of nowhere and then mutilated without having upset someone somewhere along the line.

The other two adages Henry always applied to murder investigations, though he acknowledged they were slightly corny, were also flashing across his mind like a neon sign.

Firstly: *Why + when + where + how = Who.*

Secondly: *Find out how a person lived and you will find out why and how they died.*

The old ones, he thought, were the best.

Henry read on, then moved to look at actual crime-scene photographs and a report from a pathologist who had visited the scene and subsequently carried out the post-mortem, which identified the type of knife used to murder Wright: a seven-inch one with a serrated blade, probably a kitchen knife, never found. He read further details of the progress of the investigation, which seemed to have gone nowhere fast.

Wright's personal and professional business lives seemed to have been delved into quite deeply, but had turned up nothing – no suspects, no witnesses.

Henry's mouth turned down at the corners, unimpressed by this.

He began to stiffen up, the combination of the fall and the half-healed bullet wound seeming to intensify as he sat there. He groaned as he moved, then flicked back through the crime-scene photographs.

Wright's car in a lay-by on a country road, engine still ticking over and, from the report of the first officer on the scene, with the indicator still blinking away.

Did this mean Wright had pulled in willingly, or did it have no significance?

On his pad, Henry wrote, *Someone he knew? Road rage incident?*

Henry went back on to the internet and Google-mapped his way to the scene, then switched to satellite view and then the street level one so he was actually on the road, and then, using his mouse, he travelled along the same road and reached the lay-by, where he pulled in and looked around, 360 degrees. It was a flat, agricultural area, ploughed fields on either side of the road. Henry noticed this image had been recorded two years earlier, but at least it gave him a sense of location.

He returned to the murder book and completed his skim-reading, noting that DCI Runcie had been the first senior detective on the scene on the night of the murder, obviously having been called out to it. He thought nothing more of that.

What did catch his eye was the final undated entry, written by the late Jack Culver. It was scribbled and not signed, but by now Henry recognized the dead man's handwriting.

It said simply, *What is going on here?*

The final words Culver had written in this murder book.

Henry frowned. It seemed a strange question to be asking.

He closed the book, leaned back, rolled his shoulder to ease some movement back into it, then stood up and glanced at the wall clock: 11.15 p.m.

In spite of licensing hours now almost being a thing of the past, Alison was strict about closing time for non-residents in The Tawny Owl. They were booted out of the doors by 11.30 p.m. on weekday nights, which gave Henry quarter of an hour to hobble into the bar and maybe catch a last drink with some of the regulars.

*   *   *

Chief Constable John Burnham enjoyed a pleasant early evening
meal with FB at an Indian restaurant on the A59 at Much Hoole,
a couple of miles away from Lancashire Police headquarters. He
had a lot to discuss with him, but only had time for a quick,
bullet-point chat because Burnham wanted to get going. He
intended to call in and stay the night with his widowed mother
at her house in Bacup, close to the West Yorkshire border. He
did not see her enough as his new job of breathing life into a
seriously poorly police force kept him overwhelmingly busy. But
he'd seen an opportunity to visit her on his way back and wasn't
going to renege on his promise.

After leaving FB, Burnham headed east, finally picking up the
M65, which took him into the depths of Lancashire before coming
off the motorway and taking the Grane Road over high, desolate
moorland and dropping into the Rossendale Valley. He wound
through to Bacup, took the Todmorden Road and stopped outside
the house in which he'd been born almost fifty years earlier.

It was a spacious, three-story terraced house and, as Burnham
stepped in and announced his arrival, he felt warm and comfortable instantly – and suddenly very hungry, too. Even though he'd
eaten a curry a short time ago, the aroma of his mum's baking
had its usual effect on his taste buds.

She fussed over him, served her beautiful sticky parkin and
tea, and they had a lovely catch-up before her head began to nod
after the soap operas had finished and she retired to bed.

As far as Burnham was concerned, it was still early, even
though his old bed in his old bedroom was beckoning him with
its warmth and familiarity. Though exhausted, he still had paperwork to do before allowing himself to retreat upstairs. He muted
the TV, poured himself a tot of his mum's favourite tipple – cheap
whisky from Spar – and opened his case that was bursting with
paperwork, all requiring his immediate attention, or so it seemed.

At least he'd got one thing sorted that had been preying on
his mind for too long: unsolved murders.

He remembered Henry Christie from the police training centre
– but only because he'd thought of him not so much as one of
the class idiots but as a wild young man who was more interested
in bedding policewomen (and, as in one famous, 'true' myth,
having sex with a very willing young lady cop on the bonnet of

the centre commandant's car) than taking his work seriously. Although, if he recalled correctly, Henry was pretty much a natural cop whereas he, Burnham, had to graft bloody hard at it.

From what he knew of Henry's history since then, his life had been a series of ups and downs, but the driving force behind him was his absolute dedication to catching killers and his incorruptibility: two things Burnham knew would be key to Henry's review of the murders if he took them on. He screwed his face up with a bit of discomfort, feeling slightly guilty that he hadn't been completely open with Henry about some of his worries regarding the two cases.

He put those thoughts to one side and opened a new report on intelligence-led policing in the Central Yorkshire Police (or the lack of it), and began to scan its uncomfortable conclusions. To say the least, his force was a good ten years behind all the other forces in the region.

'Shit,' he breathed, then took a sip of the harsh whisky.

Much to Henry's astonishment, the bar at The Tawny Owl turned out to be quite light in respect of the punters he liked to spend time with, so he did a swift exit and returned to the living accommodation with a tot of his own whisky.

He got changed for bed, slid between the cool covers and opened up murder book two. He began to read the report of a murder that had happened almost six months earlier.

The rather stilted way in which the *modus operandi* had been written went no way to summing up what had happened that night and, as Henry read it, he knew that, quite possibly, he would never know for certain.

Tom Salter's office was spare, an old desk, old filing cabinets, grubby mugs and a cheap coffee machine gurgling away, dripping as he stood by the window, looking through the slats of a Venetian blind on to his extensive yard below. The office was on the first floor above an industrial unit packed with HGV tractor units in various stages of repair. Corresponding low-loading trailers were parked in the yard, and beyond them were a few rows of stacked containers which could be offloaded from ships on to the trailers, their contents dispersed across the country.

Salter's fingertips opened up a gap in the blinds.

He blinked and gasped as his heart pounded remorselessly, terrified of what he was about to do.

The gate to the yard was unlocked and wide open.

Behind him, the coffee machine hissed steam, announcing the filtering had stopped.

Salter stepped back into the office, poured a black coffee and laced it with brandy. His fingers dithered as he picked up the cracked mug and took a sip. It was hot and harsh, burning its way down his chest, and he gasped again, his heart pounding.

Part of him hoped he would simply have a heart attack. At least it would give him an easy way out if it killed him.

He sat down on his office chair, feeling it rock unsteadily on its fulcrum. It needed to be replaced. One day soon, it would collapse.

Closing his eyes after another sip of the coffee, those other eyes came back to haunt him again.

Even in that short glimpse, he had seen their colour and their terror.

Brown. Dark brown. The colour that Tom Salter now associated with that terror.

He knew very little of the girl's actual journey, only that his involvement with her began in Turkey and had ended here, almost a week later, in his yard in Portsea, when the aerated container had been unlocked and prised open. Up to that point in Turkey, he could only guess at what she had endured, could only slot information together based on snippets of truckers' gossip. What he did know was that she had already been abused, and once he'd handed her over for the next stage of her journey – destination Manchester – she would become a household sex slave for a wealthy Mancunian businessman who was currently building two new skyscrapers in that thriving city.

And after that? When the limit of her usefulness had been reached?

Salter had no idea. Nothing good is all he knew.

There were five other girls with her, all from different backgrounds, countries and cultures but each sharing a similar story – hope dashed by dangerous unscrupulous villains, not all men – the life of promised riches and freedom never to materialize.

Salter was part of that.

His own foolishness had made him a cog in the wheel, but now he wanted out.

The mug trembled in his hand.

The sound of a car, a flash of headlights through the blinds, the car stopping, the engine switched off.

She was here.

He placed the cup down and walked back to the window. Her Citroën was parked alongside his car. He could see two figures in it – one in the front seat and one in the back. There was a pause, then the woman got out, followed by a man. The security lighting above the office door came on, illuminating them harshly in the yellow glow. The woman raised her face briefly, then entered ahead of the man, who did not look up. Salter frowned, unable to determine exactly what the man was wearing. His first thought was that it was a white tracksuit with the hood pulled over his head.

He heard footsteps on the wooden, uncarpeted stairs. The woman came in. Her face was set hard, like granite.

The man was just behind her.

It was not a tracksuit he was wearing. It was a full-body crime-scene suit.

'I'm glad you could come. I need to talk,' Salter said. He and the woman were on opposite sides of the desk. Her expression had not changed – it was still as cold as steel. In fact, Salter never recalled her letting that mask slip, which was a shame because she was too good looking to keep the hard look fixed all the time.

The man stayed by the door, leaning on the frame.

His face was hard to distinguish with the hood pulled tight around his head, and Salter's eyes continually flickered past the woman's shoulders, particularly now that he had worked out what the man was wearing and what was in his hand.

'You worried me; you worried us,' the woman said.

Salter nodded. 'I know.'

She gave him a, Go on, then, gesture.

'I want out. I can't go on.'

'Can't or won't?'

'*Does it matter?*'

'*There's a difference. Can't means you've got terminal cancer – won't is a self-made decision,*' she said, defining the terms.

'*All I'm saying is this: it's over. I'm out. My involvement is done. You'll have to find a new transporter.*' He said it quickly, with more conviction than he felt.

The woman sighed with annoyance, then shook her head. '*You need to remember that you owe everything to me . . . your freedom and your wealth. I saved you from going to prison for a long, long time and you owe me – us – big time.*'

'*Yeah, you're right,*' he admitted.

'*And you do not have the right to pull out of this . . . too many people are involved in this enterprise now. Too many people who do not like being fucked around with . . . especially Mr Tullane. I wouldn't have thought you needed reminding of that, Tom.*'

'*I'm presuming that guy is from Tullane?*' Salter gestured to the man by the door. '*Here to intimidate me?*'

What he could see of the man's face remained impassive.

Salter took in the man's clothing again and swallowed.

'*Here to kill me?*' he asked.

The man by the door folded his arms. Salter's nostrils flared at the sight of the automatic pistol in his hand. He could feel his chest constricting. Casually, the man pulled a surgical mask down to cover the lower half of his face.

'*Not necessarily,*' the woman said.

'*Nothing's changing,*' Salter said boldly. '*I'm out. I can't stand the suffering, can't stand being part of it. I don't like being a people trafficker among all the other stuff I do for you and Tullane. I appreciate what you did for me, but I've got a conscience and I can't go on living with this shit! I won't say anything to anyone . . . just cut me loose.*'

'*If only it were so easy,*' she said. '*Not gonna happen. Business is business, promises are promises.*'

'*And preying on the vulnerable is unforgivable,*' Salter cut in.

His eyes went to the man again, who remained immobile. Maybe he was just there as an idle threat.

As though the woman could read his thoughts, she smiled and said, '*This man kills people for a living, especially people who double-cross Mr Tullane . . . Ah, ah, ah,*' she said, raising a finger as Salter opened his mouth to defend himself. 'Letting him down, letting me down, is akin to a double-cross in Tullane's world,' she explained, defining the terms again.

'I said I won't go to the cops, the real cops, DCI Runcie.'

He saw the woman's face twitch. 'You used my name. Why did you do that?'

'No reason.' His mouth had gone very dry.

'Y'see . . . can't happen . . . this cannot happen,' she told him.

Trying to take command, Salter said, 'I'll tell you what – if you don't get out of here now, I will call the cops, right here, right now. So take your fucking scary henchman with you and go – that's it, done, dusted. Tell Tullane I'm sorry but I don't fuck twelve-year-old kids, nor do I condone anyone else doing it. I'm not part of this now, DCI Runcie.' He saw her wince at the mention of her name again. 'I made a big fuckin' mistake, but now it's over, end of.'

'You'll regret this. Not for long, but you will.'

Salter believed her. Something like this would haunt him forever.

He took out his mobile phone from his jacket pocket and placed it on the desk between them. 'I'm a fool, but not stupid. It's all been recorded.'

The woman's eyes dropped to the device. She licked her lips. 'So we can't actually trust you.'

'You can. This is my insurance. I give you my word so long as you go now.'

'I'm afraid you have commitments. Packages are en route as we speak.'

'Packages?' spat Salter. 'Is that what you call them? To distance yourself from the horror you perpetrate?' He jabbed a finger in her direction. 'These packages are people – kids for fuck's sake!' He was bereft of further words.

'And there are also goods leaving these shores,' Runcie informed him, unfazed by his tirade.

'Well, they can fucking well stay where they are,' he said and leaned back in his chair, which creaked. 'Out,' he said. 'Now.'

There was a pause as the protagonists either side of the table surveyed each other.

'You really are a fool,' the woman said at length.

She crossed to the window and stood with her back to it, arms folded.

Salter saw the miniscule jerk of her head and knew he was about to die.

The man in the forensic suit moved swiftly. No preamble, just straight to business. He was across the room in a flash, unfolding his arms, extending his right arm as he reached the edge of the desk, with the pistol pointed directly at Salter. He pulled the trigger four times, no hesitation or gap between the shots, firing into Salter's face and skull – two just above the eyes, one on either side of his nose. They were soft-tipped bullets, designed to mushroom on impact, destroy flesh, bone and organ tissue, tearing a huge exit hole in the back of his head, smashing the man against the back of his chair with blood and brain matter spraying everywhere, on the chair and on the wall behind, leaving an almost cartoonish silhouette outlined on the wall.

Salter may have slammed backwards, but there was also the forward splatter of his blood, which flicked up the killer's right arm and chest.

Runcie watched the murder without compassion.

A thin pink mist rose from the back of Salter's chair.

Runcie exhaled and crossed over to the desk, taking out a large plastic ziplock bag, which she opened and the killer dropped the weapon into it. She did not make eye contact with him.

Next, she picked up Salter's phone and deleted the recording he had just made.

Burnham didn't even know he had fallen asleep until he jerked awake having heard a noise. The heavy whisky glass thudded on to the floor from his grip, but that wasn't what had wakened him. He exhaled with a snort-cum-snore and wondered what had done so.

A creaking noise of some description.

'Ugh.' He rubbed his neck, then placed the sheaf of papers he had been reading – and dozed off over – from his lap on to the coffee table.

Then he froze, the hairs on the back of his neck prickling.

Another noise.

Burnham could not have identified the first one, a sort of

cracking sound of some sort, but the second one was obvious. The metallic clatter of the letter box in the front door.

He looked at the clock on the mantelpiece. Almost one a.m.

He rose from the chair and stepped into the hallway, looking towards the front door just at the moment the letter box flipped shut: someone was peering in from the road outside.

Burnham went completely still, wondering if whoever it was had spotted him.

Then there was a repeat of the first noise that had awoken him, and Burnham recognized it for what it was.

A jemmy or some such similar implement being inserted between the door frame and the lock, slowly splitting the wood as an intruder gently eased the wood away from around the mortice lock. It was a solid hardwood door, without any windows, that had been in place as long as Burnham could remember. The lower edge had rotted and been repaired by a joiner a few years ago, so there was a likelihood that more of it was rotten, too, even though he did try to treat it with preservative every year.

As such, it was an easy obstacle for a half-determined burglar to negotiate.

In his career as a cop, Burnham had not yet met a burglar he could not tackle.

He crept towards the door, staying close to the wall.

There was more 'crowbarring' activity, wood splintering and hushed voices, so at least two of them, he thought as his blood started to surge through his veins with the excitement and rage of the situation. It was a while since he had come face-to-face with a burglar – one of the most despicable types of criminal in his eyes, an invader of property.

And in this case, his defenceless mother's property.

He was seriously looking forward to the door swinging open and scaring the living shit out of the two shites on the other side who dared to invade this home.

He was almost rehearsing the words in his head. Something Clint Eastwood-like, he thought.

More splintering.

The old door actually moved up a little on its hinges.

And then the mortice was worked free.

The door was pushed open.

Burnham decided not to go for anything clever and simply said, 'Got you, you cunts. You're under arrest.'

He saw two dark shapes – men, not kids as he'd anticipated.

But that was all his mind really processed.

That and the blur of speed as the twenty-four-inch T-type wrecking bar (with a double-clawed head) used to gain entry whooshed through the air and was imbedded in his skull. With a blinding flash of light and pain, it penetrated his brain and killed him instantly.

Henry did not recall closing the murder book but he must have done because, when he awoke, Alison was sliding wearily into bed alongside him and the book was on the bedside cabinet, closed.

He was lying on his right-hand side in what he called his 'sleep mode', which was essentially the recovery position. Alison snuggled carefully into him and, as always, he felt a tremor of excitement as her breasts crushed softly into his back. Though battered and bruised, stiff and sore, her presence behind him overrode any of these drawbacks. The rush of blood to his genitals never seemed to be an issue – particularly when her hand snaked around him, slid over his belly and grasped him.

'I will be gentle,' she promised, breathing hotly into his ear. 'I was a nurse, you know.'

'Did you treat all your male patients like this?'

'Every single one of them.'

SIX

Henry slept heavily, the combination of tiredness, drugs and sex knocking him into a deep, dreamless sleep. He woke briefly after five hours when Alison's alarm rang and she immediately hauled herself out into the shower. He had a few moments of awe at her unceasing energy levels which put his to shame – then he closed his eyes and fell asleep again and did not even hear her come out of the shower and get dressed.

She did reappear at seven a.m. with a glass of orange juice

for him. She perched on the edge of the bed as he sat up, rubbing his face and making a strange grunting noise.

'I assume you are going to do FB's bidding?' she asked, knowing the way in which the chief constable used Henry. 'You are going to review those murders across the other side of the Pennines, aren't you?'

'In enemy territory?' Henry said, making reference to the centuries-old rivalry, sometimes murderous and bloody, between Lancashire and Yorkshire.

She nodded. 'Nothing I can say will make a difference, will it?'

He shrugged guiltily. 'I'll get Doctor Lott to sign me back on to light duties today,' he said.

Now she shook her head and said, 'What're you like?'

'Lovely?' he ventured hopefully.

He came back from Dr Lott's surgery with the necessary documentation in hand, waving the forms like Neville Chamberlain returning from his business trip to Nazi Germany. While in the surgery, Lott had given him the once-over, prodding and poking him roughly, and also had a look at the bruises sustained from yesterday's fall down the cellar steps, all of which had come out well.

'You could have been killed,' Lott muttered. 'Fourteen concrete steps, you say? Quite a fall.'

'Tell me about it.'

Henry found Alison behind the bar, polishing shelves and glasses.

'Signed me back, knew he would,' he told her. 'Now I need to give FB a ring and confirm it.'

Alison rubbed a pint glass with a cloth. 'You might not have to.'

'Why?'

She gestured brusquely to the dining room on the other side of the entrance foyer. 'Someone to see you,' she said with a clipped tone. Then she gave Henry a meaningful look which he didn't understand until she said, 'I think your chaperone has arrived. Your very *pretty* chaperone.'

'Man or woman?'

Her expression could have withered grapes off the vine. 'Female.'

'Sounds just my type.'

There were two couples from overnight having full English breakfasts in the dining room and just the one lone woman sitting at a table in the bay window overlooking the front of the pub. Her back was to Henry as he entered, and he realized she must have watched him return from the doctor's.

He helped himself to a coffee from the 'serve yourself' filter machine on the table next to the Continental breakfast selection, then approached her, noting the lines of her tightly braided hair, slim shoulders underneath a well-fitting suit jacket, then, as she turned, the amazing complexion of her black skin, the stunning beauty of her face and dark brown eyes, wide lips and perfect teeth as she smiled and stood awkwardly when Henry said, 'I believe you want to see me.'

'Oh, Mr Christie, yes, yes,' she said hurriedly, thrusting out a fine, long-fingered hand.

Henry transferred his mug of coffee to his left hand and shook hers.

'Can I help you?' he asked.

'Oh, yes, my name's Diane Daniels, er, DC Daniels, that is . . .' She pulled out her warrant card for Henry to see. 'I've just been transferred from Preston CID on to the Serious and Organised Crime Unit at HQ and Mr Bayley, the chief, asked me if I'd be interested in accompanying you over to Central Yorkshire. Apparently you've been asked to review two murder cases. He said you needed some assistance . . . like a driver . . . even though I'm not anyone's driver,' she babbled on.

Henry had been holding on to her hand as she spoke – rather liking the texture of her skin, and gripping a tad longer than absolutely necessary – but he disengaged as she finished talking.

His eyes narrowed. 'What? A driver?'

'I'm not a driver,' she insisted. 'I just jumped at the chance, that's all. Sounded interesting.'

'Not sure I need an assistant.'

'Mr Bayley was just concerned about you,' she said, unable to prevent her eyes dipping to Henry's shoulder. 'You've been shot . . . I know all about that, sir. He did also say you're a bit of a technophobe . . . I'm pretty good with all that kinda stuff.'

Henry was feeling uncomfortable. 'Mr Bayley, as you call him – let's call him FB, by the way – has never given a toss about me. Now he wants to nanny me?'

'I'm not a driver and I'm not a nanny, Mr Christie. I'm a detective and I just think this is a good opportunity for me to learn something. I've been on the Child Protection Unit and the local CID and now I'm on SOCU. Ultimately I'd like to be a murder detective on FMIT . . . It's just an opportunity,' she finished. Then re-started. 'I know you've been injured and, actually, I don't mind driving you.'

'But you're not a driver?'

'Exactly.'

'Fancy a coffee?'

As an SIO on FMIT, Henry knew many detectives across the force of all ranks, but somehow he'd missed Diane Daniels along the way. It happened. It was impossible for him to know every single one.

Henry handed her the two murder books and a mug of coffee, then, with his own brew in hand, he left her to scan the documents while he went outside and drank his on the front terrace, working in his mind's eye what The Tawny Owl might look like in the future. At the moment, the terrace was underused – just a couple of old picnic benches and a place for smokers to sneak out to – but ultimately he and Alison wanted to extend the whole thing so customers could sit out and eat.

He sat on the low wall, looking across the wide expanse of the village green and over the stream to the rising woods beyond, once more realizing how much he loved this spot and how fate had made him stagger into the village a few years earlier with his FBI friend, Karl Donaldson. Here they had found themselves in the middle of a blood-soaked standoff between two dangerous gangs. At the same time, he had met Alison, and circumstances, though tragic in the extreme, had led him eventually into her arms.

He waved at one of the villagers trudging past with a couple of gun dogs foraging ahead of him and a broken shotgun over his shoulder.

'Oh, Kate.' He sighed sadly when speaking his dead wife's name.

'Who's Kate?'

Henry spun at Diane Daniels' question. 'No one,' he said guiltily.

'Oh, OK.' She had the murder books tucked under her arm.

Henry nodded towards them. 'Any thoughts?'

She settled on the wall next to him. 'Uh . . . two very different types of killing . . . both brutal in the extreme, both against lone males. One could simply be bad luck, wrong road, wrong time; the other was very definitely premeditated, attacking a man in his office in the early hours. Both could be robbery motivated.'

'MO says that Salter's office was ransacked, though it's not known what, if anything, was taken; likewise the other guy, Wright, can't say if anything was stolen from him either.'

'The investigators seem to think Salter's was a robbery gone wrong and the other could have been a road-rage incident gone wrong.'

'Maybe, maybe not. Could be that they've been tunnel-visioned into those lines of thought, which may be why both jobs have stalled.' Henry scratched his head. 'Did you see Jack Culver's scribble – *What is going on here?* – in one of the margins?'

'Jack Culver?'

'The dead SIO.'

'Oh, yeah – yes, I did.'

'Maybe he died before he got the chance to start opening up the enquiries.'

'Could be,' Daniels agreed.

'Anything else?' Henry asked.

'Lots of things, I suppose.'

'In that case, let's chat about them on the way over, driver.'

'So I'm still going, then?'

'Yeah, why not?'

She gave a fist-punch gesture. 'I booked a hotel, by the way.'

'Really? So it was a done deal?'

'Well, uh, no, maybe . . . FB said I should.' She smiled sweetly.

'I'll give him a ring, then.'

*　　*　　*

Alison watched Henry packing a small holdall and hanging two suits and shirts in a suit carrier.

'So you're going away with another woman?'

He smiled and wriggled his eyebrows.

'Suddenly your injuries don't seem quite so serious or debilitating,' she chided him. Her arms were folded underneath her cleavage. Henry wondered if this was a deliberate ploy just to remind him what he was leaving behind. Surely not, he thought. Alison went on, 'She's very pretty. And young.'

'And, apart from anything else, wearing what looks suspiciously like an engagement ring.'

'You noticed. You checked her out.'

''Course I bloody did. I'm a man with red-hot blood coursing through my veins – although most of it did belong to someone else previously,' he said, joking about his transfusion.

She sighed. Her face cracked into a cheeky grin.

'I almost thought you were being serious,' Henry admitted.

'As if . . . look, I just don't want you to get hurt by going back to work too soon, that's all. Don't want you overdoing it.'

'I won't, promise.' He drew her tenderly towards him, nuzzling her neck with his nose. As ever, despite being on the go for hours, she smelled amazing. 'Besides which, I've got a driver now – and if necessary, she can double up as a masseuse.'

Alison punched him hard on his good arm.

DC Daniels' car was a rather battered-looking but serviceable and comfortable green Peugeot 406, probably fifteen years old, with a diesel engine that fired up first time but still sounded like a tractor.

Henry slumped into the well-worn passenger seat and looked at Daniels.

'It was my father's,' she said apologetically. 'I inherited it when he died and don't have the heart to get rid of it . . . it's only done one hundred and fifty thousand miles.'

'A mere baby,' Henry said. Then, 'Sorry to hear about your dad.'

'It's OK . . . He was only sixty-two . . . Dementia, unbeliev-ably . . . Bastard disease,' she said, and Henry saw the wounds were still raw.

'Your mum still around?'

'Oh, yeah, fit as a fiddle. On the council, busybody, nosy parker . . .'

'So that's where you get it from?'

'Quite possibly. Anyway . . .' She took a breath and gripped the steering wheel. 'How do we get to Yorkshire?'

'Head east. Aim for Kirby Lonsdale, then drive down to pick up the A59, which should just about take us in the right direction.'

'I was kidding.' She reached for something in the door pocket and revealed a satnav with a flourish. She turned it on, then looked expectantly at Henry. 'Destination postcode?'

'Don't have one,' he confessed. 'I was just going to head east until I hit the coast. When we get going I'll give Central Yorkshire a call and ask for one. In the meantime, let's just get going?'

'Have you heard back from FB yet?' Daniels asked, putting the car into gear.

Henry shook his head. 'Apparently he's been turned out to some job or other, which must be pretty serious to get him out of bed.'

Daniels reversed out of the parking space. Henry gave Alison a wave and then they were on the road, heading out of Kendleton.

Henry directed Daniels back along the twisty road away from the village and on to the main A683. Without even consulting a map, he knew the best way would be to aim for Harrogate and York first. After that, he hoped to have the postcode in his possession.

As Daniels drove, Henry asked her a few questions and she talked a little about her background. Her grandparents had come from Nigeria in the fifties with her father and settled in Preston, where her grandad worked as a coffee trader as, subsequently, did her father, building up a moderately successful import and wholesale business, together with a popular café in Preston. Her dad met her mother, who had emigrated with her parents from Kenya, although there was some Asian blood in her, she explained.

'Hence,' Daniels said, taking both hands off the steering wheel and framing her face with them, thumbs touching, 'my beautiful complexion.' She smiled broadly and re-grabbed the wheel just before the car swerved off the road.

'No comment from me on that score,' Henry said, and saw her smile shyly.

She told him she had no desire to go into the family business and it had been sold to a local chain of supermarkets as her dad's Alzheimer's became more apparent.

'Always wanted to be a cop and got into Lancashire dead easy, I suppose. Then I became a DC on Child Protection and now I'm on SOCU.'

She never revealed her age, but Henry guessed it to be around the thirty mark.

As they reached the junction with the A683, Henry's mobile phone rang.

'Detective Superintendent Christie,' he said. 'Yeah . . . just about to go to Central Yorkshire . . . What? Really?' Henry glanced at Daniels with a worried expression. 'Yeah . . . say that address again . . . yeah, we're on our way, boss. We? Me and DC Daniels . . . yep . . . forty, forty-five minutes . . . We're not far off the M6 now . . . OK, bye.' He ended the call, then turned to Daniels, who had stopped at the junction. She had waited there, picking up the gist of the conversation. 'Change of plan,' he said.

It took just under fifty minutes for Henry and Daniels to get to Bacup and find the address on Todmorden Road, which was fairly easy. Henry had spent part of his early career in Rossendale and retained a good memory of the geography of the valley, also having returned over the years to deal with murders, and he certainly knew the main routes through without a satnav, Todmorden Road being one of them.

The road rose from the roundabout in the centre of the small town and instantly began to climb. On a straight, rising incline about a quarter of a mile out of town, Henry saw a lot of police activity ahead. That half the road had been cordoned off and temporary traffic lights erected.

'Pull in here,' Henry told Daniels. She stopped. 'We'll walk in the rest of the way.'

Henry knew this was not going to be his job, but that didn't mean he wouldn't approach it in his usual way. 'Upwind, with the sun at my back,' he often quipped. Wherever possible, he liked to stroll up slowly from a distance to any murder scene, giving himself time to get his brain into gear and make early assessments.

The front of the terraced house at the centre of the police activity was screened off from rubberneckers and he could see a tent-like awning had also been erected around the front door.

'What's happened?' Daniels asked.

'I know as much as you, which isn't very much,' he told her. Then he frowned, about to ask her if she had ever been to a murder before. But he stopped himself, not wanting to appear patronizing or sexist. What would be, would be. 'Let's stroll.'

They crossed the road and walked slowly towards the property, Henry starting to get a feel for the location, which was very rural and quite wild. Less than a minute's drive from Bacup town centre, they were essentially on the moors.

The house was a stone-built mid-terrace, built over three storeys, the ground floor and first floor accessible from the road, with a third level, basically a basement, accessible from a driveway at the rear. It was a good, solid house, common in this area.

Henry walked slowly – still stiff from his fall – noting the line of police cars, vans and personnel, both uniform and plainclothes, and several in forensic suits and masks. The entry to the scene was through a slit in the screen, guarded by a PC in uniform armed with a clipboard noting all comings and goings, signing people in and out and also distributing the protective suits.

He noticed FB's Jaguar parked a little way down the road. As he and Daniels approached the screen, it slid open slightly and FB himself, dressed in one of the plastic suits, stepped out, followed by another cop Henry knew, also similarly besuited, DCI Rik Dean, one of Henry's friends and also a member of FMIT. The two men saw him at the same time and approached him with very sombre faces.

Henry knew that crime scenes were precious and, because this was not his case, he did not really want to add to the number of size-eleven boots that may have already trampled on this particular scene. But he had been asked along and therefore wanted a look, so with Rik Dean's blessing, he climbed into a forensic suit – nicknamed a Zoot suit – and invited Daniels to do the same.

Rik Dean then led them back through the slit in the screen to the front door of the house, where a crime-scene investigator was closely examining the damaged door, photographing it and dusting and swabbing the splintered wood for prints and DNA.

'Door jemmied,' Rik said. 'There's been quite a few burglaries around here recently, apparently.'

Henry paused, squatted down a few inches and peered at the marks in the door frame.

'Not a common MO for doors,' he mused. 'Does it link with the MOs of the other breaks?'

'I don't know just yet,' Rik said. 'I'm on with that now . . . but I do know that it was also the murder weapon. It's not really called a jemmy – it's a wrecking bar, apparently.' He turned to the CSI. 'May we?' The man stood aside and slowly Rik pushed the door open with his gloved knuckle to reveal the hallway and the body lying in it.

The wrecking bar was still imbedded in the dead man's head. He was lying in a large pool of coagulating blood.

Rik stepped in carefully, his feet treading on the specially laid plastic pads that everyone having business at the scene would have to use to enter, thereby preserving as much evidence as possible.

Henry and Daniels followed his footsteps.

Henry said nothing, kept his hands by his sides and just looked around. He heard Daniels emit a tiny squeak.

'Looks like a burglary gone wrong,' Rik said.

'Talk me through it,' Henry told him.

Rik cleared his throat. 'We know he came here after leaving the chief yesterday evening. He'd told Mr Bayley he was going to spend the night here before getting back to the force later today. This is his mother's house, by the way. She's with a neighbour at the moment and a family liaison officer. According to her, they spent some time chatting, then she went to bed. He stayed up. She thinks he was doing paperwork or something. It looks like he disturbed the offenders coming in through the front door and, in a panic, they whacked him.'

'Bit extreme,' Henry said, looking along the body of John

Burnham, a man he had been in conversation with not much more than twelve hours ago.

Behind him, Daniels caught her breath again.

He turned. 'You OK?'

She nodded.

'Do we know if anything's been stolen?' Henry asked Rik.

'Not yet.'

'Who found the body?'

'Some guy walking past with his dog . . . checked out, no connection,' he said, referring to the man.

Henry nodded, then looked Rik in the eye. 'Is everything in motion?'

'Yep, and the Home Office pathologist is due . . . it's Professor Baines.'

That was good. Baines was the best there was.

'In that case, I'll leave it with you.' He looked at Daniels. 'Are we done here?'

She nodded eagerly, wanting to get away.

Daniels tore off her forensic suit and threw it at the officer who was issuing and taking them back, then scurried out through the slit in the screen, leaving Henry to peel his off slowly and hand it back for auditing purposes, signing the return sheet for himself and Daniels.

He found her fifty metres down the road, leaning against the stone wall with her face buffeting the fresh wind blowing in from the moors. Her complexion now did not look so great.

'How're you doing?' Henry asked.

'I wouldn't mind, but it's not my first murder scene. Just the cold brutality of it . . .' she explained. 'How do you keep so cool?'

'I don't,' Henry divulged. 'Not really. I just know I have a job to do and there are certain expectations on me, one of which is to take it in my stride. Underneath, I remain a blubbering mess.'

She looked at him, astonished. 'Seriously?'

'Really, really.' He patted her shoulder. 'Let's go and see what the boss has to say.' He set off towards FB's Jaguar. The man himself was leaning against it, talking on his mobile phone. He finished whatever conversation he was having and faced Henry.

'What do you think?' he asked Henry.

'Well, like Rik says, it could be a burglary gone wrong – or he was targeted. This area's been hit by a few break-ins recently, so if the MO is similar to those, then we could just be looking for the local Billy Burglar who panicked, which should be a fairly easy arrest. Even if the MO doesn't quite fit, I'd still be rounding up the locals and solving those crimes as a by-product.' He hesitated.

'You don't think it was a burglary, do you?' FB said.

'I don't know what to think, though my other hypothesis is that Mr Burnham has been deliberately targeted. I have no earthly reason to speculate why that should be so, though. I'd be keeping my options wide open . . . Anyway, Rik knows what he's doing. He's had a great mentor.'

FB nodded, not rising to Henry's accolade of himself. He went to lean on the wall overlooking the fields. 'He was quite a good mate, Henry.'

'Oh, right . . . I didn't know.'

'Aye, well . . . anyhow . . . I've been ringing round as you can imagine . . . my phone's fucking red hot.'

'Does this affect what Mr Burnham wanted me to do in Central Yorkshire?'

'That's what some of the calls have been about. I've spoken to the Home Secretary, the Central Yorkshire Crime Commissioner . . . and the bottom line is that, for the immediate future, I've been given a watching brief over that force until everything's sorted in terms of a replacement for him. Short answer: yes, you can start a review of those murders, so away you go. You're on light duties, so you shouldn't even be here.'

Suddenly FB clutched his chest and the colour drained out of his face.

'Boss, you OK?'

'Yeah, yeah, yeah . . . just sometimes get bad heartburn. Go . . . you go.'

'You're going to kill me,' Henry said. He looked sideways at Daniels.

They hadn't gone far, maybe four miles at most, but Henry could see she wasn't concentrating on her driving, her mind very much elsewhere. He had directed her to drive over to Todmorden, which was in West Yorkshire, then to take the Halifax Road, which would continue to take them due east. But she was not with it.

Henry spotted a café and told her to pull in.

'Let's get a brew and recoup.'

She nodded, tight-lipped. 'I'd like that.'

They parked opposite, a little further down the road, and walked back to the establishment, which was called The Little Bird Café. It had a few chairs and tables set out on the pavement and it was just about warm enough to sit out. Henry left her and went in to order a couple of mugs of tea, which he came out bearing, and sat opposite her at the small table.

She gripped the mug for its warmth. 'I'm feeling a bit girlie.' She exhaled unsteadily. 'I've dealt with numerous child abuse cases, rapes, domestic assaults, some really horrible stuff . . . and I have been to a couple of murder scenes, so I don't know what it is. It just took me by surprise, and the fact he was a cop and in his mum's house. God!' she gasped. 'I'm really annoyed with myself. Must look a right tool . . . I've been a detective for four years!'

'No, you don't. It's only natural. Sometimes it all catches me by surprise, too . . . We do a job that sees and experiences violence first-hand. Doesn't mean you have to like it, but you do have to learn to deal with it,' he concluded gently. 'At least in the public eye. There's no time for . . . what's the word? Reactions? You have to save them for your private moments. But then again, what do I know? I've been on the edge and peered down that precipice . . . it's got to me in the past.'

A flashback: on the banks of the River Ribble in flood. Children in a bus, blown off the motorway bridge, collateral damage caused by a ruthless killer who had stuck a bomb on his target's vehicle so that when it blew up in the middle of a busy motorway, many others suffered.

It was all still with him.

His desperate, almost useless attempts to save lives, and almost drowning himself in the process.

Mostly it was boxed away, tighter than a bank vault.

Occasionally, the door opened.

His eyes glazed over slightly. There were many other closed boxes in his head and he fervently hoped they would never all open at the same time to release the demons within.

'I could very easily be a nut job,' he said, then put a finger to his lips. 'Maybe I actually am.' His vision came back into focus and he made eye contact with Daniels, who was looking at him with concern. He smiled. 'You'll be fine. The time to worry is when you feel nothing.'

'Thank you,' she said genuinely.

Henry leaned forward earnestly. 'This may seem shallow, but inside this café is a piece of carrot cake with my name on it, and one with yours on it, too.'

SEVEN

There was a certain aroma in the car. All the hours spent together without having the chance to wash properly or shave, then the diet of burgers and coffee from drive-throughs having taken its toll. And Silverthwaite's flatulence did not help matters either – so tangy Hawkswood could almost taste it, even with the windows open.

They had parked on some spare land a good two hundred yards further up and on the opposite side of the road from Burnham's mother's house on Todmorden Road, partially concealed by a huge mound of chippings dumped by the council which would ultimately be used to resurface the road. Angling the car so they had a decent but restricted view of the front of the house, they settled down to watch the proceedings unfold, confident that if they were challenged in any way they would be able to bluff their way with a flash of their credentials and come up with a cock-and-bull story to explain why they were here. They did not expect to be challenged anyway.

The activity at the house started with a man walking his dog down the road and glancing in through the open front door to see Burnham sprawled out in the hallway. It had not taken long for the first patrol cops to arrive, all coming up the road from the direction of the town centre, none driving down past the two detectives.

They were sure they were in a good position.

They were on a large tract of spare land between the last terraced house on their side of the road and the next houses, probably a quarter of a mile further on. Opposite, across the road, was a dry stone wall with fields beyond, running up to the higher moors.

Hawkswood was using a tiny pair of binoculars to watch the comings and goings and the speedy build-up of cop activity: firstly uniforms, then CID, followed by a CSI van, the erection of screens and the tent at the front door.

All as it should be.

Throughout the morning, Silverthwaite kept in contact with Runcie, updating her when there was anything to report.

Such as, after a couple of hours, the arrival of the chief constable in his fancy Jag.

They watched, eating cold burgers and drinking coffee.

'We probably need to get back now,' Silverthwaite suggested.

Hawkswood quickly placed his burger on his lap and jammed the binoculars to his eyes. 'Shit.'

'What is it?'

Slowly, he handed the binoculars to Silverthwaite and pointed with a wavering finger.

Silverthwaite refocused to suit his eyesight.

'Shit.' Henry Christie had arrived in a green Peugeot driven by a young black woman. Silverthwaite's chin wobbled. 'What's he doing here?' He watched Henry get out and walk slowly towards the murder house. 'More to the point, how can he even be walking?' Even from that distance, with Henry reduced in size by the lens, he could see Henry wasn't just strolling along. 'Why isn't he dead? Or at least in hospital?' He turned accusingly on Hawkswood. 'You did push him down those steps, didn't you?'

'As sure as you stuck a jemmy in Burnham's head.'

'It was a wrecking bar,' Silverthwaite corrected him. 'He must bounce, the bastard. Looks like he's in pain. Walking like an arthritic monkey.'

He continued to watch Henry, feeling his stomach churn for

more than one reason: the very unsettling feeling of seeing Christie rock up to this crime scene after believing he might never walk again this side of Christmas (or ever again). Despite his snide remark to Hawkswood, he had been behind him when he launched Henry down the cellar steps, so had seen him nosedive down.

'We should've made sure.'

The other unsettling feeling in his guts was because of the horrendous diet he'd been living on for the last day, the meal at The Tawny Owl excepted. His stomach was all griping pains and escaping wind from both ends, and the realization that sooner rather than later he would need to pay an urgent visit.

Henry and the woman were met by Fanshaw-Bayley and the detective who seemed to be in charge of the scene.

After a chat, they were led through the screen.

Silverthwaite took the binoculars away from his eyes and handed them back.

'We didn't leave anything incriminating, did we?' he asked. Hawkswood shook his head.

Silverthwaite took out his phone and called Runcie with an update, readying himself for the rant that would surely – and did – come. He held the phone away from his ear as she raged at his and Hawkswood's ineffectuality. Many expletives accompanied the abuse before she hung up.

Silverthwaite looked at his phone. 'I've never known a woman use the word "cunt" so many times,' he said. 'Especially when she was talking about you.'

'She certainly doesn't mince her words,' Hawkswood said, ignoring the jibe.

'Seems to think we should've killed Christie.'

'I heard,' Hawkswood said sourly, lifting the binoculars to his eyes again.

Silverthwaite's guts gurgled.

Christie and the woman – obviously another detective – reappeared after a few minutes and talked to Fanshaw-Bayley at his car, then made their way back to the car they had arrived in.

At which moment, Silverthwaite could not hang on any longer.

'Jeez, I got to go – now!'

The Peugeot pulled away from the roadside.

'He's setting off, coming in this direction,' Hawkswood said. 'And I need a shit,' Silverthwaite said urgently. He grabbed the door handle and opened it, almost falling out on his knees as he scrambled around to the back of the car, struggling to undo his belt but just managing to yank his trousers down and squat low as the Peugeot drove past; Hawkswood had slithered low and out of sight behind the steering wheel. Silverthwaite peeked diagonally across the boot, and as Henry and the woman drove past, his bowels evacuated themselves in the most horrible, spectacular manner.

'I don't believe this,' Hawkswood said. He and Silverthwaite had given Henry about a ten-minute start before they set off, starting to think it would be unwise to remain in the vicinity of the murder when two Support Unit vans drew up and disgorged over a dozen bobbies who would be deployed on initial house-to-house enquiries and maybe some searches of land before a real, concerted search was undertaken. Whatever, they would no doubt encompass the two detectives and their car. Knowing they would only be able to bluff that one so much, they set off back over the hill and into West Yorkshire, down into Todmorden and east on the A646.

Hawkswood's outburst was as they travelled in slow traffic past a café and saw Henry and the female detective sitting outside with brews and large chunks of cake.

'This fucker's gonna haunt us,' he said.

'Eh, what?' Silverthwaite was still in recovery from his urgent call of nature, which included the embarrassment of not having slid his underpants off enough and having a further accident in that respect, hence he'd had to ditch the garment in the pile of chippings. Nor could he rid himself of the memory of watching Christie drive past, his eyes just above the level of the boot of his car. He was also seriously worried that his stomach had not finished playing up.

'Get down,' Hawkswood said suddenly. He himself slid low behind the wheel and Silverthwaite did not have to be told twice, even though he wasn't sure what was going on.

With just their eyes showing above the dashboard, they drove past the café as Christie and his companion shovelled in cake.

* * *

Henry settled into the battered car seat next to Daniels and they set off towards Halifax, virtually circumnavigated the town and dropped on to the M62.

Progress was slow on this motorway, but Henry did not mind too much. He spent the time rereading the murder books, although his thoughts continually flipped back to Burnham's death, which did not sit at all right with him as a burglary gone wrong. Few burglars he had encountered in a long career of catching them had the courage to stand up to the occupants of houses, unless they were frail grannies, which Burnham was not. Most would flee first. Yes, there were the bad ones, the ones intent on causing harm or rape, but they were the headline-grabbers and the minority. Mostly they were weedy losers.

He tried to concentrate on his assignment: two very different killings, seemingly not related, but as he read through the pages, one similarity did hit him.

'Nothing much about mobile phones for either of these guys,' he commented. He'd already noticed this with regards to Mark James Wright's murder – the guy stabbed near his car, whose file he had open on his knee. There was no phone listed on the inventory of his property, and though there was one listed for Tom Salter, there did not seem to be much information from it. However, Henry knew the murder books were not meant to be an extensive record of property seized.

'I noticed that,' Daniels said.

'Bit odd.'

'Could the offenders have made off with them?' she asked.

Henry shrugged and posted the query to his mental clipboard. It was something to ask of the lead investigator, DCI Runcie. He checked the name again. Yep, that was the guy.

'I'm not saying that the phones are relevant, but the movement of both victims prior to their death could be crucial, and a bit of phone triangulation could be useful to tell a story. That said,' Henry went on philosophically, 'the chances are that all we'll get in both cases are screenshots – no real detail, or feel for them . . . that's how it is with a review. We may never get anywhere near the truth, just hopefully point out the directions the investigators might not have thought to take.'

'Funny how we seem to be faced with a series of crimes that

have gone wrong. Two burglaries – if you include Mr Burnham's death – and a road-rage incident,' Daniels observed.

'Or, if they haven't gone wrong, it means they've gone exactly to plan,' Henry mused, 'but I'm sure the investigators will have thought of all that. I know for a fact that Rik Dean will have.' He closed the murder book and eased himself back. The seat might have been battered but it wasn't half comfortable.

For a while, he had forgotten his aches and pains. The job did that; the focus of investigating a murder tended to channel the mind and put physical and other problems to the back of the queue but, as he leaned back, they all started to pulse again. His shoulder, which he was fortunate not to have whacked too badly on his tumble down the steps, started to tighten up and the fall injuries began to feel painful again. He knew he'd been lucky on that fall. He frowned, annoyed that he hadn't been as careful as usual on that top, mossy, greasy step. He should have power-washed it ages ago.

Yet down he went.

Idiot.

He tried to recall the incident. Had he been pushed? It seemed stupid to think so, yet was there a feeling of something in the back of his mind? He wasn't sure.

'Wouldn't it be funny,' Daniels speculated, 'if the deaths of that detective – what's he called? – Culver and Mr Burnham were linked in some way?' She shrugged. 'Y'know?'

'Highly amusing.'

'And if the two deaths we have to review are linked to each other and to the deaths of the two cops?' she went on relentlessly.

'Now I'm in stitches. Stop it.'

'Just a thought,' she said. 'That would be some web to weave.'

Henry stared blankly through the windscreen, watching the road whizz by. Not long now and they would be in the county of Central Yorkshire, then, another hour after that, on the coast.

His mobile phone rang: Rik Dean calling.

'Hi, what's happening?' Henry asked.

Henry listened, asked a couple of questions then ended the call, turning to Daniels, who glanced at him.

'Just a quick update from DCI Dean. The MO of the other
break-ins in that area – and there've been thirty of them in the
last two months – does not quite match the entry method for
Burnham's mum's house.'

Daniels digested this.

'Puts a whole new spin on it,' Henry said. 'And another spin
on it is that two houses on the other side of Bacup were broken
into last night, same MO as the prolific burglar.'

'Which makes you think . . . what, exactly?'

'That Burnham was targeted,' Henry finished for her. 'And
although one or two objects were tipped over in the house and
some things were stolen, there is no sign of Burnham's attaché
case with all his work in it.'

Eating carrot cake and drinking a large mug of tea may well have
had a rejuvenating effect on Henry and Daniels, but it also meant
that he needed Daniels to make a stop at the first motorway
services they reached on the M62 – Hartshead Moor – pleasantly
screened from the sound of the motorway by trees and landscaping.
Henry didn't want to have to explain that his bladder wasn't what
it once was; however, after he'd relieved himself, he decided he
needed more coffee. Daniels went for some flavoured tea of
the type Henry had tried but failed to make himself like. At heart,
he remained a simple man with simple tastes, and fruity tea wasn't
ever going to be one of them.

Daniels had settled now, recovering nicely from the shock of
the brutal murder.

She knew what Henry had said was true. The thing about being
a cop was you had to have the ability to deal with anything, then
power on and put aside personal issues until later – maybe never,
sometimes – otherwise you'd be no use to anyone, including
yourself.

Ten minutes later – and after another quick visit to the loo by
Henry – they were ready to roll again and were probably a good
hour and a quarter from their destination.

They walked out of the services to the car. Daniels went to the
driver's door and Henry to the passenger side. He noticed that
the front tyre on that side was completely flat. Daniels saw his
shoulders slump.

'What, boss?'

Henry pointed. She came around to look, by which time Henry had bent over and was running the palm of his hand across the tyre tread and wall, feeling for a nail. What he did find was a knife cut in the rubber wall.

'Slashed,' he said.

Daniels swore in anger, stood up and looked for a culprit. Henry looked along the vehicle to the rear wheel. It too was flat. He tapped her and pointed. Daniels swore again as Henry went to it and checked it with his hand. 'Also slashed,' he said, diagnosing the problem. 'But at least they're only flat on the bottom.'

Silverthwaite and Hawkswood were past masters at slashing people's tyres, having targeted many vehicles in Portsea belonging to local low-level crims. They usually did it under cover of darkness and in places unlikely to be overlooked by CCTV cameras, but they took a chance this time, coming on to the motorway services about a minute behind Christie and the woman, just in time to see the pair walking across to the services building. Christie was still hobbling, but going quite speedily.

They pulled in beside a campervan for cover, then the younger and more agile of the two, Hawkswood, waited a few moments before sliding out of the car. He crouched between parked vehicles, drawing out his flick knife. The Peugeot had been parked fairly tightly against a van, providing even more cover, and he squatted at the front nearside wheel and slid the sharp blade into the tyre wall, then duck-walked to the rear wheel and did the same. He could hear the hiss of both tyres as they deflated.

He was back with Silverthwaite seconds later, and moments after that they were back on the motorway, giggling like a couple of immature yobs after committing a crime that would cause severe inconvenience as much as anything.

Silverthwaite reported in to Runcie, who could not believe her ears.

The only luck that Henry and Daniels had was that, as she phoned the AA, a mobile tyre service truck rolled on to the service area. Henry waved him down, snaffled his services and was delighted to discover that he had two tyres of the correct size in the back of his van and was able to fit them straightaway. The repair man confirmed, by showing Henry and Daniels the inner tyre wall, that a knife had been used, making the tyres irreparable.

'Someone don't like you,' the guy said.

Henry paid for the new tyres with his force credit card and, just under an hour after the incident, they were back on the motorway.

Daniels was clearly brooding.

They had tried to access the security cameras on the service area, but the cranky security guard who had obviously clambered out of bed on the wrong side that morning moaned that he needed to get permission from his boss, who was somewhere between London and Birmingham at that moment, so he could not allow the detectives to see any footage.

'Data protection an' all that,' he said as an excuse.

Henry and Daniels withdrew before she came to blows with the man, who, as Daniels became more aggressive with him, was more defiant.

'How the hell? Why the hell?' she said repeatedly while Henry tried to contact the security guard's boss via the mobile number he had been given. He had to leave a voicemail.

Henry tried not to speculate.

But Daniels did. 'Is it a race thing? Some effin' yob see me park up?'

Henry did not respond, but doubted the hypothesis.

She thumped the steering wheel.

'Next junction,' he reminded her.

With her mind having been elsewhere, she was forced to swerve across two lines of traffic to get on the exit ramp and join the M6121 that would take them on their final leg of the journey, through the middle of Central Yorkshire, straight to Portsea on the east coast.

They made no further stops until they arrived.

Portsea police station was a very big, old and decrepit four-storey Victorian building in the city centre, built at a time of great prosperity when the port was booming. While the port itself had survived many ups and downs since, and was currently experiencing a surge of business, the police station had lived through all these times with very little money having been spent on it over the years. Recent government cuts to capital budgets and some money mismanagement by the police and the county council had meant that, since 1996, the station had been left virtually untouched and was starting to crumble.

Some parts of the building had seen some refurbishment, one of which was DCI Jane Runcie's office which, somehow, had been redecorated and kitted out recently with new office furniture and triple-glazed windows that overlooked the main street.

Her office, though, was not the location in which Runcie was talking to Silverthwaite and Hawkswood that evening.

Being such a huge old building – the spider web of a cell complex connected to the adjacent magistrates' court – there were many nooks and crannies where private conversations could take place without fear of being overheard.

She had asked to meet the two detectives in one such place, a small, unused anteroom that had access to the magistrates' private chambers through a door that was always locked. It was just off one of the first-floor corridors on which the CID offices were located in the station. It was very private and virtually soundproof. There was one high window, only accessible by standing on a chair, overlooking an inner courtyard where, legend had it, prisoners used to be hung.

Runcie and Saul possessed the only two known keys for the room.

It was always set up as a small meeting room, large table in the centre, that could have once been in a courtroom, four chairs around it.

Silverthwaite and Hawkswood watched Runcie stalk the room like an angry ostrich.

'You slashed his fucking tyres,' she said.

Hawkswood nodded.

'So . . . let's work this back . . . he plummets down a set of steps, gets up and brushes himself off . . . survives, yeah? Then his tyres are slashed . . . don't you think he might start adding a few things up?'

'No connection, no connections whatsoever,' Silverthwaite said with certainty.

Runcie stopped in front of him, hands on her hips. 'You dick,' she said.

'Well, there isn't.'

She very much wanted to slap him round the room, smash his face into the wall. She reined in this urge and sat down calmly, opening a ring binder, forcing open the rings with a click, taking out two files – one for each man – and keeping a third for herself.

They were all exactly the same and were entitled, *Henry Christie*.

'This is everything I have been able to pull together about this man,' she explained. 'Read it and weep.'

They eyed each other, then opened their files.

Runcie watched them before reaching into her handbag, finding a packet of cigarettes and a lighter. The cigarettes were long and slim, the filters a cream colour with a gold band. She lit one, inhaled deeply, then exhaled a plume of smoke, knowing that the sensors would not reveal a smoker in the building because the one that had been fitted in this room had been ripped from its moorings on the ceiling.

They read their Henry Christie bios.

Silverthwaite finished first. 'So he's an SIO with a history,' he said indifferently.

Runcie blinked at his crass stupidity but said nothing.

Hawkswood closed his file.

'Despite your best efforts, this man is coming into this force and he is going to examine two murders we really do not want examining. The chief constable of Lancashire, Fanshaw-Bayley, has now assumed short-term charge of this force and this fucker Henry Christie is going to delve into our investigations whether we like it or not. We have no idea what Jack Culver managed to say to Burnham – or even really how much he knew in the first place – nor what Burnham told Fanshaw-Bayley and Christie. Hopefully not very fucking much. All we really know is that Culver was not happy with the way things were going and had his suspicions, shall we say, about us . . . and now we're going under the microscope.'

'But Christie's just a fuckin—' Silverthwaite began.

'A fucking what?' Runcie cut in furiously. 'I'll tell you what he is. He's a guy who makes connections. A standalone incident is one thing; two standalone incidents are something else. He'll start thinking, start musing . . . that's what people like him do. Two oddballs show up at the pub, he goes down concrete steps, his car gets vandalized and he is coming here, slashed tyres notwithstanding, poking around with his black sidekick.' She eyed Hawkswood for a reaction but got nothing. 'And guess what, you two are redundant because you've shown your stupid faces to him by having tea with him and pretending to be sales reps.' She rubbed her face ferociously with her free hand, then pinched the bridge of her nose to try to alleviate the dull, stubborn throb across her frontal lobe.

'Blind him with science,' Hawkswood suggested.

'Or just fuck him and video it,' was the older man's idea, but off the look Runcie fired at him, he raised his hands, palms out, and said, 'Just spitballing. Surely he's corruptible?'

'Have you actually read a single word I've put in front of you? This guy has dealt with everyone from the Mafia to serial killers to God knows who, so no, no, he's not corruptible.'

'Always a first time,' Silverthwaite persisted.

Runcie rolled her eyes, but was actually thinking along those lines. Then she made an announcement. 'Tullane's due in.' Both men cowered visibly. 'So we'd better think of something fast. We have a lot of things we need to protect.'

The hotel Daniels had booked was on the old waterfront in Portsea, named the George. Thirty rooms spread over four floors all nicely refurbished with en suites and Wi-Fi connections. The ground floor consisted mainly of a couple of bars, a lounge and a dining room, all done in dark wood with a nautical feel in keeping with the location. It seemed a good choice to Henry, not far from the city centre yet out of the way and close enough to the police station to make it easy.

They booked into their rooms, which were adjacent but not connected on the second floor, with views over the waterfront.

Henry was glad to get in and splay out on the double bed for a few minutes. He roused himself before falling asleep and called Alison on the landline number of The Tawny Owl because of the poor mobile signal back there. She didn't pick up, so he left a message for her to call.

Then he called DCI Runcie on a number he'd seen in the murder books. That went to automated voicemail and he left a message saying he had arrived with DC Daniels and they would present themselves at Portsea police station at nine the following morning. His next call was another attempt to speak to the boss of the security guy at the motorway service station. This time he connected.

The boss – his name was Newsham – was nowhere near as cautious as his employee in guarding the security camera footage. When Henry gave him the short timeframe to work with, he promised Henry he would send him the split-screen images the cameras recorded on site but that it would take him a couple of hours to sort. He would send it to the email address Henry provided for him.

Then he called Daniels in the room next door. No reply.

Not having an awful lot of luck, he decided to freshen up by way of a shower and, when he emerged, damp, he saw two missed calls on his phone from Daniels and a text from DCI Runcie. He called Daniels back first and they arranged to meet in the hotel bar at 7 p.m., then decide where to eat, although Henry assumed they would stay in the hotel. He'd glanced at a sample menu in the room and it looked extensive yet reasonable.

Then he read the text from Runcie. *Sorry missed ur call. In bar of George Hotel now for quick intro.*

EIGHT

Henry rapped on Daniels' door but got no reply. He stuck his ear to it and heard the shower and some music playing, so he sent her a text then made his way along the creaking corridor, down to the bar.

It was quiet.

A couple of old guys were sitting at a brass-topped table, deep in conversation. The only other person was a tall, long-legged woman sitting alone at the bar, hunched over a cocktail of some description.

Henry went to the bar and ordered a pint of Stella Artois,

necking about a third of it in a couple of long gulps, wiping his lips with the back of his hand as he turned and leaned on the bar, wondering if he had missed Runcie. He peered into the darker alcoves in the bar, all empty, then checked his watch. It was a minute past seven.

As his head moved he became aware of the lone woman further along the bar, eyeballing him.

'You're looking for a man, aren't you?' she asked him. Instantly Henry booted himself mentally for allowing his deep-rooted assumptions to lead his thoughts. Runcie was a female officer, not a man.

All that equality training gone to waste, he thought. He turned smoothly to her and said creepily, 'Not now.'

'No harm done . . . coppering's still a man's world at heart.' She held out a slender arm with long, tapering fingers. 'Runcie, Jane Runcie, DCI Jane Runcie.'

'Got it,' Henry said embarrassedly, shaking her hand and feeling the soft warmth of her skin. 'Christie,' he countered. 'Henry Christie . . .'

'Detective Superintendent Henry Christie,' she completed for him, and gave a wonky but attractive smile. 'I know. You're here to investigate me.'

She cocked her head slightly, still wearing the same grin, and allowed Henry more than a moment to evaluate her. Even seated, he could tell she was tall and slim and elegant, with a quite long, pointed nose and long, shiny auburn, almost red hair that cascaded down her shoulders and back. Her shoulders were square with a masculine edge, and her body was slender rather than shapely, but Henry being Henry did notice that her bosom was pleasantly ample as her silk blouse was unbuttoned to her cleavage. Her eyes were steel grey with a hint of the Far East about their shape. She wore a tight, knee-length skirt. Henry estimated she was in her early forties.

He swallowed and found the power of speech. 'Just to check all is well, as I'm sure it is – not to investigate as such.'

'To poke around, then?'

'Where any poking is necessary,' he said, seeing her eyes sparkle with the mirth of the exchange, and he knew he needed to quit with the double meanings right now, so he did.

'Sad news about your chief,' he said. 'Your force must be reeling.'

'Yeah, yeah.'

He thought she seemed strangely unmoved or concerned.

'I never really met him,' she added. 'The news hasn't really gone in yet. But I think he was a good man.'

'I visited the scene this morning. It was very nasty.'

'Really? You were there? It sounded grim from what little I know. However,' she shrugged, 'life and the cops still goes on and we will do our best to ensure you can do your job while you're here. We'll offer as much assistance as possible.'

'That's good to hear.'

'Can I buy you a drink? Home turf and all that?' she offered.

'Er.' He looked at his lager. 'I'll finish this first, thanks.'

'OK.'

Henry did just that and the lager seemed to clear away the grit of the journey across the country. Runcie ordered another for him and a Martini for herself, olive included.

'Shall we sit in one of the booths?' Before he could answer, she collected her drink and clutch bag and led Henry across to some empty seats. They settled across from each other. 'Hope your journey was OK, all the way across the country.'

'Fine,' he said, not wanting to share the tyre-slashing experience. 'Longer than I thought it would be.'

'Any idea how the investigation into Mr Burnham's murder is progressing? Early days, I know. Early day, in fact.'

'The SIO has some leads, I think,' he said vaguely.

'Good, good,' she said – and not really sounding genuine to Henry. 'Anyway, how do you want to proceed? What can I get ready for you?'

'I'll just have a look at everything, slowly and surely, from the discovery of the bodies onwards and including victim profiles, forensics, post-mortem results. All I want to do is tick boxes and, if there's anything I feel you might have missed – not saying there is, by the way – I'll let you know. That's all. As far as I can tell, everything seems to have been covered . . . I've read through the murder books.'

'I believe so.'

'And it all seems fine.'

'But sometimes murders don't get solved. Rarely, but occasionally.'

'I understand that.' Henry paused. 'There are two of us, by the way. Me and my colleague, DC Daniels. Just freshening up. Be down shortly, I guess.'

'DC Daniels. Man or woman?' Runcie teased.

Henry grinned at the jibe. 'Woman.'

'Ah, right . . . I believe your chief, Fanshaw-Bayley, is taking over the helm of Central Yorkshire for the short term?'

'He is.'

'What's he like?'

'Ruthless.'

'Really?'

'Really.'

'Interesting.' Runcie sipped her drink, her eyes playing over Henry's face, and he had to admit that if he had been doing this ten years ago, he would probably have followed his erect penis and tried to bed this woman sitting opposite him. Nowadays, he just thought about it for a while, then forgot it. Time had moved on, and Henry's desire now was to ditch his bad old days and be and remain a better man. He had spent too much of his past life putting his wife, Kate, through hell, and there was no way he would repeat his shenanigans with Alison.

Runcie's gaze shifted, looking beyond Henry's shoulder, and suddenly her shoulders seemed to tense, her eyes narrowed and a hard-edged mien came on to her face, transforming the soft lines into harsh ones.

Henry glanced around to see Daniels coming in from the bar door, making Henry blink. She had more than freshened up, had re-braided her hair and changed into a blouse which was tied underneath her breasts, leaving a gap of skin before the waistband of a colourful knee-length skirt.

'This must be your colleague,' Runcie said in a way that chilled Henry.

'It is,' he said, rising to his feet, hardly able to take his gaze off Daniels. 'This is DC Daniels.' He made the introduction. 'Diane, this is DCI Runcie, the SIO in the two cases we'll be having a look at.'

'Hi, boss,' Daniels said brightly, and offered a hand to shake

Runcie's, who did not respond, other than with a curt nod. She did not get to her feet and Henry almost felt a wave of unnecessary antagonism radiating from Runcie like a force field via her posture and expression, both of which had changed subtly. Henry wondered where it was coming from.

Daniels looked at Henry, showing how unimpressed she was in a more obvious way. However, she smiled and said, 'Can I get either of you guys a drink?'

Runcie's eyes were half-lidded and contemptuous. 'Not for me,' she said brusquely. She tipped the remains of her Martini down her throat, then rose to her feet and seemed to tower over the slightly shorter Daniels, who had to look up into her face. Henry then realized that Runcie could be very intimidating. 'Tomorrow at nine,' she said to Henry. 'Just come to the public enquiry counter and announce yourselves. I'll send someone down to fetch you . . . You do know where the police station is, don't you?'

'We'll find it,' Henry said, and then she was gone.

The two Lancashire detectives watched her leave.

'What's that thing in the Harry Potter films?' Henry asked. 'You know, when someone can change from one thing into another?'

'What, like from a cougar into a bitch?' Daniels suggested.

'Mmm, sort of. There's a word for it . . . trans something.'

'Let's not go there . . . I'm going to get a glass of wine. Do you want anything, boss?'

Henry glanced at his second beer and shivered. 'Not just yet, thanks.'

He did not drink any more alcohol other than a nightcap at ten p.m. They had a good meal in the hotel dining room and chatted about the way forward, how the review should be handled and other personal stuff about families and loved ones, with Daniels revealing that her engagement ring was a relic from a broken relationship and couldn't really say why she was still wearing it.

He hit the 'wall' at ten p.m. and decided he needed to get to bed as his aches and pains were worsening. He needed painkillers and sleep.

Daniels said she would have another glass of wine before retiring.

In his room, Henry stripped, cleaned his teeth and slid into the cool double bed where, from his prone position, he called Alison again. This time he got through. For once, she was having a fairly easy night at The Tawny Owl, with only a handful of diners in and few regulars. She and Henry had a pleasant conversation, after which he sat up again, reached for his laptop and logged into the free Wi-Fi to check his emails. He had expected a response from the security guy at the motorway services, but there was nothing, which he found frustrating.

'Well, he's definitely going to make connections with this,' Runcie said, shaking her head in utter disbelief at Silverthwaite and Hawkswood. Both had showered, changed and managed to get a couple of hours' sleep before coming back in via a McDonald's drive-through. Silverthwaite, in spite of his earlier stomach problems – dealt with by means of Imodium – had happily bought burger and chips and a large milkshake, which he wolfed down with gusto, stuffing the food into his mouth.

'You can't really see me properly,' Hawkswood said.

Runcie's mouth sagged open as she looked at the two detectives. 'Oh, let me think . . . no, you can't, but you can see a Vauxhall Insignia drive on to the service area and you can clearly see what appears to be a black man – you,' she pointed at Hawkswood, 'slashing the tyres. A bit of enhancement and the number plate will be read and your mush' – again she pointed at Hawkswood – 'will be on bloody *Crimewatch*.'

They were in their 'private' room within the police station, which, other than the areas occupied by uniformed patrols, was quiet, all the office staff having gone at five p.m. They were sitting around a laptop computer watching the footage obtained from Newsham, the security manager of the motorway services.

'It's a bloody good job I had the foresight to get hold of this guy before he sent these images to Christie, isn't it, boys?' Runcie said sarcastically. She had shed the glamorous veneer she'd tried with Henry and reverted to her more comfortable persona. She'd realized that any detective worth their salt would have been in contact with the security company to get footage from the cameras on the service area forwarded to them for scrutiny. 'Not rocket science,' she'd told her two detectives. 'Common bleeding sense, that which you two don't seem to have much of.'

The security manager, Newsham, had initially baulked at Runcie's request, but when she'd explained – lied – that the detective who had made the initial request was under investigation and was likely wanting the footage to attempt to cover up a crime he himself had committed, he'd been only too pleased to send the video to her instead. She'd warned him that Christie might call again and threaten him with grief. If that happened, she'd instructed him to tell the officer that the cameras had not been working correctly and had failed to record; he was then to immediately inform her of the harassing call. She'd assured him that he would not become embroiled in anything.

'Where do we stand?' Silverthwaite asked.

She sighed heavily down her long nose. 'Well, we now don't have a meddling Detective Superintendent Culver – dead – or a meddling chief constable – also dead – to worry about. But in their place we have a meddling Henry Christie with his glam sidekick.' Runcie's face twisted. 'And, for some reason, Christie didn't even bother telling me about the tyre-slashing incident, which I find odd and worrying . . . Anyway, somehow we have to deal with these two individuals, play them and send them off with a pat on their heads, having discovered nothing untoward. We have too much to lose on this, guys. Too much invested, too much to look forward to in our dotage.' She rubbed her thumb and forefinger together, meaning 'money'. 'Give 'em what we have, what they want to see, be nice and they'll be gone before we know it. That's the key – and I have an idea on that score. As for you two, you'll have to keep out of the way because if Christie spots you . . .' She drew her finger across her throat. 'So you'll have to leave them to me and Saul . . . OK.' She looked at Silverthwaite folding the last of his chips into his mouth and jerked her head at him to get lost. He shook his head cynically, collected up the fast-food wrappers and left the room.

Runcie lit a cigarette, eyeing Hawkswood through the slowly rising smoke.

She turned down the lighting via the dimmer switch to just a glow, came across to him and eased herself in front of the detective. Their eyes seemed to grip each other's gaze hotly. She grabbed his jacket and hauled him to his feet, tipping up his chair in the process. Then she stubbed out her cigarette on the table top and both her hands went to his belt and zip, unfastening both roughly and diving in behind his boxer shorts with her right hand, taking hold of his already engorged cock.

They pirouetted around. Hawkswood raised her on to the table, shook off his trousers and hoisted her legs around him as he bunched up her skirt, already knowing she was not wearing panties.

Henry took a call from Daniels.

'Just checking you're OK, boss. You looked a bit tired.'

'I'm fine, thanks, tucked up safe and sound,' he told her.

'Me too.'

Despite knowing it was wrong, he could not prevent himself imagining her lying in a bed maybe less than twelve feet from where he was, thankfully separated by a thick stone wall and a locked door.

'Have you heard from the security guy?'

'No. I left a message, though,' Henry said.

'OK.' Henry heard her yawn. She said, 'You're not like other bosses.'

'Is that a good thing?'

'Yeah . . . I was talking to someone about you before I set off for The Tawny Owl. Jerry Tope; he's a good friend of mine.'

'Ah, the lovely Jerry.' Henry knew Tope well – a gifted intelligence analyst and computer nerd whose habits of hacking through firewalls had almost once cost him his job when the FBI came knocking because he'd been interrogating their systems like a kid in a sweet shop. Henry used him often and relentlessly on murder investigations.

'He speaks highly of you,' she told him.

'That'll go to my head.'

'And even though I've only just met you, I can see why people are prepared to follow you so keenly. I get it.'

Henry wasn't sure what to say.

'I know I will,' she said softly. 'I think the carrot cake is what did it for me.'

'Always works. I do it with every member of my staff. Costs a fortune.' He was still imagining her in bed but knew that if he asked her what she was wearing (secretly, he hoped nothing), her perception of him would change rapidly.

'Anyway, thank you.' Her voice sounded dreamy.

'It's a pleasure.'

'Good night . . . see you at breakfast.'

'Good night.' Henry thumbed the end call button and said, 'So what *are* you wearing?' only to realize his thumb had missed the key and the line was still open. 'Holy shit,' he said, fumbling with the phone. He heard her chuckle. 'Oh, God, you didn't really hear that, did you?'

'Oh, yes.' Her voice was now mischievous and husky. 'Nothing, by the way.'

This time Henry's thumb did find the correct button, even though his digit was dithering.

'So that's my career done,' he muttered as he tabbed through the menu of his phone: one last call to make. He found the number and dialled.

'This better be good,' the grumpy voice at the other end of the line answered.

'Evening, Jerry,' Henry said.

'Evening? Middle of the night! And anyway, you were supposed to be off sick, but I hear the chief has coerced you to come back in.'

Henry was speaking to Jerry Tope, the aforementioned detective who was an analyst within the Intelligence Unit based at Lancashire Constabulary's headquarters. Henry always accepted that Jerry was a curmudgeon, old and grumpy beyond his years, but because he was so good at his job (so good Henry had had to talk the FBI out of headhunting him after finding out he had been hacking their mainframe) he gave him some leeway, but not too much.

'Yes, I'm back,' Henry declared, 'and I'm on the wrong side of the Pennines.'

'I believe so. Anyhow, what can I do for you? I'm just disinfecting my materials,' he said – giving Henry a mind's eye picture of Tope in his spare bedroom where he home-brewed his own beer and wine.

'I need you to do some background checks, Jerry.'

'I'm not at work.'

'But I know you can access the Intel database from your home.' Henry also knew that Tope had the skills and knowledge to access the computer systems of virtually any police service or law-enforcement organization the world over from his battered-looking laptop at home.

'Go on,' he said resignedly.

Henry gave him the names and dates of birth of the two murder victims, Tom Salter and Mark James Wright. 'Just see what you can pull out on these guys, will you? All I've got is the murder books at the moment, so not much background. Hopefully I'll get more in the morning, but see what you can find.' Grudgingly, Tope said he would try. As an afterthought, Henry added, 'Will you have a look at DCI Jane Runcie, too . . . she's the SIO in charge of the two cases.'

'Why?' Tope asked dubiously.

'Just do it . . . Oh, and Detective Superintendent Jack Culver. He was the SIO on both murders before he got wiped out in an accident. See what you can discover about the circumstances of that, will you?'

'Don't Central Yorkshire have an Intel Unit?'

'Yeah, but not as good as you, pal.'

Henry rung off, only for his phone to ring again almost immediately. It was Rik Dean.

'Rik, I was going to call you,' Henry said, though it was going to wait until tomorrow.

'Hi, Henry, how's it going?'

'Nothing to report just yet. You?'

'I'm at Blackburn Police Station custody office and I've just been talking to one of Rossendale Valley's most prolific burglars. I've cleared up about three hundred jobs and I'm absolutely certain this isn't the guy who killed John Burnham.'

NINE

Since the body of Chief Constable John Burnham had been discovered murdered early that morning at his mother's address in Bacup, DCI Rik Dean had been working flat out, as is expected of an SIO in charge of a murder enquiry.

Rik would one day probably become Henry's brother-in-law as he was engaged to Lisa, Henry's wayward sister. The relationship was topsy-turvy at best and Henry wasn't at all certain it would reach wedded bliss, but he knew both parties were good for each other. Since Henry had taken the bullet in the hospital storeroom, Rik had been covering for him on FMIT but not as a temporary superintendent, just in his rank of DCI. Henry suspected, even though he and Rik were close friends, that Rik would also one day happily step into his shoes if the opportunity presented itself.

However, until that day came . . .

Rik had worked and controlled the murder well and, having ensured he got the scene under the firm hand of a crime-scene manager he trusted, he started to fast track the investigation which led to him exploiting local intelligence to identify burglars believed to be active in the area and deploying two pairs of keen detectives to haul in the ones most likely to have committed the numerous burglaries that had taken place in the Bacup area over the last few months.

Two arrests were made and one of them easily discounted because he had a broken leg and an ankle tag. The other one, a scrawny male aged twenty from a notorious council estate in Bacup, was detained, but the officers had been told to be slightly cagey about exactly which houses he had been arrested on suspicion of breaking into.

Rik wanted to talk to him.

He had been conveyed to Blackburn Police Station, where all detainees from Rossendale were now housed, however inconvenient that might be, the days of prisoners being bunged into cells in their home towns being very much a thing of the past as police stations closed down following budget cuts. He was searched and shown to a cell; when Rik eventually arrived, the prisoner – surname Mullen – was ushered into an interview room, where he was represented by the on-call duty solicitor.

'Bin arrested fer nowt,' Mullen said after the tape had been switched on and interview formalities completed.

'Not true – you've been arrested on suspicion of committing a series of burglaries in Bacup over the last few months,' Rik told him, keeping his eyes level with the prisoner. 'Right now, officers are searching your flat, your sister's flat, your mum's flat and your best mate's flat.'

'Whatever.' Mullen was unimpressed.

'But I'll be honest,' Rik said, leaning forwards, 'I'm really more concerned about the man you murdered last night.'

That statement seemed to get his attention.

Rik saw Mullen's eyes flash and his throat visibly contract.

'In fact, you are now under arrest for murder. You don't have to . . .' Rik began to caution him again, but Mullen broke in.

'Whoa, whoa, whoa.' He shot up from his folded arm slouch. 'What the fuck?'

'Fuck is you broke into a house on Todmorden Road, Bacup last night and killed the man you disturbed in the house, didn't you?'

'Is this a fucking joke?'

'I'm deadly serious, Mr Mullen. I'm investigating a murder, and you are my prime suspect.'

Mullen looked desperately at his brief.

'What were you doing between the hours of ten p.m. and six a.m. last night stroke this morning?'

'I was at home.'

'Have to do better than that.'

Mullen twitched. Rik knew he was a drug addict, burgling and then fencing the stolen property to fund a serious habit.

'I think you were breaking into that house, were disturbed and, in a panic, maybe, you killed the guy by whacking him with a wrecking bar, because I know you use a similar tool when you break into houses, don't you?'

'No,' he replied stubbornly.

'What do you use, then?'

Mullen looked blankly but challengingly at Rik.

'This is a murder enquiry, Mr Mullen; at this moment in time you are right up here' – Rik gestured with his hand as flat as a blade, reaching high – 'and it's looking like you.'

'I don't use a jemmy. I use a screwdriver. Flat-bladed. Wide.'

'Thank you. Now, let's start to make some progress,' Rik said, glad this would not be a protracted process. Deep down, he knew that Mullen probably wasn't the killer, but he had to be ruled out. A short time later, Mullen started to blab and reveal he had committed two burglaries overnight in Rawtenstall and was nowhere near Bacup. Once he knew this, Rik left the two arresting detectives to continue the interview. This ultimately involved Mullen taking them to an address where he kept his burglary kit, consisting of two flat-bladed screwdrivers, a Maglite torch, a small hand drill and masking tape, plus the property he had stolen overnight. This led to further admissions and the revelation he had burgled over three hundred houses in the valley that year.

Rik Dean then had a post-mortem to attend.

'How did that go?' Henry asked Rik, continuing the phone call.

'He was killed by the wrecking bar with a double-claw head, which was still imbedded in his skull. One blow, major trauma, probably died instantly according to the pathologist. You could see the hole in his cranium, all the way through, and the damage to his brain. One hell of a blow. Cold and brutal.'

'And the property stolen from the house? I know you've told me, but remind me again.'

'A couple of items from the mantelpiece, figures, an old clock, plus Burnham's briefcase and laptop. I've had house-to-house and search teams in the area all day, but nothing as of yet. It'll all resume at first light tomorrow.'

After a few more words, the conversation was over.

Henry leaned back against the pillows in the soft, wide bed. His painkillers were having some effect. When his phone next rang, it was Alison.

'You've been busy chatting.'

'Speaking to Rik and Jerry Tope.'

'About what?' She knew who both Rik and Jerry were, but

she didn't know that Henry had called in on a murder scene on his way to Central Yorkshire that morning.

'Just stuff,' he said nebulously.

'I thought I'd phone you again,' Alison said. 'Just wanted to hear your voice.'

Henry glanced at the time, already close to midnight.

'I've cleared the pub – no one more drunk than usual.'

'That's good.'

'You settled now?'

'For the night. All alone in a fluffy bed.'

'I should bloody think so.'

TEN

Henry and Daniels met on the hotel corridor at eight a.m., the former not quite able to look into her eyes.

'Sometimes I say things I shouldn't,' Henry said, and apologized for his remark last night when he thought he'd ended his call to her. She smiled. 'I'm taking so many drugs that I become delirious sometimes.'

She held up her hand to stop his blabbering. 'That'll do. It was funny and I'm not offended or harassed. I'd have been more hurt if you hadn't been thinking those thoughts. Breakfast.'

Henry had woken just before six a.m. One of the perils of living life in the fast lane of a country pub/hotel was that days started early and finished late and his body clock had made the adjustment. He called Alison and had a muzzy conversation with her, after which he rooted out his running gear he'd managed to stash in his small holdall – just a pair of screwed-up shorts, a creased T-shirt and old trainers. No Lycra.

Outside, it was chilly on the old waterfront. A fine mist hung over the harbour. Steeling himself after stretching carefully to loosen off, he set off for a short trot around the port and city, inhaling the wonderful aroma of the sea deep into his lungs.

He followed the quayside of the old port, now mainly populated

by day-trip cruisers and a few fishing boats. On the quay itself
was a vast array of fish-and-chip shops, cafés and amusement
arcades, and a few old pubs which would bring in the summer
crowds. As he jogged along the river, the tourist area petered out
and the landscape became much more industrialized, with berths
long enough for container ships, a series of cranes, their tips just
visible through the mist, and one medium-sized container vessel
alongside the dock, looking empty, maybe waiting to be loaded
up with the containers stacked alongside it. Henry hoped its
journey would be to somewhere exotic.

As he ran, keeping the river to his left as he went upstream,
there were even more containers stacked up – certainly hundreds
of them on areas of flat land. The sight was nowhere near as
extensive as big ports like Felixstowe, but still quite impressive.

He jogged on.

And then came to the entrance to a large, high-fenced business,
a haulier by the name of Tom Salter Ltd.

Henry stopped, amazed to find this here, so close. He wasn't
sure where it could have been in his imagination, but he
wasn't expecting to be running past the scene of the crime of
one of the murders he was reviewing.

The fence was his height, the double gate locked, secured by
chains and padlocks, remnants of police cordon tape flapping in
the breeze. He peered through the mesh and saw more stacks of
containers beyond, and a few HGV tractor units and trailers
parked neatly, like huge snails awaiting shells to be fitted.

Beyond them was an industrial unit, ground floor and first
floor. The big, corrugated door was high and wide enough to
allow the HGVs to drive inside. The first floor was, he presumed,
the office in which Salter had been shot to death.

The scene of the crime.

Henry took it in, gave the gate a thoughtful rattle, then jogged
slowly back through the city – a nice blend of old and new –
back to the hotel, where he went straight into the shower and
slithered down on to the floor because he was sore and exhausted.

'Yes, breakfast,' Henry said. They walked down the corridor side
by side.

'Did you enjoy your run?' Daniels asked him.

'How did you know I went for a run?'

'I saw you set off, just as I circled back from mine in the opposite direction.'

'You've been for a run?' Henry was respectfully astounded.

'Why break the habit of a lifetime? Just a five-miler. I'm presuming you must've done the same, judging by the time you took?'

'Yeah, yeah . . . much the same, I'd estimate,' Henry fibbed with a white-ish tinge. 'Just trying to get back to some modicum of fitness, but it's graft.'

'I can imagine.'

In the dining room, they secured a table at a window over-looking the harbour. Daniels helped herself to what Henry thought looked like very dry and unappetizing cereal with skimmed milk, some fresh fruit and a large glass of orange juice.

He ordered the full English, a real ventricle slammer.

The only similarity was that each had a cafetière of strong, fresh coffee.

Henry brought her up to date with what he had learned from Rik Dean last night, then Daniels asked about the plan for the day ahead.

He admitted it would consist mainly of winging it.

Daniels grinned.

Henry said, 'What?'

'She was after you. I'd be on my guard,' she told him.

'Who was?'

'You know, that giraffe-like woman, Runcie. She would've had you pinned down if I hadn't arrived.'

'No way.'

'I'm a woman. I know how we operate, and she was operating.' She spooned a mouthful of wheat and oats into her mouth and crunched them. 'Watch her, Henry . . . she has an agenda.'

'I'm a big boy.'

'That's what she's depending on.'

Henry tried to look thoughtful as he placed a slice of Cumberland sausage into his mouth. He frowned. There was something in his brain he couldn't quite seem to access, some-thing unsettling, and it concerned Runcie.

It was Daniels' turn to say, 'What?'

But he could not rake it out, so he made a bacon sandwich with his toast and ate that instead.

They left the hotel at exactly 08.42 hours. This fact was transmitted to DCI Runcie from the back of a very old surveillance van, a Ford Transit fitted with a chemical toilet, no aircon and only the most rudimentary ways to keep an eye on a target, such as one-way mirrors fitted in the back doors and false flip-up air vents in the vehicle side panels. Inside, it had two rudimentary wooden benches, one either side of the vehicle, and no other creature comforts. An old-style aerial lead hung down from the roof, so old it was impossible to plug into the new-style police radios used by the two miserable detectives now sitting in the van.

They had been on the harbour side a couple of hundred yards away from the hotel since five a.m. and had seen both Daniels and Henry set off for their early morning runs, then return. Daniels looked as fit as when she'd set off, but Henry had lumbered back looking as though he was ready to collapse.

'Looks like they're on their way,' Hawkswood radioed through to Runcie on the dedicated encrypted radio channel only their little team used.

Henry and Daniels had walked down the narrow drive leading to the hotel car park at the rear of the building. About a minute later, the old Peugeot stuck out its nose and turned into the traffic that was beginning to build up.

'Received,' she acknowledged.

'Want us to do anything?' Hawkswood asked. He hoped the answer would be no because Runcie's insatiable sex drive had completely wasted him. He looked over at Silverthwaite on the bench opposite, looking weary and unpleasant.

'No, just stay out of sight,' was the order back.

The Peugeot came towards them and both men crouched low in their seats, even though it was impossible for the occupants of the car to see them.

'Roger that,' Hawkswood said.

Daniels found a space in the visitors' car park at the front of the police station and she and Henry walked into the public enquiry desk and presented themselves. The Public Enquiry Assistant (PEA) had been briefed and told them to take a seat while she called up to the CID Serious Crimes office.

Henry and Daniels moved away from the desk and stood at the back of the foyer, saying nothing, just watching as the PEA used the internal phone. She finished the call, slid open the toughened glass screen and beckoned to them.

'I'm afraid something's come up, apparently. I don't know what, but DCI Runcie has turned out to something. But someone will be down for you shortly.'

'OK,' Henry said stonily. He didn't like to be kept waiting and Daniels noticed his body language change. He'd assumed his all-business role of being a top cop now and she guessed he would not put up with being messed around. Although he had a reputation for not pulling rank, she knew that, if he did, you were in deep shit.

Fifteen minutes later, they were still waiting, at which point a stern-faced Henry approached the desk and tapped on the screen. The PEA slid it open and he leaned in, invading the woman's space. Daniels did not hear what was said, but a look of horror came over the lady's face and she quickly picked up the phone again.

Henry pushed himself away from the counter and stalked back to Daniels, who now realized she would not like to get on his wrong side. He could certainly put on the mantle of 'superintendent' when he had to. There was a definite core of steel running through him.

He arched his eyebrows at her.

A few moments later, the door next to the desk that led through to the innards of the police station opened and a sour-faced man wearing a loose-fitting suit appeared, held open the door and called, 'Mr Christie?'

Henry strutted across with Daniels in tow and the man stepped aside and gestured for them both to enter.

Once inside, Henry turned to the guy, who held his right hand out to shake.

'I'm DC Saul. I'll be looking after you, boss.' He spoke directly to Henry, not taking in Daniels at all. She knew already that, to him, she didn't exist.

Henry shook his hand and peered at him. 'Don't I know you? Weren't you on a CID course I once lectured to?'

'You have a good memory, boss.' Saul looked uncomfortable.

'Yes, I do.' Henry indicated Daniels. 'This is DC Daniels – and you can shake her hand, too.'

A look of outrage came to Saul's craggy face and his lips tightened as he withdrew his hand from Henry's grip then held it out to her. Daniels took it with a genuine smile and made Saul wince when she clasped his hand with the other and said, 'Pleased to meet you.'

He couldn't extract it quickly enough.

'This way.' He led them through the station.

'Where's DCI Runcie?' Henry asked.

'She's had to turn out to a job . . . a suicide, we think, but she went anyway.' Saul didn't turn as he spoke.

Henry grinned at Daniels. 'What are the circumstances?'

Henry could see the man's shoulders tighten. 'Guy drove over a cliff,' he said unwillingly.

He led them through a series of tile-lined corridors, reminding Henry of the old-fashioned swimming baths he used to go to when he was a lad – cream, grey and green tiles. Then they went up some stairs by the entrance up to the first floor where the CID offices were located. On that level, he took them to a small room with a table in the centre of it, together with four chairs around it. There was a window high on one wall through which Henry could see other high walls, which he presumed belonged to the police station. Essentially, though, there was no natural light, the illumination provided by three long fluorescent tubes hanging on metal frames from the ceiling.

Lined up in the middle of the table were four loose box files, two marked with the name Tom Salter and two with Mark James Wright. They were murder boxes containing everything connected with the two deaths under review.

'I made sure all the shit's here for you.' Saul waved an indifferent hand towards the files. 'Help yourself, guys.' He looked deliberately at Daniels on the word 'guys'. Then he was gone.

'I get the impression we're not really welcome,' Henry observed, narrowing his eyes at Daniels. 'How do you feel about letting me borrow your car?'

'I don't have a problem with it.' She shuffled the ignition key out of her pocket and lobbed it to him. 'What're you thinking?'

'That I might just go and look over DCI Runcie's shoulder at the job she turned out to. I might be able to chat to her about these two jobs while her mind is slightly distracted. In the meantime, you start with the Salter murder, if you don't mind staying here?'

'No probs with that.'

Henry gave her a nod and left the room, finding his way along a corridor to the main CID office, where a couple of shirt-sleeved jacks were working at desks. Across the room was a door marked *Serious Crime Team*, to which Henry headed.

It opened out into a large open office with a couple of doors off, one marked *DCI*. Saul was chatting to a woman at a desk and his head turned rather like the Devil's, slowly and frighteningly. Henry beamed disarmingly at him.

'Can I help yuh?' Saul asked with great effort.

'I want to catch up with DCI Runcie. I realize she's on a job, so I thought I'd join her.'

'She's probably busy enough, I'd say,' Saul answered.

Henry paused a moment, then crossed over to him and whispered, 'See me in the corridor please.'

In the space of a few minutes, Henry Christie had been made to feel very annoyed and unwanted. His skin was beginning to prickle at the back of his neck as he spun away from Saul and walked back out through the CID office into the corridor, feeling the eyes of the detectives on him. He waited a few moments before Saul appeared.

As Daniels knew, Henry rarely pulled rank. He preferred to use what people skills he possessed to guide others, and the belief that most members of staff really wanted to do their best.

Plus, any bollockings he did care to dish out always came from him. He never distanced himself from any uncomfortable tellings-off.

This time, he had a point to make.

Saul appeared, his expression sullen.

'Let me tell you this, DC Saul. I'm here at the request and with the authority of your chief constable, and although that man is now unfortunately dead, that authority still stands and is reaffirmed by my chief, who is now in charge for the time being. So, though you may not like me being here – and I get the feeling you don't – here I am, and here I'll be staying until my job is done.' Henry paused. 'Now, into that little mix, I hold the rank of superintendent, and I fucking well expect full, complete and unfettered cooperation from you, your colleagues and DCI Runcie, busy or not. Do I make myself clear, DC Saul?'

'Yes, boss,' he said unhappily.

'So in that case, this is what I want. I want you to provide DC Daniels with more mugs of tea and bottles of water than she can possibly imbibe; I want you to be nice and kind to her and afford her the respect she merits. She is a very experienced detective, and don't you forget that. Then I want you to provide me with a CID car, OK? And I want you to tell me exactly where I can find DCI Runcie and give me directions. Got that?'

Saul nodded.

'So, tell me, what do I want?'

'Refreshment, respect for DC Daniels and a car for you.'

'Oh, and friendliness.'

'And friendliness.'

Henry returned Daniels' car key to her then found his allocated car in the police car park at the back of the nick. It was a battered Ford KA, as basic a model as was possible to find, and had all the accoutrements of a CID car down to the fish-and-chip wrappers in the door compartments and an empty can of Red Bull rolling about in the passenger footwell. It also had the aroma of sweaty detectives and ground-in grime – and 102,000 miles on the clock.

Using the satnav app on his phone, coupled with the directions given to him by Mr Reluctant (Saul), Henry drove out of Portsea north along the coast road, suddenly realizing he was in fact driving along the same stretch of road on which Mark James Wright had been dragged out of his car and stabbed to death in a field. He recalled it from the Google Earth search he'd done previously. He pulled in and called Daniels, asking her to check through Wright's file to see if he was correct.

He could hear her riffling through papers as he waited.

'What did you say to DC Saul?' she asked.

'Why?'

'He's suddenly as nice as pie. Coffee, bikkies.'

'I told him tea, actually. Does that guy not listen?'

'Well, whatever, a sea change has come over him. He's almost human.'

'Good.'

'Ah, here we are . . .' Daniels read out the road number and location of Wright's murder and he thanked her, then realized he had stopped in the exact lay-by in which Wright's car had been left running, the body found in the adjacent field. Henry climbed out of the KA, leaned on it and surveyed the scene.

He sniffed, then looked further afield, turning a slow, full circle, seeing how remote the location was, how few vehicles there were on this stretch even at this time of day. Late evening and into the night, he guessed, the place would be deserted. It was literally in the middle of nowhere.

And, confirming his previous conversation with Daniels, it was a good place for a killing, especially if it had been premeditated, but just as good if not.

He didn't spend too much time there. The murder, after all, was months old and there would be little to gain from a re-inspection of the scene, although he wouldn't necessarily rule it out. He continued following the satnav, which was taking him further north, then sharply east towards very rugged coastline where the road became narrow and winding until he arrived at an area of police activity at the entrance to a wooded track. He found a parking spot for the KA in some bushes so as not to block the road, then walked back to the track, where a marked police car was parked across the opening and a fairly scruffy bobby slouched next to it, looking at his mobile phone. His flat cap was tipped on the back of his head, bus conductor style.

On seeing Henry, the cop pushed himself reluctantly off the car and raised his eyes from the screen of his phone. 'You can't go down there,' he said, raising a hand.

Henry produced his warrant card. 'I'd guess that DCI Runcie is expecting me by now,' he said.

*   *   *

The call had been logged at 6.30 a.m. from a farmer out tending livestock on his land that encompassed Salterforth Cliffs. He had spotted a gap in his fencing, through which several of his sheep had already ventured and were precariously negotiating the cliff face with much less finesse than the mountain goats they were clearly trying to emulate.

He had aimed his ATV towards the break, noticing tyre marks running right across the field from the gate near the woodland to the cliff edge, but he hadn't really thought much about them. He'd been having problems with youngsters in cars driving on his land for a while now.

What he hadn't expected to see was the car at the bottom of the cliffs, smashed to smithereens, and a hand sticking out of the window.

DCI Runcie had been awake most of the night in her swish waterfront apartment in a block close to the river. It had cost her in excess of half-a-million pounds but she'd blagged that she'd got it at a knockdown price of just over £200,000 because a sale had fallen through and the developer was desperate for a sale. Not true, but she had to keep nosy people away from her business.

She'd stalked around, vaping and smoking, irritated and not a little concerned by Henry Christie's arrival.

From what she'd read about his background, she knew his reviews would be detailed and searching, and that she'd have to prepare herself for some awkward questions.

Sleep came about five a.m., instantly deep and dreamless, but interrupted by the bonkers ring of her iPhone, jerking her back to wakefulness.

The car – and the body – had been found at the bottom of the cliffs.

The further unsettling news of Henry Christie's imminent arrival at the scene of the 'suicide' had, while not totally unexpected, made Runcie glad she had turned out immediately and not left it to some lackey not under her direct control.

Under normal circumstances, she would have taken her time, but Christie's presence in town gave her the impetus to get there and start to cover up any problems there might be – such as explaining away two sets of vehicle tracks across the field to the broken fence, one set going over the cliff, one set returning.

On her way, she called into comms and asked them to urgently turn out a mobile crane operator she knew, thinking that if they got to the cliffs quickly enough, the crane tracks would obliterate any tyre tracks and any requirement to field awkward questions.

When, at the scene, she took a rather frantic call from Saul about his frosty encounter with Henry and Henry's decision to turn out, there was no surprise there.

'You just keep an eye on the black bitch. I'll take care of Henry.'

Henry walked down the country lane seeing police cars, an ambulance and a fire engine parked right in the trees, then saw the reason why they'd been shoved to one side. They had been moved to allow a mid-sized low-loader to reverse down and pull up where the lane widened out. There was nothing on the back of the truck and the ramps were down.

Henry went on to the end of the lane. It widened out slightly and the woods ended where they met a big, wide field.

He stopped and saw the activity on the far side which he guessed would be the cliffs, as beyond he could see the grey North Sea.

A small mobile crane on tank-like tracks had obviously been offloaded from the low-loader and was at the cliff edge with its jib jutting out to sea. A gathering of people surrounded it, peering over the edge. Henry could hear lots of shouting in the wind.

He stopped at the gate, looking at the deep indentations made by the heavy crane tracks across the field and just thought, 'Hm.' He contorted past the stone gate post, keeping well off the tracks, and headed towards the activity at the cliff edge.

ELEVEN

D aniels had a good eye for detail, as any good detective should have, and she was happy to settle down in the small, strange room with the two murder files in front of her and start to read while making notes on a pad.

An hour into the first file on Salter's murder, she realized she hadn't altered position and found she was stiffening up. She stood up and stretched her arms and legs, then rolled her neck and hips, just to loosen off.

DC Saul came in, knocking but entering without being beckoned in, at a point where she was halfway through one of her hip rolls. His creepy eyes took her in. Having removed her jacket, her curves were easy to see as her clothing strained against her with the exercise.

She stopped immediately.

'I thought you might want a break,' he said. His eyes lingered on her breasts, then ascended slowly up her neck to her face. His expression did not falter, even though he knew she'd clocked his gaze. He did not know that she was not remotely intimidated by him, but she guessed that was how he wanted her to feel. 'Been at it for a while now, haven't you, lass?'

'Yeah, could do with a leg stretch.'

'Want me to show you where the dining room is on the top floor? Coffee and snacks always available.'

'Point me in the right direction and I'll find it.' She grabbed her jacket from the back of the chair, then paused to look at him. 'You were one of the detectives on the Tom Salter murder, weren't you? You took some witness statements.'

'I did.'

'What did you make of the whole thing?'

'What d'you mean?'

'I mean,' she half-shrugged, 'nobody gets killed like that for no reason, do they?'

'Robbery, maybe. He supposedly had a couple of grand in

the office safe. Probably stumbled on some low-life trying to rob it.'

'Still . . . a strange time for him to be in the office anyway, wasn't it? Gone midnight.'

'That's my point of view,' Saul said abruptly, bringing any further speculation to a dead halt. 'Dining room.'

Henry peered over the dangerous cliff face to see members of the local mountain rescue team scaling the rock face and running steel harnesses through and around the body of the car, securing them with hooks and giving the thumbs up to someone also on the cliff edge in a hi-viz jacket, who then thumbed-up the crane operator, who began to lower the hook. This was attached to the harness around the car. It took the weight, and the crane began to haul the vehicle upwards. With the crane jib extended, the operator managed mostly to keep it away from the cliff face, bringing it up slowly and surely, then rotating and depositing the mangled car on the field.

Henry could see the equally mangled body of a man behind the steering wheel.

Not a pretty sight.

Runcie came towards Henry, who had kept his distance while the cops and CSIs worked around the car following instructions given by Runcie. As she approached him, she was deep in conversation on the phone, and Henry caught the last few words just before the mobile crane's engine revved up, turned 180 degrees where it stood, churning up more ground under its tracks, then commenced its slow journey back across the field to the low-loader.

'Yes, that's right,' Henry heard Runcie say into the phone. 'If you can do it as soon as possible, that would be good . . . So, yes, shall we say three p.m. at the local mortuary?' Words were then drowned out by the crane and Runcie ended the call, watching with a scowl on her face as it churned away until it was finally quiet enough to talk.

'You didn't need to come. I'm a big girl,' she said sourly. 'Quite capable.'

'I'm sure you are,' Henry agreed. 'I don't doubt your abilities.'

'And yet, here you are.'

'Thing about me is this: I can't resist turning out to jobs. It's in my blood. Why sit reading a dusty old murder file when I can leave someone else to do it and get out to the sharp end?'

'I thought you might be spying on me.' She was wearing Wellington boots chopped off at the calf and they looked incongruous against her smart trouser suit. 'That's what you're here for, isn't it?'

'No, but I thought it might be an opportunity to talk.'

'To be fair, I don't think I'll have much time,' she said. 'The ambulance crew are going to help us, somehow, get this poor, mashed-up guy out of the car and get him to the mortuary. I want to watch all that for evidential continuity, and then I'll accompany the body to Royal Portsea Infirmary. By that time I might want to have my lunch – I always eat alone – and then it'll be time for the PM, which I've just arranged.' She held up her phone.

'I'll stick with you,' Henry said with a fixed grin, knowing when he was being held at arm's-length. 'It's a while since I've been to a post-mortem.'

Runcie's chin almost crashed to the grass.

'Look, I do know you're busy, I get it,' Henry said.

'Well, then?'

Henry didn't take her up on that, but instead asked what this job was all about.

'Suicide.'

'Do you know him? The dead man?'

'Pretty sure I do.'

Henry waited.

'Martin Sowerbutts. He was in police custody yesterday. I was the officer dealing with him.'

'For what?'

'Suspicion of abducting, raping and murdering four young girls.'

Henry was taken aback.

'He admitted nothing and we could find nothing but some circumstantial evidence against him, so he was released without charge. It looks like he did do it, and this shows he's committed suicide in his remorse.'

'Not a great way to go about it. Car over cliff.'

'I'd guess his mind was in turmoil, not thinking straight. Not thinking, full stop.'

'It's a theory,' Henry admitted.

'It's a fact, sir.'

'Not until it's proven.'

'What exactly are you getting at?'

Henry turned his head and his eyes followed the churned-up track in the field. 'Forgive me for saying "bread and butter" here, DCI Runcie, but what is the first thing you should be thinking with something like this, until the evidence shows otherwise?'

Henry watched a red rash rise up her neck.

'Murder,' he answered for her. 'I only hope that, at the very least, the CSI managed to take photographs of this field before that dumb piece of machinery ploughed the shit out of it.' He paused. 'I'll see you at the post-mortem . . . three p.m. at the infirmary, if I heard correctly?'

Henry drove back to Portsea police station, calling Jerry Tope on the way to see if he had anything from the searches Henry had asked him to carry out. The detective was evasive and finally admitted that his services had been snaffled by Rik Dean to do the Intel work relating to CC Burnham's murder in Bacup. Henry chuckled at this, and understood. Tope was the in-demand analyst of the moment and Henry wasn't surprised by Rik's move. He would have done the same. Henry asked him to do it when he found a moment to spare.

At the station, he found Daniels hard at work in the room provided for them, deep into the Tom Salter murder, making copious notes.

'Boss. How did it go?'

Henry slumped on a chair. 'Not impressive.' He was going to say more when he clamped his jaw shut. 'Let's go get a coffee. I've noticed a Costa just down the road. Let's wander out, get a feel for the town.'

'Will this stuff be OK left here?' Daniels swept her hand at the murder files.

'Let's tell the delectable DC Saul we're leaving the room for a while, get him to lock up. I'm sure he'll have a key.'

Ten minutes later, they were in the café on the high street. Henry had a medium Americano (he refused to say Medio when ordered) and Daniels had a medium tall and milky latte.

'What have you got?' he asked.

She'd brought her notebook with her. It was on the table, but not open. She sipped her coffee thoughtfully, then wiped away the line of froth from her top lip.

'Gaps,' she said, her mouth twisting. 'Two major ones, I'd say. What exactly was he doing from his last sighting until he was killed? And I can't find a major analysis of his phone records, which must surely exist somewhere. His property does include a mobile phone. Who did he call, who called him and what was he doing in his office at such a godforsaken hour? None of these things have been answered.'

Henry listened.

She said, 'Like you, I'm not impressed.'

'What about the ballistics on the weapon?'

Daniels opened her notes for this one. 'No actual weapon was recovered but he was killed by nine-millimetre bullets, probably from an automatic pistol of some sort. The rifling . . .' she looked quizzically at Henry, '. . . I'm not exactly sure what that means – I'm not a firearms buff.'

'It's the pattern the bullet takes from inside the barrel of the gun as it spins out when it's fired. They're a bit like a fingerprint – all vary slightly, even on the same model of weapon.'

'I knew that.' She smiled. 'Anyway, the rifling links to a bullet fired in an armed robbery committed last year in Portsea, when a security guard was wounded in a cash-in-transit robbery at a post office on the edge of town. Again, the weapon wasn't recovered and one male offender made good his escape. Never been caught.'

'Just one offender?'

'Seems so.'

'Unusual for that sort of job; it's usually a gang.'

Daniels nodded and sipped her latte. It was decaffeinated because she was essentially coffee'd out now.

'Coming back to Salter,' she said, 'I'd say those gaps are what really need to be scrutinized – his whereabouts, who he contacted, etc., and his phone records.'

'Do the files show what work was done in those respects?'

'Very little.'

'Anything about use of bank cards? That could pin him down to a time and place maybe?'

'Nothing.'

'It's often the last person to see the victim alive who is the killer,' Henry said. 'Who was that?'

'His wife, according to the file.'

'So maybe she has a story to tell that hasn't been told?'

'Maybe, but I have read her statement and it does seem a bit . . . meh . . . if you get my drift. Woolly.'

'Let's get a copy of it and go see her, shall we?'

Back at the station, Saul let them into the room. Henry asked to be given a key, which he almost slammed into Henry's palm.

'I'll keep hold of it from now on,' Henry informed him. 'Not that for one moment I think it's the only key.'

'It is, actually, so don't lose it, sir,' Saul lied.

'I'll keep it close to my heart.'

Henry and Daniels watched him leave the room.

Daniels said, 'Do you think this lot have something to hide, other than general incompetence?'

'No one likes other people rooting about in their underwear drawer . . . I know I don't, but then again, I don't give anyone cause to do so.'

'I'll bet it's a sight for sore eyes.'

'Cheeky.' He smiled at her, liking her a lot: professional, serious yet fun. 'However, it might be worth—' He stopped talking abruptly, wondering if he was being excessively paranoid. He dropped his voice to a whisper and continued, 'Copying everything that might be of interest to us.'

Daniels nodded and whispered back. 'I'll find a photocopier and do the whole lot.'

DC Saul was extra whiny when they told him of their intentions. Firstly, he wasn't happy about them copying anything so sensitive and confidential, and secondly, he didn't want to provide them with his code for the CID copier because, in an effort to save money, all copying of documents had to be accounted for. The days of free photocopying had long since gone, and the same applied on the other side of the Pennines.

'I'll pay a fiver to finance if you want,' Henry offered.

'Be 'right,' he said, leading them to the copier in its own little room.

Daniels copied both sets of files, watched half-lidded by Saul.

'On your head if any of this gets out,' he warned them both, drawing a scowl from Henry, who toyed with having a dig at him for insubordination but held back. He had a feeling that, somewhere along the line, this nasty person would trip up.

So they ignored him and, when completed, Daniels took the stack of warm paper back to the room and began to sort it.

'We'll need a stapler. With staples,' Henry told Saul. 'Obviously I'll fork out for the staples.'

Later, in Daniels' Peugeot, Henry skimmed through the file on Salter's death again and read the statement from his wife (Karen Salter, née Bolton). It told him very little about her or Salter or their life together, just that they'd been married for fifteen years, he ran a haulage business, they were happy, she knew of no enemies, and the last she saw of him was when he left the marital home at about eight a.m. on the day before his death, in the early hours of the morning after. He had gone to work, and it wasn't unusual for him to work excessive hours. She believed the business was doing OK, wasn't aware of any problems. There was no mention of his mobile phone.

Salter's house was in the countryside about eight miles inland from Portsea, set in a stunning, rolling landscape of green fields and woodland. It was a converted barn with a huge, quadruple garage and a covered swimming pool. From a distance, the property looked beautiful, but as Daniels approached up a narrow driveway, it became obvious it had seen better days.

Henry wondered if the house was a clumsy metaphor for a marriage on the rocks. Or was he reading too deeply?

Daniels negotiated several speed humps and drew in outside the front door behind an old BMW.

As they climbed out, a woman came to the door.

She looked to be in her late thirties, close-cropped hair dyed a strange shade of henna red, though Henry thought the label on the bottle might describe it as something more exotic. She was thin, her face gaunt and her dark eyes were unhappy, yet she was still very pretty.

Daniels was closest to her.

'Mrs Salter?' she asked, and the woman nodded. Daniels produced her warrant card as Henry joined her, also with his card in his hand. 'I'm Detective Constable Diane Daniels from the CID and this is Detective Superintendent Henry Christie.'

He flashed his card.

'We'd like a word with you, please.' Daniels was pleasant but firm, stating what she wanted as a statement and not giving her any wriggle room.

'What about?'

'Your husband's death.'

Henry had seen the reaction on the faces of many relatives of victims of terrible violence he'd had to re-interview about cases over the years. Usually they were sick of the cops, sick of answering questions, just somehow wanted to believe their loved ones were really still alive and they could return to normality – or, having come to the point of accepting the death, just could not bear having the wounds reopened.

The three of them sat at the kitchen table.

Mrs Salter had made them a mug of tea each.

'Mrs Salter, we're so sorry to have to go through this with you again,' Daniels said.

She looked resigned to the inevitable. 'That's OK, I suppose.'

'Can I call you Karen?'

'Yes, that's fine.'

The two detectives, Henry suspected, were about to open an old wound.

They spent an hour with her going through Tom's movements, but there was nothing she could tell them about after he set off for work that fateful day. He did have a mobile phone and she gave them the number, though Daniels knew it was in the file. Beyond that, there was very little information. The marriage was one of those 'brother and sister' things, and his business was very much hand to mouth, chasing money all the time, and she saw little of him.

They thanked her and left. Henry asked Daniels to drive him to the infirmary so he could find the public mortuary.

'So what have we learned?' he asked Daniels.

'Er . . . middling marriage, business kept him busy . . . and still a yawning gap that's unexplained. He had a phone, but no info on that as such, so that needs to be clarified with Runcie, I'd say. And Mrs Salter is a sad woman who did not love her husband, just tolerated life.'

'Female intuition?'

'Just obvious.'

'Let me ask you a question.'

'Go on.'

'How many people, even serious business folk, leave for work at eight in the morning and are still working after midnight – legitimately?'

'Very few, I'd say.'

They had reached the end of the long drive at this point.

'Over sixteen hours,' Henry said, and they looked at each other. 'Nothing to say where he was during that time? Was he a man covering his tracks, do you think?'

'That lady back at the house isn't telling us everything.'

Daniels reversed all the way back up the drive. The two detectives knocked on the door again but got no reply.

Daniels tried the door handle: locked.

'Maybe she's having a bath,' Henry said.

Daniels knocked harder, louder, then crouched down at the letter box to peer in. 'Nothing.'

They walked the perimeter of the house, shading their eyes to look through ground-floor windows, but could not see her.

'Odd,' Daniels observed.

Henry swivelled slowly and looked at the garage block which might once have been a hay storage barn, he guessed.

Daniels set off ahead of him, aiming for the side door of this building, leaving the less-than-agile Henry hobbling in her wake. She pushed open the door and stepped inside.

Daniels' scream for help made Henry forget his aches and pains, and he turned his hobble into a sprint.

The disfigured body of Martin Sowerbutts lay naked on the mortuary slab. His face was mashed beyond any way of identifying him, though fortunately he did have his driving licence with him, and Runcie confirmed that he had been wearing the same clothes he'd had on when he'd been released from custody the day before. Dental record checks would come later.

That clothing had been stripped from him and bagged up.

Henry saw that Sowerbutts' chest had been crushed, probably by impact with the steering wheel of the vehicle he'd driven over the cliff.

When Henry had entered the mortuary, Runcie was in hushed conversation with the Home Office pathologist. She saw Henry's arrival but continued the conflab with the pathologist, and Henry assumed she was briefing him on the circumstances of the death.

Eventually the conversation ended. Runcie turned to Henry, who asked, 'How's it going?'

'Progressing. He had no known next of kin, so the coroner has accepted my ID of him for the sake of the PM,' she said. 'I'm told you had an incident with Tom Salter's wife,' she accused him.

'You could say that.'

'I thought you were here to review two unsolved cases, not go raking muck and driving already unbalanced people to attempt terrible things. If you'd asked, I could have told you she was on the edge.'

'I'll pretend I haven't heard that, DCI Runcie,' Henry said frostily.

Their eyes had a fleeting moment of fiery jousting, then both turned away as the pathologist began speaking into the microphone dangling above the body on the slab.

'My name is Professor David Wrackham and I am a Home Office pathologist. I am about to commence a post-mortem on Martin Sowerbutts. The circumstances of his death, as outlined to me by the police, are as follows . . .'

TWELVE

D iane Daniels sat beside a hospital bed in one of the bays in the A&E department at the Royal Portsea Infirmary, looking wretchedly at the sleeping form of Karen Salter. A drip fed into the woman's right arm and an oxygen tube ran under her nostrils, assisting her rasping breathing.

Daniels could still vividly see Karen's body hanging from the noose slung over one of the steel rafters in the garage, the upended chair on the floor below her dangling feet, which she had climbed on to before putting the noose around her neck, the plastic bag over her head and then kicked it away from underneath herself.

Daniels had opened the door as the chair tipped over and Karen's slim body dropped on the noose, drawing a horrific gasp from the poor woman. Almost instantly, her legs began to dance the jig of death by hanging. The fall of the noose wasn't enough to break her neck but she would have slowly strangled herself and suffocated from the plastic bag, which she sucked into her face.

In all, a very serious attempt at suicide.

Daniels screamed for Henry as she raced into the garage, grabbed Karen's legs, encompassing them with her arms, trying to take her weight and raise her.

Henry clattered through the door a moment later, instantly took in the scene and hurtled across.

'I'll do that,' he said. 'You sort the rope and the bag.'

He took over from Daniels, embraced Karen's legs at her thighs, then braced himself, knowing this was going to hurt a lot. Daniels pulled the chair upright and clambered on to it, whipping the plastic bag off Karen's head, which made her draw breath involuntarily. Her eyes shot open like some sort of zombie doll, and she moaned, 'Let me die.'

Daniels suddenly had a small pen knife in her hand, which was attached to her keyring.

'You got her?' she asked Henry.

'Yeaaah,' he groaned, the pain in his shoulder ferocious.

Daniels reached up behind Karen's head and began sawing at the cord, which was a length of washing line, not easy to hack through with the tiny knife blade because of the inner thread of flexible steel cord, but she kept at it until she cut through, then caught Karen's upper body and, between her and Henry, they lowered her to the ground. Daniels eased the cord from around her neck.

Karen sobbed uncontrollably.

Daniels propped her up, took hold of her and gently embraced her, stroked her, telling her everything was going to be OK.

Meanwhile, Henry was dialling treble nine, asking for an ambulance.

In the hospital bed, Karen opened her caked-up eyes slowly.

'You should have let me die,' she said. 'I have nothing to live for.'

Henry watched the post-mortem, one of many he had attended from his early days as a young probationer, all the way through his career to becoming an SIO. He had learnt many things about the human body from these.

Usually during a PM he would be watching closely, asking questions of the pathologist, showing interest. But he stood back from this one. It was not his job, nor had he been offered any protective clothing. He did, however, stalk a full circle around the slab in the centre of the room as the pathologist began his investigation of Sowerbutts' chest, eventually exposing and lifting out the cracked, crushed ribcage and broken sternum, injuries consistent with having been at the wheel of a vehicle going over the edge of a cliff. The bones reminded Henry of an archaeological dig.

He stood a little further back as the professor cut out the lungs and lifted the sloppy organs across to the dissecting table, placing them there like a huge, dead bird, talking as he did so, explaining his process as he sliced the lungs section by section.

Henry saw the blood seep from the sponge-like tissue, trying to hear what the man was saying.

He also watched Runcie, who was standing close to Wrackham, accidentally, Henry supposed, but regularly obscuring the view.

She was asking questions softly, persistently, but Henry could not hear them.

The next major thing was to investigate Sowerbutts' skull, an operation which entailed – after Wrackham had closely inspected the facial injuries – paring away and peeling back the skin to reveal the bone structure underneath, then removing the clearly very badly damaged skull itself using a bone saw that reminded Henry of a pizza cutter, slicing off the top like a boiled egg and revealing the visibly damaged brain underneath.

Sowerbutts was a terrible mess.

Yet there was something playing on Henry's mind.

After just over two hours, a mortuary attendant threw Sowerbutts' organs back into the empty cadaver he had become, then refitted the sliced-up brain into his head, put the skull cap on and pulled the skin and scalp back over it. He then replaced the ribcage and sewed up the chest. Now, with his features even more distorted, and the criss-cross sewing, Sowerbutts looked something like Frankenstein's monster, just on a smaller scale.

'Cause of death,' the pathologist declared as he washed off, 'massive brain trauma consistent with having been involved in a serious vehicle accident.'

'Consistent with having taken his own life?' Runcie asked.

'Unfortunately I cannot tell you what his mental state was,' Wrackham said. 'That will be up to the evidence collected around the tragic event and the outcome of a coroner's inquest.'

'Thanks, Professor,' Runcie said, then looked at Henry. 'No mystery then, and a dangerous child killer off the streets without recourse to a costly trial.'

Henry's mouth twisted sardonically as something unsettling flitted through his thoughts like a dark shadow.

Now he had a couple of things on his mind that he could not quite seem to grasp. He put it down to the ageing process, the slowing down of his faculties, though he still had a strange faith in himself that he would get there in the end.

Something Runcie had said previously.

Something he'd seen during the post-mortem.

Unsettling 'somethings'.

He bumped into Daniels in a corridor close to the A&E department. She looked relieved to see him.

'Henry, I hope you don't mind this,' she said, and without warning gave him a quick hug, through which he could feel tension judder out of her. As she pulled away, she said, 'Is it always this much fun working with you?'

'Sometimes it has its moments,' he admitted. 'How is Mrs Salter?'

'Sleeping now. Been very emotional, as you'd expect.'

'And was our unsaid assumption correct?'

Daniels nodded and puffed out her cheeks. 'She thought her husband was having an affair but doesn't know with whom.'

'Does she have a suspect?'

'Yeah, Salter's accountant. But how have you gone on?'

Henry jarred as one of those elusive 'somethings' clicked in his brain. 'I need to make a phone call,' he said. 'An urgent one.' Then, reacting to Daniels' puzzled expression, he said, 'I'm no pathologist, but I'm pretty sure Martin Sowerbutts was murdered.'

It was almost six p.m. when Henry and Daniels met in the hospital corridor and decided they'd had enough for that particular day, to get showered and change their clothes, then meet in the bar for a drink and a meal.

Henry planned to stretch out on the bed in his underpants and ease his aching body and soul for half an hour, which became an hour before he jerked awake when his mobile phone rang.

'Henry, my man, you left a message for me to contact you.' It was his old friend Professor Baines, the Home Office pathologist who covered the Lancashire area and who, Henry knew, had performed the post-mortem on John Burnham. The two men went way back and had developed a good relationship verging on friendship, and they'd had many conversations over many a pint after post-mortems to discuss sudden death. Baines had also always been interested in Henry's once very complicated love life, but since he had turned over a new leaf, Baines seemed to find him a little dull. That said, Baines obviously knew of Henry's current situation. 'You need some advice from an old tom cat?' Baines asked, which Henry thought was quite rich: Baines wasn't even a kitten. 'A few days away with a young lady? I'd say go for it – you only live once. What happens in Central Yorkshire, etc., etc.'

'No, I'm not after any advice along those lines,' Henry chuckled, 'and if I was, you'd be the last person I'd ask. No, look, I want something to happen very quickly . . .'

The next phone call he took was from Jerry Tope, who'd been able to do some background checks on the two murder victims. Henry took a few notes and asked Tope to email him details he could scrutinize at leisure.

For a while, Henry felt like he was operating in a call centre, making and taking calls, but the final one he made was to FB to bring him up to date with the state of the review and to ask him to intervene in something else, and also to share some of the doubts he – Henry – was already beginning to have, although he warned FB that none were really founded in anything other than arse-twitching gut feeling – that 'thing' he got that had served him well over many years. That thing called instinct.

FB listened, hummed and hawed in all the right places and said yes in the right places too, and finally, after a pause, said, 'Henry, there is one thing you do need to know . . .'

She knew that when she wanted them to be, Jane Runcie could make her eyes into orbs of pure evil. As they scanned the faces of the three people sitting across the desk from her, each one shifting uncomfortably under their glare, she knew she was having the desired effect.

Her eyes took in the three detectives, Saul, Silverthwaite and Hawkswood. She was certain the skin on the back of their necks was crawling just a little.

The power she could muster gave her a good feeling.

They were seated in her actual office, door locked, and the three men under her scrutiny sitting like little boys on plastic chairs while she remained high and regal on the leather chair behind her desk.

She had listened to their reports.

The one from Saul detailed his interactions with Christie and the gooey-eyed lady detective, DC Daniels, and their insistence on copying the murder files and wanting a key to the room they had been allocated, plus Christie's pathetic attempt at being the big 'I am' superintendent after Saul had purposely kept him waiting that morning.

'So he's liable to pull rank,' Runcie sneered. 'The last bastion of a weak manager.'

'I wouldn't say he was weak,' Saul responded, but clamped his mouth shut tight when Runcie's eyes seemed just about to fire a death ray at him and evaporate him where he sat. As he crumpled, she looked at the other two. 'And what have you idiots been up to?'

'Keeping out of the way, like you said,' Silverthwaite told her.

She considered something for a moment. 'Tell me about their early morning runs.' Silverthwaite told her again: Daniels was up first and away, Christie almost an hour later. 'So they didn't set off together or come back at the same time?'

'No, her first, and she was back before he set off.'

Her eyes narrowed. 'OK. What route?'

'How would I know that?' Silverthwaite asked. But, under her stare, he said, 'Down the river, I'm presuming.'

'OK.'

'What are we going to do, boss?' Hawkswood asked worriedly. He was also wondering if she would be expecting him to perform again for her. Not that the sex wasn't fantastic, just that he didn't enjoy being dominated so overpoweringly. He felt like a dog on a leash, being jerked around by a nasty owner, and it made him squirm . . . yet acquiesce at the same time.

The three underlings exchanged glances.

'Firstly,' she said, looking directly at Silverthwaite, 'Tullane arrives in Manchester just after four p.m. tomorrow. You need to be there to pick him up and bring him across. He's booked into the Metropole. Look after him and I'll make arrangements to see him sometime in the evening.'

'Tullane?' he said.

'Tullane,' she confirmed.

'OK. Transport?'

'Hire a decent car.'

He nodded.

Her attention moved to Hawkswood. 'You keep our two friends under surveillance tonight . . . yes, all by yourself . . . but there is one thing extra.' She paused for effect. 'You know how you didn't manage to put Henry Christie out of the game?'

Hawkswood shifted uncomfortably.

'I need you to make amends.'

'How, exactly?'

'If the pretty little lady goes for her early morning jog, you go along too – yeah? And put the bitch in the river.'

A half-smile of anticipation brightened his face. 'With pleasure.'

Runcie said to Saul, 'While we indulge in a great deal of subterfuge and misdirection at the same time as solving a murder.'

She opened a drawer in her desk and removed a clear plastic bag, which she laid on the desktop.

It was the Makarov pistol.

'A gun with provenance.'

After a contact call to Alison, assuring her he wasn't overdoing anything and that all was well, Henry changed into his jeans and a T-shirt and went to meet Daniels in the bar, where she was already a few sips into a glass of white wine, sitting in one of the alcoves and reading the murder files.

Henry joined her after buying a pint of Stella and another wine for her. After a clink of glasses, he took a long draught of his lager and enjoyed the cool sensation of its ice-cold fingers reaching down into his chest.

'How are you feeling?' he asked her.

'I'm good,' she promised him. 'You?'

'Apart from taking the weight of a hanging woman which hurt my poor shoulder, I'm good too.'

They sipped their drinks.

'I don't like these people,' she declared. 'Runcie, Saul . . . not the most helpful of folk.'

'Maybe they're just feeling under pressure. I always get jumpy and defensive when one of my cases is under review. Human nature.'

'It's more than that,' Daniels said, 'unless I'm just being over-suspicious. An undercurrent. I can't work out if it's something sinister.'

'Well, you're good at reading people,' Henry complimented

her. 'You did well with Mrs Salter . . . it's a good job we went back.'

'She doesn't think so.'

'She will, in time.' He had another mouthful of lager, then nodded at the reading material Daniels had slid to the edge of the table. 'Anything more?'

'No. Still the gaps and the mobile phone issue . . .'

'I've been sent some information from Jerry Tope to peruse. Maybe later, if I forward it to you, perhaps we can have a look at it – after we've eaten.'

'Sounds like a plan. I'm famished.'

'Me too.' He hesitated. 'I also asked Jerry to look at anything concerning the accident Jack Culver was involved in – the stolen car thing. Turns out, and it wasn't revealed to me at the time I spoke to Burnham – and FB has only just seen fit to tell me – that Culver was on his way to see Burnham having told him he had misgivings about two murder investigations he was overseeing. Kinda wish I'd known that when we went into bat here.'

Daniels sat upright. 'What misgivings?'

'I don't have the answer to that.'

'Coincidence?' Daniels punted.

Henry shrugged. 'Anyway, let's eat. I think we have a busy night ahead.'

'Why would that be?'

'Oh, did I not mention?' he said innocently. 'There is every chance we might be attending a post-mortem in the next few hours. I'm not sure of the collective noun for a number of autopsies on the same person. A "cut-up", maybe?'

Before he could explain, his phone rang. It was FB calling. There was a short conversation and straight after Henry made another call, which was also short, then looked at Daniels and gave her the thumbs up.

'FB came up trumps,' he said. 'Let's eat and I'll reveal all.'

They ate steadily, no rush, at a pub further along the waterfront. Henry explained his plans and what he hoped to achieve over the next few hours (just to put his own mind at rest, he told her). After this, they fell into an easy conversation again about their personal lives, though not in any great depth.

Henry found her to be pleasant company, funny and incisive. He got the impression she did not know how good looking she was, and he noticed a lot of sidelong glances from the men in the pub. Part of him wondered if it was just curiosity – seeing a black girl with an older, white man, and them drawing the wrong conclusions.

They were back at the hotel two hours later. After a drink in the bar, Henry suggested they went to his room, that she brought her laptop and he sent her what Tope had sent him, so they could spend time examining this information and rereading the murder files.

Daniels looked coyly at him. 'Will I be safe?'

'As houses, trust me. I'll sit at the desk and you sit on the bed.'

Hawkswood was pleased that Silverthwaite had been given another job, even if it meant he was alone in the back of the old surveillance van on the quayside. At least it meant he would only be troubled by his own farts instead of having to inhale the odious clouds that seemed to continually seep out of Silverthwaite from both ends.

This time he had repositioned the van almost directly across from the George Hotel and, by peering through the side-vent peephole, he could see straight through the front window into the bar. Though there were quite a few people coming and going, he clearly saw Daniels arrive in the bar and take a drink over to an alcove, then Christie join her a short time later. He watched both leave on foot and saw them walk down to a pub a little further away. He would have liked to follow them but knew his cover had been blown by his and Silverthwaite's ill-considered appearance at The Tawny Owl; plus, though he hated to admit it, his skin colour didn't help matters.

He had set up the van to have a few more creature comforts by way of cushions, a flask of coffee and one of soup, some nice bought prawn sandwiches, crisps and chocolate.

It was going to be a long night.

The two detectives strolled back a couple of hours later, chatting and laughing amicably, the sight of them turning Hawkswood's lips into a snarl of hatred and concern because he was grudgingly afraid of these two people who, if allowed, could topple a very lucrative enterprise meticulously built up over several years. Not to mention his unofficial pension pot.

'Bastards,' he hissed, watching them through the one-way glass.

He saw them in the bar again, taking up a couple of empty chairs right in the big window.

Hawkswood itched for a Heckler & Koch MP5 to strafe the window and take them both out.

That would be the end of the story – a blood-soaked drive-by shooting.

Part of him thought it might actually come to that.

When they'd finished their drinks, they stood up and went out of sight. Hawkswood checked his watch. It was still quite early.

He called Runcie, who speculated. 'Henry Christie, by all accounts, finds it hard to keep his cock in his pants. See if you can find out what they're up to . . . maybe they're going to fuck.'

Hawkswood slid unobtrusively out of the back of the van, jogged over to the George and flashed his warrant card at the young lad manning Reception. Hawkswood had been wondering how best to get information on the guests, and when he immediately recognized the lad, his heart began to sing melodiously.

He had arrested him twice before for being in possession of cocaine in one of the city centre clubs and, as the lad looked up at Hawkswood, his face dropped while Hawkswood's grin was evil.

'Evening.'

Five minutes later, Hawkswood was on the phone to Runcie as he sat in a small office at the back of the hotel reviewing security footage from the camera on the first-floor corridor where Christie's and Daniels' rooms were situated. He slowed down the image to one frame at a time, saw Christie's door open and allow Daniels into his room.

'She's in his fucking room,' Hawkswood said gleefully.

'Capture it, download on to a disc if you can, just for safe-keeping. I have a phone call to make.'

'You old dog, Henry,' Hawkswood said appreciatively, then looked sideways at the very scared hotel receptionist.

*   *   *

Runcie found the number for The Tawny Owl from the internet website and rang it after firstly withholding the number on her phone.

It seemed to ring for a long time, then it was answered by a woman.

'Hello, Tawny Owl, Kendleton, can I help you?'

'I'm after Alison Marsh, please.'

'Speaking,' Alison said brightly.

'Oh, great. Alison, you don't know me, but I need to tell you something.'

THIRTEEN

Henry stretched, yawned and stood up from the uncomfortable chair at the desk in his room, arching his lower back to get movement into it. Daniels, sitting propped up on the bed with her laptop on her lap, had fallen asleep after nearly two hours of reading.

The time had been fairly productive in terms of getting more understanding of the murder victims, but they still had no real understanding as to why either had been killed. Henry was pleased that a possible affair had been discovered in relation to Salter, and he would point Runcie in the direction of re-interviewing the suicidal Karen Salter in greater depth because now, in Henry's eyes, she had to be a suspect.

Mark James Wright's murder wasn't much clearer, but to be honest, Henry's mind wasn't completely focused on that one just yet.

Daniels' eyes flickered open. 'Did I fall asleep?'

'Yeah. Maybe time to hit the sack now.'

She closed her laptop, collected all the various documents and stood up. Henry followed her to the door, leaning on the door frame as he watched her walk along the corridor to her room. She gave a little wave, then was gone.

Henry reversed into his room and quickly undressed, eager to rest his bones for a while, and slipped under the duvet in just his underwear.

For a moment, he considered calling Alison, but instead sent her a lovey-dovey text, placed his phone on the cabinet and switched off the light.

Before he could even close his eyes, the phone rang.

'Hi, sweetie.'

There was a pause. Henry wondered if the signal had dropped off, but somehow sensed Alison was still on the line.

'Babe?'

'Where are you, Henry?'

'Uh, in bed. Why?'

'Who's with you?'

It was his turn for a pause. Then: 'What do you mean?'

He was sitting up now, not remotely liking the tone of Alison's voice. It was giving him the creeps.

'Who is with you is what I mean.'

'No one. Why would there be?'

'OK, who has been with you?'

'What are you getting at, Alison?'

'Has she been in your room with you?'

Henry heard a sob catch in Alison's throat. She went on: 'I'm giving you the chance to tell me straight, Henry.'

By this time Henry was fully upright and his skin was crawling with dread. His stomach felt like worms were wriggling in it. 'I have nothing to tell you,' he said, though this wasn't strictly true.

'Yes, you fucking do,' Alison said, reverting to her aggressive level of vocabulary to which she descended when enraged. Also – scarily – she did not raise her voice.

He swallowed. 'Yes, DC Daniels has been in my room.'

'I fucking knew it! It is true!'

'Hang on a minute – there is nothing to know here. Yes, she has been in my room – we were reviewing the cases. It was more practical and private than sitting in the public bar and doing it. She's gone to her own room now.'

'Did you fuck her?'

He knew he should not have hesitated with his answer because that tiny gap made him appear truly guilty. It just did.

'You did, didn't you?' Alison cried.

'No, I did not. I'm here to work. I'm here to do a job and not screw some woman I've only just met. I'm certainly not here to screw up my relationship with you. I love you. I'm going to marry you. I'm going to spend the rest of my life with you – bottom line. Why would I jeopardize that? Not only that, I'm a superintendent and she's a DC . . . I've been stupid in the past, I've told you about it all, but now I've got the most beautiful, most wonderful, most caring woman in the world . . . Jeez! So, no, I didn't, Alison. Got that?'

'I'm sorry.'

'That's OK, but you know what my next question is, don't you?'

'An anonymous phone call from a woman. The number was withheld.'

'I'll bet it was.' Henry's heart was thudding hard against his chest.

His mind swirling, Henry did not get to sleep quickly. He spent some time doing what he called tiger-pacing the room, wondering if he should phone Daniels or knock on her door.

In the end, he did neither.

After a quick raid on the minibar where the best thing on offer was two miniature bottles of Bell's whisky (combined price as much as a seventy cl bottle), he poured them side by side into a glass, added a few drops of tap water, then sunk them in a couple of gulps.

Sitting upright on his bed, he then dozed off.

The persistent knock on the door at two a.m. just about roused him. Groggy, he lurched to the door, almost expecting to find Daniels there looking sexy with a fingertip on her lips.

This pathetic male fantasy was doused by the gangly figure standing in the corridor, dressed rather like Sherlock Holmes.

Henry shook his head to clear his brain. 'I wasn't expecting you until a bit later.'

Professor Baines looked at Henry and said, 'I decided to get this over with. You sounded harassed on the phone, and as the coroner has given us permission – something arranged by your chief constable, I believe – I thought it appropriate to get it done speedily.'

Henry stood back and let him in the room.

'How did you get into the hotel?' he asked Baines.

'Parked at the back, rang the back doorbell for access.'

Henry thought this through as he pulled his jeans on. 'OK, you in your E-type?'

'No, I brought my assistant with me and dropped her off at the infirmary, so I'm in the Mark X.'

'Great.'

'What do you want exactly, and why?'

Baines, now acting more like Inspector Clouseau rather than Sherlock, stood at the back door of the hotel, looking furtively both ways to check if the coast was clear. When satisfied, he put his head down, scuttled across the car park and jumped in the very old, pristine Mark X Jaguar, second only in his pride and joy stakes to the E-type he also owned and cherished. The engine started smoothly and he drove close to the back door, where he stopped briefly and allowed Henry to dart out and fling himself across the back seat.

Baines pulled out and headed towards the city centre.

'Do you see anyone or anything suspicious?' Henry asked from his hiding place.

'No, no one about . . . just a trannie van parked across the road, that's all.'

'OK. So you have an assistant?' Henry asked.

'All self-respecting pathologists do. She doubles as my mortuary assistant too. Very helpful.'

'A flexible woman, then?'

'Very,' Baines confirmed. 'She should have everything sorted for us, but from what you say, this shouldn't take long.'

'I could be wrong,' Henry said.

Having possession of the written authority of the local coroner with her meant that by the time Baines and Henry arrived at the mortuary, Baines' PA had indeed prepared the way.

The corpse of Martin Sowerbutts was again laid out on the slab, ready for Baines to carry out a further examination.

Henry looked at the stitched-up body, hoping he was right. The thought of unnecessarily having another PM performed went dead against Henry's beliefs. He knew it happened but should be avoided if at all possible, because it was another knock at someone's dignity in death. On the other side of the coin, though, he knew his uncertainties had to be explored. Even if the man on the slab was a child murderer, he still deserved to have his own death properly investigated.

'This is Steph, my PA I was telling you about,' Baines said as he walked into the room, heaved his work bag on to the side and began removing his tweed jacket.

Henry gave Steph a wave, not surprised she had a grey tinge to her young, pretty face.

Baines took out his protective surgical gown, hat, mask and gloves and fitted all four items after having carefully washed his hands. Once he had done this, he unfurled a tool rack in which the implements of his trade were lined up in the slots. He fitted a microphone to his face and linked it by Bluetooth to record on his phone.

Henry saw that Steph had already set up two digital cameras on tripods to record the PM.

Baines looked at Steph from over his mask. 'Are we in a position to proceed?'

'Yes, Professor.'

'In that case . . .' He removed a scalpel and held the blade up to the light. It looked very sharp.

Henry sat, watched and listened from a chair in the corner of the room, not wanting to interfere in any way, just to let Baines carry on and find what he had to find. He half-expected the axe to fall on his preposterous notion that Sowerbutts had not actually died in a car accident, but had been dead before plunging over the cliff.

He was prepared to look stupid.

Baines removed the ribcage once Steph had unpicked the stitches and, after placing it gently alongside the body, he carefully picked out the already dissected lungs and carried them across to the inspection table to examine them, speaking softly into his mike while Steph took a video of the procedure with a Go-Pro digital camera.

Henry's mouth was dry from his unwise decision to down the double whisky from the minibar.

Baines and Steph stood over the lungs. He pointed out things to her, and even picked up a slice of a lung and squeezed.

It oozed blood.

Baines glanced at Henry, then returned his attention back to the lungs.

Henry was beginning to feel a bit silly.

Baines crossed back to the cadaver and inspected Sowerbutts' bashed-up face closely, then unpicked the stitching around the scalp, folded the skin back over the face and removed the skull cap. Gently, he picked out the brain and carried it to the table, placing it next to the lungs. He opened it carefully.

It took him ninety minutes, after which he and Steph reassembled Sowerbutts and slid his body back into the chiller cabinet.

'Let's find a coffee machine,' Baines said to Henry.

Henry handed one, then another coffee to Baines and Steph. The three stood in a little triangle in the corridor just behind the A&E department.

Henry waited, wondering what an axe felt like when it fell.

'There are injuries consistent with being involved in a very serious road traffic accident, as you have described. Facial and chest injuries,' Baines explained.

Henry closed his eyes and thought, *Shit*.

'But not all his facial injuries fit with his head having hit a steering wheel. There is no doubt that his face was pounded into something flat – a wall, maybe. Hard to say. That is as well as having hit the rim of the steering wheel. I'm sure it would be possible to match up the pattern of the injuries with the pattern on the wheel itself. But' – Baines sipped his coffee – 'the man's face was essentially battered to a pulp before it hit the wheel.'

'So he'd been assaulted before the accident?'

'Either that or been involved in another accident where his face hit something very flat and hard, repeatedly. The face is a mess, but when you know what you're looking for, it's all easy to read. There is some form of indentation on his left temple which could have been caused by an iron bar, maybe, or a police baton . . . just saying.

'His chest injuries are consistent with the accident you described to me. If he wasn't wearing a seat belt it is possible he was thrown against the steering wheel as the vehicle crashed down the cliff, but I would argue that it's unlikely he would receive injuries to both his face and chest consistent with having impacted on the steering wheel during that descent. Obviously it was a rough ride, but it doesn't seem physically likely he would bash his head and chest in the same manner. I won't stake my life on that.'

Henry thought about the words, visualizing the vehicle going over a cliff: a tumble dryer.

'Another but,' Baines said significantly. 'The injuries to his face and chest are both post-mortem, sustained after he died.'

Sometimes Henry could not stop his bottom lip from drooping, which it did. 'You mean . . .?' he began, trying to grasp this.

'I mean his face was bashed on the steering wheel after he was dead, as was his chest, but like I said, it is unlikely they both occurred when the car was going down the cliff. I'd say the chest injuries came with that but not the facial ones. I can determine that from the nature of the bruising. His face, I think, was bashed into the steering wheel before the vehicle went over the cliff, but he was dead at that time.'

Henry tried to compute this. 'You sure?'

'Just as sure as an oncologist can look up your bottom and tell you you've got bowel cancer. It's my job, it's what I do.'

'I get it. But how did he die, then?'

'Well, you were right in your suspicions – his lungs were filled with an excessive amount of blood, so he suffocated in it. I would say he was unconscious from having had his face smashed against something flat, and then he was left lying face up, and the blood from these facial injuries – from his broken nose, cheekbone, teeth knocked out, et cetera, was inhaled and he died.'

Henry pursed his lips. 'He was dead before he went over the cliff?'

Baines looked pointedly at him.

'OK, I get it.'

Baines patted him on the shoulder. 'Best of luck with this, my old friend.'

Baines had to leave immediately to get back across the Pennines with Steph to carry out a PM scheduled for later that morning.

They would get very little sleep. He promised Henry a full report of his findings later that day by email. He dropped Henry back at the hotel by the same devious means as he'd picked him up. He asked Baines to report any suspicious vehicles outside the hotel, but there was just the same, the old Transit van.

Henry thanked him profusely and promised a catch-up soon, then slithered out of the car and in through the back of the hotel up to his room, his mind churning with the vivid memories of attending the cliff-top accident and the subsequent – first – post-mortem, during which Runcie had a hushed conversation with the pathologist, then Henry's own doubts about the PM itself – the fact that he saw the lungs saturated with blood. *Too much blood.*

He walked past Daniels' room, seeing a light under the door, then on to his, which he entered, paranoia setting in, without turning on a light.

It was just after five a.m. and, although he hadn't slept, he wasn't feeling tired at all as he tried to work out what his next steps should be.

He drew up a chair next to the window, put his feet up on a footstool and looked out over the quayside as a slow dawn began to creep in from the east.

His mobile phone was in his hand and he tapped it thought-fully on the palm of his other, then made the decision. Scrolling through his contacts page, he found Jerry Tope's home number again.

Diane Daniels had not slept well, but lay awake tossing and turning on the big soft bed.

Her mind, too, was cluttered with thoughts of the investigation on which she had found herself.

When she had volunteered she had expected it to be a by-the-numbers review of a couple of slow running, unsolved murders. The chance to sit by Henry Christie's shoulder, enjoy and learn from the experience was all she had wanted.

It had become much more than that very quickly, not least because she had not expected Henry, still in recovery from the gunshot wound, to be so proactive and willing to ruffle feathers. He seemed to revel in making people feel uncomfortable.

The last thing she thought she would do was go out and speak to a murder victim's wife, and then rescue her from suicide.

Daniels smiled. Actually, it had all been pretty good. She looked at her phone for the time. Just gone five a.m.

No point in even thinking about sleep now. She threw off the duvet and padded naked into the bathroom. A pee, and then a run to set up her energy levels for the day ahead. Somehow she knew she had to be on tip-top form.

'That's odd,' Jerry Tope said.

'What is?'

'I was just about to send you a text for you to phone me.'

'At this time in the morning?' Henry was amazed to find the normally grumpy-at-any-time-of-the-day Tope almost jovial – well, certainly amenable at this hour. Over the years, Henry had learned that whatever time he called Tope, he was bad-tempered.

'Yep, been surfing all night.'

Henry held back from making a quip. Just asked, 'Why?'

'You have a victim over there, the one called Mark James Wright? Stabbed to death.'

'Yep.'

'Well, I've looked into his business. As you probably know, he was a bit of a one-man band working in the construction industry. I've looked at all of his accounts online, but they're a bare minimum – there's not a lot of information. He provided heavy plant machinery for building sites and demolition projects and all that, but you know all this.'

Henry did, but didn't want to interrupt Tope, which could have had fatal consequences. Tope usually liked a dramatic set-up followed by a denouement, and anything that got in his way usually resulted in heavy sulking.

'So I don't know if this is helpful or not. I've been reviewing crimes for Central Yorkshire, Portsea Division, and come across a few undetected fraud cases.'

Henry leaned forwards, looking through the window at the quayside. It was still quiet.

'Two quarter of a million scams.'

'OK . . . and . . .'

'Two legitimate companies hired out their machinery to

companies who were supposedly about to begin some demolition projects in Portsea.'

'What type of machinery?'

'Crushers and screeners – big effing things that crush stone then sort it. Worth over a hundred grand each. Thing is these companies found out too late that they were dealing with artificial companies – all set up and sophisticated, with mobile phone numbers, offices in Portakabins – that didn't actually exist. The legit companies provide plant machinery on rental, supposedly, then deliver it, only to discover that when they go to seize it back because none of the rental fees have been paid, there is no sign of the plant – or the companies, 'cos they didn't exist in the first place. Probably exported to Europe and sold over there.'

'Is this machinery not traceable or trackable?'

'Yes, they do have GPSs fitted but any half-good engineer can remove them. The GPSs still emit signals, which made the owners think the machinery is where it was delivered, but it's long gone. Two companies have been bankrupted.'

'Crikey,' Henry said.

'I just wondered if Wright was somehow involved in the scam, that's all. Just doing my job as an analyst. Why were you going to call me?'

'How good are you at accessing bank accounts on the sly?'

Henry leaned forward again as a figure jogged across to the quayside from the front door of the hotel. It was Daniels out for her early morning jog.

She paused, running on the spot, fitting her earphones before trotting off up river. Stretching and rolling her muscles, she settled into an easy pace. Henry had no intention of running that morning. He fancied a couple of hours in bed.

That changed as the back door of the Transit van that had been parked up all night opened and a black-clad figure climbed out with a hood pulled over his face and set off behind Daniels.

FOURTEEN

The music from her iPod enveloped her, pulsing a steady beat that translated to her feet as Daniels jogged gently along the path by the river. It was a good pace, one she knew she could maintain for about four miles with ease, which is, give or take, as much as she wanted to do three or four times a week. Added to a couple of focused gym sessions, which she hated, it was enough to keep her sometimes bad diet at bay. She liked her food, liked sweet things, and knew the payoff was moderate exercise.

She was aware of her body as she relaxed into the pace. The way her feet connected with the ground, the muscles in her legs and her arse tightening, her boobs gently bouncing . . . All felt good.

Until she became aware of something else.

A sixth sense kicking in, but too late.

A sudden rush. The feeling of someone behind her, approaching quickly. A shadow. A change in the air pressure.

She tried to twist.

And the gloved hand went around her face, covering her eyes, nose and mouth, instantly gagging her, and she felt the strength of a man – she knew it had to be a man – yank her to a stop and drag her sideways to try to pitch her to the ground. Her hands grabbed at his forearm, digging her nails deep, although she knew the barrier of the material of what he was wearing made her sharp nails ineffective.

'Interfering bitch,' the man growled into her ear.

She began to struggle violently, kicking back with her heels and stomping down in the hope of smashing the man's toes.

But she was off balance and could feel herself teetering over.

She twisted again, right round, facing him, and saw with terror he was wearing a balaclava mask with slits for the eyes and mouth. It was a terrifying glimpse that sent a shockwave of fear through her whole being, making her think, *Killer, rapist . . .*

As she pirouetted to face him, her right hand thrust up between their bodies. She wanted to slam the heel of her hand up into his nose to try and drive the shard that was his septum up into the frontal lobe of his brain, but she misjudged the trajectory and instead slammed her hand on to the underside of his chin, which had a great effect.

He screamed, reeled backwards and let go of her.

'You bitth.'

He had bitten his tongue. She had managed to ram his teeth together with his fat juicy tongue between them.

His hand came up to his face, then came away as he spat blood, a terrible sight coming out through the mouth-opening in the mask.

But he did not hesitate for long.

He came at her like a wild animal. The difference this time was that she was ready for the attack, had regained her balance and, as his arms came together, she danced out of reach of them and he grasped fresh air where she had been standing a microsecond before.

Again, he recovered quickly from his setback, swung his fist and caught her on the side of the face, sending a tremor through her brain and knocking her down on to her hands and knees.

She tasted blood inside her own mouth now, where her cheek had been cut on her teeth.

'You're going in the river, bitth,' he promised, unable to say 'bitch' properly.

She was not going anywhere without a fight.

He was standing perhaps four feet away from her, and she could see the lower portion of his legs from the knees down. She dived for them, propelling herself like a runner from the blocks, intending to wrap her arms around them and bring him down.

He sidestepped nimbly aside and slammed the sole of his trainer against the back of her head, driving her into the gritty ground.

She rolled away and he was suddenly towering over her.

From his outline, she saw he was wide and muscled, and knew that if he managed to grip her properly it would be almost impossible for her to break free and she would be in the river. As fit as she was, she knew she could not match his strength.

She crabbed backwards in terror but he came at her relentlessly and determinedly, spitting blood, his hands reaching towards her.

Henry hurtled out of his room and spun down the corridor using the door frame for propulsion, tearing his shoulder as he did so, jolting pain searing through him. He ran down the stairs four at a time, using the rails to assist take-off and landing, crashed through the residents' door and sprinted through the hotel lobby, much to the consternation of a cleaner holding a dustpan and brush. He was out through the front door and landed on the waterfront.

For a moment, he was conflicted about what to do.

The number plate of the Transit van was obscured by another parked car. He knew he needed the number but his first instinct was to go after the jogger, although he hoped he was very wrong in his assumption that Daniels was in danger.

The protection of life had to be his priority, so he set off up the river, hoping he was on the right path. He had his phone in his hand, trying to find Daniels' number as he ran, which he did.

'Answer it, answer it,' he insisted as he heard it connect, ring, then go on to voicemail.

Daniels scrambled away, but he lurched for her and grabbed the back of her running vest, stopping her abruptly and dragging her towards the edge of the path and the river flowing just beyond, the tide sweeping out and high. While holding her with one hand, he punched the back of her head and neck with the other, but though his blows hurt they were mainly off target and ineffective because she wasn't going quietly. Then she broke free and rolled sideways toward the bank. He followed, kicking out at her, catching her lower gut and driving air out of her with an agonizing, 'Unph!'

Once more, he hauled her to her feet, dragging her up by her T-shirt front, though she was raining blows to the side of his head. Suddenly he had full control as he spun her round then jammed his left forearm across her throat and used the palm of his hand on the back of her head, pushing forward with his palm, his grip ever tightening.

She tried to dig her nails into his arm, but she was weakening.

And now his cheek was close to the side of her head by her ear. She could hear his breathing, feel the heat of his breath, the reek of his sweating body, and began to realize these were the last things her senses would experience before she died.

Then there was the impact.

Like a steam train thundering into the pair of them.

The grip came loose. Daniels staggered away, sucking fresh air into her lungs as she sagged to her knees, not understanding what had just happened.

Henry knew he was witnessing a death embrace.

The jogger was attacking Daniels, had her pinned against him, trying to strangle her and, in some sort of macabre waltz, force her towards the river.

Up to this point, Henry had run almost three-quarters of a mile and was flagging, but the sight ahead spurred another rush of adrenaline into his system and he simply went for the frontal assault, sped up and barged into the pair of them, hitting the man hard in the ribs as he connected.

The man released Daniels and rounded on Henry, who saw the blood spluttering out of the mouth of the balaclava mask.

He came at Henry, his body language showing his intent. The man's shoulders seemed to swell and his fists seemed as large as oranges.

Henry knew this would hurt a lot.

The man sped up and raced towards Henry, who braced himself, turned sideways-on and dropped his left shoulder in preparation for the clash while trying to protect his right shoulder as much as possible.

At the very last moment, Henry ducked sideways. The man skittered past and, as he did, Henry swivelled, swung his left fist in a wide arc and planted it on the back of the man's head at the point where the skull met the spine. Not the greatest punch in the world – Henry had never been a hitter – but it sent the man on his journey for a few steps before he stopped, turned and launched himself back at Henry.

By which time Daniels was back on her feet.

She was behind Henry, ready to engage, a snarl of rage on her face.

Henry sensed she was there and that, hopefully, the pair of them made an impressive crime-fighting duo, not to be messed with, even though one was a pretty unfit bloke and the other had just been half-strangled.

Henry raised a finger at the black-clad man.

'I'm a cop, she's a cop' – he jerked his thumb at Daniels – 'and you're fucking under arrest. So c'mon,' he went on bravely, wriggling his fingers to encourage the man on, 'let's continue this.'

The man turned and fled.

Daniels stood in the shower room, looking at her reflection in the mirror. She'd cleaned herself up, dabbed Savlon on the grazes on her cheek and chin, but the pounding swelling on the side of her face could not be treated by anything other than time, though she had downed a couple of Henry's strong painkillers.

She rubbed her neck gently, raising her chin to inspect the red welt across her throat.

Then she glanced at the reflection of Henry Christie.

He was leaning on the door frame, just outside the bathroom, watching her do the repairs, slightly uncomfortable that she'd shed her outer clothing and was now just clad in her running bra and – it had to be said – fairly generous knickers, which he assumed were used when exercising only.

He had offered to leave, but she'd asked him to stay. Now he was very, very conscious of her lovely smooth back. He swallowed.

'What the hell's going on, Henry?'

He had just told her about the phone call he'd received from a very angry Alison. Daniels had listened with a cold look on her face but, when he finished, she smiled and said, 'You know I'd never sleep with you, don't you?'

He accepted that information with a shrug.

'So she has nothing to worry about on that score.'

'I get it – no need to rub it in.'

'I mean . . . look at the age gap, for one thing.'

'Yeah, I'd never sleep with a younger woman,' he said.

'So what is going on?'

'They're watching us. They're on the run and they're dangerous.'

'What you're saying is that the guy who went for me – that wasn't just opportunism?'

'He was in the van outside. It's gone now and I didn't get the number. He got out and followed you, attacked you.'

'Shit.'

'I should've had my suspicions after Alison called, but I didn't tell you then because I thought you'd be asleep.'

'Some hope. Anyway, like I said . . .' She turned and faced him. 'What are we into?'

Henry shrugged. 'Fucked if I know.'

'He was a black man, this guy.'

'I know . . . and in the last, what, twenty-four hours, I've encountered a black man at The Tawny Owl and you've been attacked by one. Same one?'

When both had showered and medicated, they met in the dining room for breakfast, at which point Henry brought her up to speed with the post-mortem he'd attended in the early hours. Daniels listened but said nothing, and because they were ravenous, they both had a full English. They knew they would need as much stoking up as possible for the day ahead.

'I know we haven't had much sleep and it's going to be a long one. I think the best course of action will be to carry on as though nothing's happened, collect information – and evidence if it presents itself – see where we are at the end of the day and take it from there.' Henry dipped toast into his fried egg. 'Let's go and do what detectives do, eh?'

'Detect things?'

'Talk to people. That's always the bottom line for a good jack – the interaction with people and the ability to drag stuff out of them.'

'What are you going to do about the post-mortem results? You won't be able to hide that for long.'

'Not quite sure yet. I'll speak to the coroner first thing and ask him if he'll put a hold on any movement of the body – or move it somewhere it won't be interfered with . . . you never know. Then I'll wait for Baines to email me, speak to FB – with you – and discuss how to move on. FB'll want quick answers. But again, it could simply be a case of incompetence on the part of the local pathologist and moving forward on that will be very delicate and maybe not for us . . . But if there's collusion between him and DCI Runcie . . .' Henry screwed up his face.

Daniels kept listening, liking what she was hearing, and the bit about including her in his plans. 'What about the assault on me?'

'If you don't mind, let's just keep a little lid on it. We've got photos on your phone of your injuries and of the scene, plus – big plus – we've got some splats of the offender's blood and saliva on your clothing.'

'OK, I'll go with that.'

Henry's phone rang. Jerry Tope.

'You do know that accessing bank records is dead easy? It's covering your tracks that's the hard bit,' Tope said.

'Fortunately you're a past master.'

'I am, I am,' he said proudly.

'Get on with it Jerry. I'll pat your back when I get home.'

'Professor David Wrackham, Home Office pathologist? Jeez, d'you know how much these guys are on? No? I'll tell you – a lot. That said, an extra few quid is always welcome, I suppose, especially when most of your debit card payments are to online bookies. He's a bit of a gambler.'

'Not a crime.'

'No . . . I've found a few of his accounts, actually, but nothing I'd say was untoward, other than the overdraft figures, which are high . . . anyway, I flagged them and got a "ping" this morning, meaning a deposit has gone in.'

Henry looked at Daniels and pursed his lips.

Tope continued: 'The "ping" was a deposit from an unknown source – which I'm working on. Two thousand pounds dropped into his current account this morning, maybe five minutes ago.'

'But you don't know where the "ping" came from?'

'Not yet . . . I'm working on it. Could take some time.'

'Well done. Look, let's back off for the time being . . . we don't want to get caught out ourselves.'

Here he heard Tope say, 'As if.'

'Come out, cover your tracks and I'll put in a request for a warrant later today, then we can access his accounts above board.'

'OK, whatev.'

Henry hung up and shrugged at Daniels, who had managed to earwig most of the conversation. 'Could be nothing.'

He poured two coffees from the cafetière, then sat back feeling weary again, but the strong coffee did hit the energy button, which was good because as he drank it his phone rang again: DCI Runcie.

'How hard could it have been?'

Runcie held Hawkswood's face between her forefinger and thumb and squeezed.

'I said how hard can it be?'

Hawkswood jerked his head out of her grip and spat out a gob of blood on to a tissue from his still-bleeding tongue that he'd bit into like it was a chunk of rump steak when Daniels had driven her uppercut into his jaw.

'How hard can it be to dump a prissy little bitch into the river, dead? You are a fucking big bloke and you're not stupid,' she said scathingly.

'She fought back.' He defended himself.

'Of course she fought back, but that shouldn't have been a surprise.'

'And then he turned up.' He had more blood accumulating in his mouth, warm and salty, from a wound that was struggling to heal. He swallowed it and gagged a little.

'You should've chucked both of them in.' Runcie gripped the top of her head with her hand and stalked around the office. 'They didn't ID you, did they?'

'No, I'm sure.'

Now she rubbed her eyes, so tired they squelched, and shook her head, completely at a loss for words.

'Look, just piss off and make yourself scarce. You're neither use nor ornament at the moment.'

He left, only to be replaced by Saul. 'Ready to roll, boss.'

'Good. I'd better call our guest and see if he wants a ride-along.'

Runcie arrived ten minutes later in a battered, plain car and pulled up outside the hotel. She didn't get out but stayed on the double yellows and waited for Henry to come out, which he did, and got in alongside her.

Runcie looked puzzled. Henry read her confusion. 'Just me.'
He said, 'DC Daniels is busy. Doesn't take two to watch what
you're up to, does it?'

'No . . . what's she doing?'

'Just some enquiries for me,' Henry said vaguely. 'So what've
you got planned for me?'

Henry let her tell him as she drove away, and he wondered
if he should broach the subjects of his phone call from Alison
last night and this morning's assault on Daniels. He certainly
wasn't going to reveal the early-hours post-mortem – even
though he was aware word could get easily back to her through
other channels – so he decided to see how the day would reveal
itself. He didn't want to make any move that would come back
and bite him on the backside, or, as he looked sideways at
Runcie, unleash a tiger he might not be able to control. He
knew he was out on a limb here on the other side of the country,
and would be surprised if there was anyone around here willing
to back him up.

Daniels watched them drive off from the cover of the dining-room
window, then she drank the rest of her coffee before returning
to her room and spending more time going through the murder
files again.

For the first time, she began to wonder if there was any connection between the killings, even if they seemed dissimilar as regards
the MO. But both were extremely brutal in their nature. Both
victims were essentially one-man-band businesses, though the
two businesses did not seem to have any connection.

Yet neither had been solved, and both were investigated by
the same team, so was it just one of those things? Bad luck.

She did an internet trawl, looked at Central Yorkshire Police's
website and saw that the previous year's murder clear-up rate
was a cracking ninety-nine per cent, so despite a lack of funding
and investment in the force, they still seemed pretty hot as regards
solving murders. She also saw that there were two other murders
in Portsea last year, solved by Jane Runcie's team. So they could
do it.

But not these two.

What were the 'misgivings' the now-deceased chief constable

had? Did he give FB more information than FB subsequently shared with Henry?

If nothing else, that was a connection.

Two murders investigated by the same DCI. The two murders that senior officers had misgivings about.

She scribbled notes as she thought through these things: *Henry tripped and fell. Car tyres slashed. Me assaulted. CC Burnham murdered. Jack Culver dead – accident? Phone call from Alison!*

Then she wrote, *Fuck!*

'OK,' she said lightly, 'first things first.'

Her first call was to the man called Newsham, the head of security at the motorway service area where her tyres had been slashed. She had checked with Henry and the promised CCTV footage had not arrived, so this was an easy thing to tick off.

She stood at her hotel-room window watching the quayside outside getting busier and a small container ship edge slowly up river towards the main docks. Her phone was to her ear.

'Ronnie Newsham,' the man answered, his voice harassed in just those two words.

'Mr Newsham, this is DC Daniels—'

'Sorry, sorry, I'm busy,' he said straight away.

'I know. We all are, but you promised to forward some footage from your cameras to Detective Superintendent Christie. It's not yet arrived.'

'Er, no, I know.'

'Could you do it, please?'

'Well . . . well,' he said, becoming flustered, 'it's just that the footage was corrupted for some reason . . . Happens occasionally . . . Hello? Hello? Can you hear . . .?'

'I can hear you loud and clear, Mr Newsham.' Daniels' voice was icy. 'We need that footage.'

'Hello . . . hello . . .'

The connection failed and Daniels was left holding a dead phone.

'Bastard,' she snarled.

She called him again and the phone rang but wasn't answered; it went straight to voicemail. Daniels left a terse message and, as soon as she hung up, the phone rang. Expecting it to be Newsham, she said, 'I'm so glad you called back Mr Newsham . . .'

'It's not Mr Newsham, whoever he is,' a voice she knew well cut in.

'Oh, Mr Bayley . . . what can I do for you?'

'Sometimes even *Crimestoppers* comes good,' Runcie said. She drove on to the edge of a large council estate of a type Henry knew well. Much of his career had been spent prowling such places on the other side of the Pennines. It was extensive, rundown, looked to be overwhelmed by despair and belied its happy name. 'Welcome to Sea Vista estate,' Runcie announced, 'home to dead legs, dead ducks, deadbeats and dead-end streets.'

Henry grimaced internally at the unflattering description, which was not good coming from a high-ranking cop.

'All human shite is here,' she said.

Henry's lips formed a tight line. One thing he did know from experience was that the majority of residents in such places were decent and law abiding, often cowed by the minority who weren't. It was those few who gave estates like this their reputations, and sometimes cops came on to them expecting trouble from everyone.

'Harsh,' he said.

She shot him a look. 'But true.' There was defiance in her voice.

'Where are we going?' Henry asked, moving the subject on, not wanting to provoke an argument just yet but knowing it would come at some stage.

'To catch a killer.'

Using her satnav, Daniels negotiated the streets of Portsea, heading for the outer edge of the town and finding a fairly recently built private housing estate with the usual modern range of properties, two bedrooms to five.

She found the address she needed on a small cul-de-sac of about a dozen large houses, one of the newest sections of the estate. She parked in the turning circle and walked to the front door with her warrant card ready in the palm of her hand.

A big dog barked and Daniels could see through the patterned frosted glass in the door as the beast rushed down the hallway and went upright, two huge paws slammed themselves against the glass and the dog's black snout came into contact with it, smearing a wet trail.

Daniels took an involuntary step back. Dogs were not her favourite animal. She was more a budgie girl.

A woman shouted a name and the dog dropped out of sight, then the door was opened by the female holding the dog's collar tightly.

Daniels immediately held up her warrant card so no mistakes could be made, and introduced herself. 'I'm DC Daniels from Lancashire Constabulary . . . are you Melissa Phillips?'

The woman was in her early thirties, Daniels estimated, nice looking, casual but smartly dressed.

'I am. What can I do for you?' Already Daniels picked up a slightly uneasy tone in the voice.

'I believe you're an accountant?'

'Yes, why? Do you want your books doing?'

'No.' Inside, Daniels chuckled at the thought of the miniscule net profit she had after deductions and spends from her salary every month. 'Do you work from home?'

'Yes, mostly . . . Look, I'm online now and everything. Got a website you can look at.' Still defensive, a bit aggressive. 'So what can I do for you? I'm quite busy – the dog needs walking and I have tax returns to file.'

Daniels never allowed anyone to rush her. 'I'm in Portsea reviewing an unsolved murder case.' She kept her eyes firmly locked on Melissa's. 'The death of a man called Tom Salter. I believe you kept his books for him?'

There was a moment of hesitation, a weighing up of how to respond, then the decision was made. 'You could say that, I suppose – in as much as I filed his returns for him.'

'So you were his accountant?'

'An accountant is someone who does much more than that,' she said. 'Look, I really need to walk the dog.' She pulled him back, ready to close the door on Daniels.

'No, no, no,' Daniels said. 'I need to talk to you.' Her face and voice meant no backing off or dog walking. The sag of Melissa's shoulders said she had got the message.

*   *   *

Henry could not deny a certain thrill when Runcie turned into a high-walled back alley and drew in behind two police personnel carriers, a dog van and a couple more less-identifiable cop cars. Henry spotted armed officers chatting in a small group, all dressed in protective overalls, ready for an assault. Henry had led and been part of many such operations, and they always got his adrenaline pumping.

So far, Runcie had not revealed anything to him, but then she turned to him.

'Last night we received an anonymous call from *Crimestoppers* – from a female and that's all we know – that a certain Jamie Milner, well known armed robber of this parish, is the man who shot and killed Tom Salter in his office in a robbery that went disastrously wrong.' She smiled wickedly. 'So we're going for him today. Supposedly he has a gun hidden at his property.'

Henry was stunned. 'Was this guy ever a suspect?'

'Never on the radar,' she admitted. 'He's a hold-'em-up, cash-in-transit kind of guy, but clearly not averse to diversifying his MO. Let's go get him and see what transpires.'

She was out of the car before Henry could say anything more, going round to the back and lifting the hatchback. Henry joined her and she tossed a bulky ballistic vest to him.

'Might want to sling this on,' she said. 'Milner's a real handful.'

Henry slid his arms into the vest. It was one of the old style – heavy ones with plates of steel. The one Runcie put on was one of the new, sleeker ones, and lightweight.

'Have this lot been briefed? Henry asked as he tied the Velcro fastenings.

'Yep, first thing. They know what they're doing. In, out, shake it all about.'

Although James Martin Milner was a professional career criminal, always ready for a knock on the door from the cops, in truth he wasn't actually expecting them to pour into his house that morning. The last job he'd pulled months ago, all the way down in New Cross, London, had netted him enough cash to live comfortably for a year, and he was just starting to weigh up his options for the next job, which could simply be some smash-and-grab raids on money being delivered to hole-in-the-wall cash machines. A nice, fun way to top up reserves.

He was in bed with his girlfriend after a night on the 'lash'. He hadn't slept well under the influence of drink and, although he was in the twilight zone between sleep and waking, he knew he needed to pee but couldn't be bothered to stagger to the toilet. It wasn't unknown for him to piss the bed, something he thought entirely reasonable if needs must. He was just that kinda guy.

What prevented him from doing that was the presence of the woman in the bed next to him. She was having a good influence on him, making him a better person, within the boundaries of his profession, and when he had once wet the bed with her in it, her look of horror and disgust had been a quite effective deterrent since.

So, displaying a huge hard-on caused by the requirement to pee, Milner reluctantly flipped the sheet off and, naked and proud, made his way out of the bedroom to the toilet down the landing, holding his cock and knowing he would have to spread his legs wide and contort over the loo like a giraffe at a watering hole if there was any chance of hitting the porcelain as opposed to the ceiling.

He was half asleep as he spread his legs, holding himself upright with one hand on the wall behind the toilet, and began to urinate.

This was when the crash happened. His front and back doors were booted open and the shouting and screaming started. The pounding of boots up the stairs. Part way through the emptying of his bladder, Milner was smashed against the wall by a helmeted cop yelling in his ear, pulling his arms around his back and cuffing him.

After the dog had been locked in the kitchen, where it whimpered pathetically, Melissa showed Daniels into the lounge and gestured for her to take a seat. In spite of the whining of the dog, Daniels thought she heard someone else moving upstairs in the house. She smiled at the accountant.

'I'm here reviewing the progress of the murder case on behalf of Central Yorkshire Police, and that process will obviously entail re-interviewing key witnesses and finding new ones if at all possible.'

Melissa shrugged that she understood.

'Can I confirm you were Mr Salter's accountant?'

'In as much as I did his returns based on the figures he gave me year end. Other than that, not really.'

'What exactly do you mean?'

Melissa marshalled her thoughts. 'Let's say I'm aware he submitted the minimum required to keep the Inland Revenue off his back.'

'And what does that mean?'

'Mmm . . . don't suppose it matters now . . . and I'd deny knowing this . . . but most of his business was cash in hand and he skimmed more than he banked.'

'What exactly was his business?'

'Haulage mainly. Shipping, that kind of thing.'

Daniels nodded. 'Was he a wealthy man?'

'Not according to his tax records.'

'How long had you been doing his returns?'

'Five years.'

'So you must have known him reasonably well?'

'Only as well as I needed to.'

'But you are aware of the nature and circumstances of his death?'

'It was all over the papers and local TV news.'

'Have you any idea why he died in such a violent way? Did he have any enemies that you knew about?' Daniels probed.

'None that I know of . . . But, y'know, his line of work was pretty rough . . . it just is,' Melissa said. 'But no, I don't know of any enemies.'

'Could he have had any personal enemies, rather than those from his line of work, maybe as a result of his private life?'

'What do you mean?'

'Well, the thing is, Mrs Phillips . . . one of the things I've noticed in my review of this case is the big gap between Mr Salter leaving his wife at home and his actual murder, and I'm struggling to fill it with activity, if you will. It's almost like he was covering his tracks.' As Daniels spoke, she watched Melissa's face working out what the agenda was behind the words.

'Can't help you, I'm afraid.'

'Where were you on that day, evening?'

Melissa's face became hard. 'What are you insinuating?'

'OK, there's some suggestion that Mr Salter was seeing another woman.' Daniels left it dangling like that.

'And you think it was me?'

'I'm trying to discover Mr Salter's movements in the time leading up to his death. I don't really care one way or another about his personal life as such, unless it has a direct bearing on his murder. You know, jealous husband/wife, that sort of thing. I'm just trying to find the truth.' She paused. The dog in the kitchen whined and scratched the door. 'So, were you having an affair with him? If not, you still might want to think about what you were doing on that day because, one way or another, I will find out what he was up to.'

'I wasn't with him. I wasn't having an affair, either.'

'All right,' Daniels said, not convinced. 'Do you know if he was seeing someone, and if so, who?'

She shook her head too vehemently.

Daniels ploughed on. 'Because I'm going to discover who he was with that day.'

'Not me.'

'Right, thanks for your time, Mrs Phillips.' Daniels stood up and extracted a business card from her pocket. Her contact number was on it and she'd scribbled Henry's on the back. She handed it to Melissa. 'If you recall anything, or decide you want to tell me anything at all, ring me or my boss – his is the number on the back. There's every chance we'll be chatting again at some stage,' she concluded with a veiled warning.

From behind her blinds, Melissa watched Daniels drive away.

The living-room door opened and a slightly younger woman entered and stood behind Melissa's shoulder, just catching the back end of Daniels' car as it turned out of the cul-de-sac.

'Did you hear all that?' Melissa turned to her younger sister. 'Did you hear that, Miriam?'

Her sister's face was pale and afraid. 'Yes,' she said meekly.

'She'll be back. She knows. I'm not a good liar.'

'Yeah, yeah.'

The living-room door opened again and a frightened-looking young girl entered, thin-faced, pretty.

Her eyes were dark and haunting.

FIFTEEN

'I want my brief, I want my phone call, I want my rights and I want some *fuckin' clothes*,' Jamie Milner demanded, screaming the last two words into the face of the young female custody sergeant across the wide desk, who remained unmoved and unafraid of the prisoner's outburst.

Flanked by two burly cops in overalls, Milner stood at the custody desk covered by a harsh woollen blanket and wearing nothing else, because when he'd been arrested he had become instantly and terribly violent. It had taken five cops to subdue him and he'd been dragged naked out of his house, a cop on each limb, one holding his head in a vice-like grip, and thrown like an old carpet into the back of the section van. He had been pinned down for the journey to the nick, biting and spitting like a deranged wild animal.

Once in the station, ten more minutes were spent calming him down while he was still pinned to the van floor, until he eventually capitulated and allowed the cops to walk him into the custody office and present him to the sergeant.

'You'll get all those things when I say,' DCI Runcie said. She was leaning on the end of the desk, watching with a smirk. Milner scowled at her.

'You won't find fuck all,' he snarled. 'I've done nowt and I certainly ain't involved in no fucking murder.'

'We'll see,' Runcie said and looked at the sergeant. 'This man has been arrested on suspicion of the murder of Tom Salter, some six months ago.'

Milner's head tipped back as he laughed at the allegation. 'Fuck I did.'

The sergeant said, 'But you understand why you've been arrested?'

'I understand the words, lass, but they're not true.'

'Whatever.' She began to tap in the details on the booking-in computer but, while she did this, she said to the officers with the prisoner, 'Take him to interview-room two and get him a forensic suit, then we'll look at sorting out some clothes for him from home. Bring him back when he's decent.'

The cops pushed him away, leaving her and Runcie at the desk.

Henry Christie had observed these proceedings from the rear of the custody office and only moved forward when Milner had been taken away.

'So what's happening, boss?' the custody sergeant asked Runcie.

'He can have a solicitor but no phone calls just yet. I've got a search team at his house and at a garage he owns.' Runcie produced a printed sheet of paper. 'This is the search warrant for both premises. You can have copies for the custody record. I've already left copies at his home. I want to have an initial interview with him, then take it from there. No phone calls because I don't want to give him the chance to alert any co-defendants he might have. The searches are crucial here.'

'OK, boss.'

Runcie looked at Henry. 'It's not through want of trying we haven't got anywhere with this, sir. Sometimes you have luck, sometimes you don't. Today we just had a stroke of it . . . you know how it rolls.'

Henry nodded, but thought, *What a coincidence! I know what I think about coincidences.*

The custody suite at Portsea was extensive: a dozen female cells, forty male cells, interconnected to the adjoining magistrates' court with a couple of holding cells underneath the court itself. It reminded Henry of some of the old-style custody suites in Lancashire he'd known as a young cop but which had all been gradually phased out and closed down as new police stations were built. In custody terms, Portsea was a dinosaur, badly in need of either shutting down or heavy investment for refurbishment.

Just through his innate curiosity, Henry wandered through the cell corridors, seeing old-style cell doors, sniffing up the atmosphere of a hundred years or more of prisoners. As he walked back to the desk, Milner was being taken to an interview room with Runcie and Saul and a duty solicitor who had already been onsite representing another prisoner.

The custody officer was in a small office behind the desk, putting on a kettle. Henry didn't blame her.

He'd been a custody officer for a while, as all newly promoted sergeants were required to be back in those days. He often recalled coming on duty half an hour early just so he could make himself a cup of tea, because he knew he probably wouldn't get one for another six hours. Often, though, all those hours later, he would find that same brew still standing there, untouched and cold. A custody officer had to take the breaks as and when they presented themselves.

Henry sidled up behind her.

She said, 'Hi.' Then peered at his ID badge and added, 'Sir. I'm not sure who you are,' so he introduced himself properly.

'Why are you here?'

'Just reviewing a murder case.'

'Tom Salter's, I presume?'

Henry nodded.

'Today's seen good progress, then?'

'Hopefully.'

She poured boiling water into a mug containing a tea bag and offered one to Henry. He declined.

There was a buzzing noise. The sergeant looked at a TV monitor giving a view of the entrance to the custody office. On it, two cops were holding another prisoner. 'Never stops,' she said, leaned towards the counter and pressed the door release button.

Henry watched her deal with the processing of a man who had been arrested on suspicion of theft. On shelves under the custody desk was a row of ring binders containing hard copies of all completed custody records for the last week or so. Henry helped himself to the binder covering the last three days and took it to the office behind the desk.

He quickly found and read through the one relating to Martin Sowerbutts, who had been arrested on suspicion of murder and kidnap and then, following a series of interviews in which he denied all the offences, been released without charge.

There was nothing untoward on the record or in any of the handwritten entries thereon.

At the desk, the latest prisoner was being taken to a cell. Henry looked at the custody sergeant. She was the same one who had authorized Sowerbutts' detention and then release. Her head was down, concentrating on writing something on the new record she had just started, then entering details on the computer. She seemed young, but maybe that was because Henry was feeling old.

Lifting the ring binder across and planting it beside her, he said, 'Got a quick minute?'

She pulled her face as if to say, *Yeah, right.*

Instead, she said, 'Just a sec, boss.' She completed her task and turned to him. 'What is it?'

'You were the custody officer the other day when this guy' – Henry indicated the open file in the binder – 'Martin Sowerbutts was brought in. You were also on duty when he left.'

Something tightened in her face. Just minutely. 'That's right.'

'You know he committed suicide, don't you?'

'I'd heard. Couldn't have happened to a nicer guy,' she said nastily. 'Maybe his conscience got the better of him.'

'How was his time in custody?'

'What do you mean?'

'Was he any bother?'

'Don't remember him being. It'd be in there if he was.'

'Did he say anything to you?'

'Such as?'

Henry was about to ask when the buzzer on the back door sounded again – another prisoner being brought in, and suddenly no one could interrupt a custody officer. Henry didn't envy her, so he lifted the binder off the desk and retreated back to the office for a more detailed read. The problem he had with Sowerbutts was that – besides him and only a select few knowing the man was dead before he went over the cliff – the time gap between him being released from custody in one piece then being found at the foot of the cliffs was a blur. Henry didn't like blurs any more than he liked coincidences.

He flipped through the other custody records on either side of

Sowerbutts to find who was in custody at the same time as him. He found several names, took notes of what cells they had been in, then closed the binder.

Then he had a second thought.

Not that he was paranoid or anything.

Not that he didn't suspect everyone.

He was.

He did.

He took the binder under his arm and, while the sergeant was busy booking in the latest prisoner, he left the office, calling for the door release, and went into the police station proper. The custody sergeant didn't even look up as she reached for and pressed the buzzer.

He made his way through the complicated building until he found Admin on the second floor, introduced himself and demanded access to a photocopier.

Permission was given and he copied Sowerbutts' record and the front sheets of four other prisoners' records who were in custody at the same time. He then asked someone who looked after all the CCTV footage taken from the cameras in and around the custody suite. He was told that all those details were stored on a computer in the custody office itself.

He pouted at that news, then made his way back down to the custody office to find the sergeant was busy with even more prisoners. He checked the interview rooms and saw Milner was still being interviewed, so he returned the original custody records, and then it was time for a brew.

He linked up with Daniels at a newly opened Starbucks in the city centre, and both brought the other up to speed.

'Overall gut feeling?' he asked her when she'd finished her bit.

'She was adamant she wasn't having an affair with Salter,' she said regarding Mclissa the accountant. 'I believe her.' Then she added, 'But I don't believe anything else, just as I don't believe a word anyone else has told me since we've been here.'

'I know what you mean,' he agreed just as his name was called out by a barista. He went to collect two lattes and brought them back to the table they had bagged by the window. 'Anyway, how are you feeling?'

'Me?'

'After this morning's fracas by the river.'

'I'm OK. Sore, grazed . . . I am angry about it but I'm not going to let it bother me.'

'I'd get it if you did.'

'Hey, you're recovering from being shot, you've tumbled down steps and you haven't had any sleep, yet you're still functioning. I got a bit of a slap – so what?' She shrugged and picked up her coffee, but before she took a sip, she said, 'A lot's happened in two days.'

'You're telling me.'

'What about the man they arrested this morning?'

'Milner? He's in denial. He's a good suspect. Violent. Uses firearms. Could easily kill someone but he looked as shocked as anyone. I know, I know, people are good actors and you can usually see through them, but I'm pretty convinced by him.'

'One of the few people around here telling the truth?'

'That would be ironic.' Henry placed the copies of the custody records he'd just made on the table.

'What're these?'

Henry explained, then asked, 'How d'you feel about visiting these people, see if they can remember anything about Sowerbutts?'

'Is there anything to remember?'

'Dunno.'

'What will you be doing?'

'Keeping my enemies close.'

The initial interview with Milner lasted almost two hours. Henry was waiting in the custody office as Runcie came out and presented the prisoner to the custody sergeant before he was taken back to his cell. She came up to Henry, looking stressed and not a little concerned.

'He's a lying cunt,' she said, and beckoned him into the office behind the desk where Saul was standing. 'Shit, shit . . . mostly no comment. To be honest, I don't really have much to link him to the murder . . . it's all dependent on what we find at his property . . . Fuck!' She stared at the ceiling, rolling her eyes. 'You don't know how much I've wanted to crack this, Mr Christie. It's always here, on my mind,' she said, tapping her head. 'I was hoping this might be the key . . . comes of trusting anonymous information to *Crimestoppers* . . . but I'm sure he's the one.' She clenched her fists.

'I'm assuming it's a blank at his house?'

'As yet, yes. Fucking worrying. Search teams have found nothing.'

'They might yet,' Henry said reassuringly.

Runcie watched him leave the custody office with her eyes in predatory mode. When she was certain he'd gone, she looked at Saul.

'Was that a good enough act? The desperate detective? All that shit?'

'You were very convincing,' Saul flattered her.

She gave him a wink. 'Now it's about time that gun was found, don't you think?'

Then she turned to the custody sergeant, who was standing there with one of those expressions on her face that made Runcie say, 'What?'

'Him,' the sergeant said, gesturing to where Henry had just disappeared.

'What about him?'

The fact was, as much as Daniels' assessment of his staying power made him bristle with male ego, Henry was flagging.

Guilty though he felt about it, he walked out of the station, then through the city to the quayside, and returned to the hotel. He went to his room and flopped on the bed. He wasn't quite as good at all-nighters as he used to be and as soon as he hit the bed, energy flowed out of him.

It was an effort to stay awake, then drag himself over to the desk and log on to his laptop to see if anything more had arrived from Tope. Nothing had. Slightly disappointed, he turned his attention back to the murder books, but something made him pause.

It concerned the books themselves.

Something about them.

A reference to them.

He felt he was on the verge of realizing something quite simple but vital . . . Then it was gone as his mobile phone rang and severed his line of thought.

He answered absently, irritated.

It was Rik Dean.

And all thoughts went out of the window as he concentrated on what his old friend had to say.

'Believe you chatted to my intelligence analyst this morning?' Rik teased.

'Yeah. Nice guy, but Mr Grumpy.'

'He mentioned you asked about how we were doing with Burnham.'

'I did.'

'Not that well, to be honest, though we do have one thing we're trying to bottom. Two guys in a car seen hanging around. This from a woman who lives near to Burnham's mother. Might not be connected but we'd still like to trace them.'

'That it? Two guys in a car.'

'Pretty much, although there is one other thing: it was a white guy and a black guy, she thought.'

Henry tensed up. 'A white guy and a black guy?'

'Yeah. Why – does that seem interesting?'

Henry swallowed. That 'something' that was eluding him now suddenly morphed into a concrete slab.

Henry had a quick, reviving shower, then returned to the police station on foot and settled himself in the small room he and Daniels had been so generously allocated. It looked as though nothing had been disturbed, but he would not have been surprised if it had been riffled through.

He reread the murder books, knowing that all he could do for the moment was bide his time, gather information and then make decisions. He didn't want to do anything too rash, just allow things to brew.

Firstly with the gun issue.

He needed to see where that would lead.

It wouldn't be hard to find a weapon of some sort on or some-where near a guy like Milner. It was just whether any weapon found was the right one, but if it was, then it looked as though the Salter murder could be solved, so great.

But that left Mark James Wright's brutal stabbing and the circumstances surrounding the alleged suicide via a cliff of Martin Sowerbutts, and the fact that a Home Office pathologist had declared the cause of death to be something other than it really was. And if there was some collusion with Runcie, what was that all about? Sowerbutts had been in custody some hours before his death, been released, then committed suicide.

Simple.

Henry's skin crawled.

He'd expected to come along to Central Yorkshire, look at a couple of murders, make a few recommendations, then go home.

Instead, simple had become complex, and the attitude of the Serious Crime Team here was, to say the least, unsettling.

He looked at the note Jack Culver had made in one of the murder books: *What is going on here?*

What the hell did that mean? Henry asked himself.

Unfortunately he couldn't ask a dead detective.

'I didn't see owt, saw nuffin', not frickin' interested in talking to cops, 'specially black uns.'

Daniels smiled warmly at a man called Bernard Williams who she had managed to track down to a bedsit by the cathedral in Portsea. He was one of the prisoners who had been in custody at the same time as Sowerbutts. He'd been arrested for minor public order offences and drunkenness, and Daniels guessed he would have spent most of his time in custody asleep and sobering up.

'That's not very pleasant. A bit racist,' she said.

'And yer a woman. I don't talk to women, just shag 'em. White uns, that is.' His cider-tainted breath made its reeking way into Daniels' face.

'Lucky ladies,' she said. She assumed he was one of the city-centre drunks. 'I'll be off then. Thanks for your time.'

'But I did see one thing,' he relented, suddenly changing tack. 'After they'd taken the two-pence piece off the peephole.'

'The what off the what?'

'You 'erd.' He described a small circle with the tip of his forefinger. 'Two-pence pieces . . . peephole.'

'What do you mean?'

'The peepholes in them cell doors, yeah? Just a big bigger than a two-pence piece. Stick a two-pence piece in one an' you can't see out.'

'Right.' She screwed up her nose, wondering what the significance of it was. 'So what did you see?'

'Blood – an' a lot o' moppin' up goin' on.'

Daniels hurried to her car, calling Henry at the same time.

'Where are you, boss?'

'In our cubbyhole at the nick.'

'I'll be there in five.'

'You sound rushed.'

'You'd better believe it.'

Henry placed his phone on the table just as there was a knock on the door and Runcie poked her head in.

'Boss. Development. You got a minute?'

Henry followed Runcie to her office. Once inside, she turned to him and her face was transformed as she gave a triumphant dig with one of her fists.

'Good news, I take it?'

'Found a gun,' she said almost breathlessly.

'Oh, wow! That's bloody good news.'

'Well, yeah,' she said, tempering her victory with caution. 'Early days, but it looks good. Found in a plastic bag underneath Milner's shed in his back garden. A nine-millimetre Makarov . . . and nine-millimetre bullets were taken out of Tom Salter's head. Obviously going to need analysing but, whatever, this guy has some serious questions to answer. I'll request a fast-track analysis. Could be done in three or four days if I get a traffic car to run it down to the lab today.'

'Very nice.'

'Here – look.' Runcie scooped her iPhone from her desktop and showed it to Henry. It displayed a photograph of a gun in a plastic bag.

'Really great stuff. If this cracks it, bloody marvellous.'

'I'm going to re-interview him now, see what he has to say. If necessary, we'll bail him to come back in a week. Some really tough questions coming up.'

SIXTEEN

'I'd either like to be in on the interview or be able to watch it on an A/V feed if possible,' Henry told her, and the request seemed to stun Runcie. 'I assume you have an A/V feed?'

He knew she was considering saying no – he could see that possibility cross her mind – but she also realized it would be a lie he could easily see through. She composed herself quickly.

'I'd rather you weren't in the interview room. Myself and DC Saul have this covered. We've got a bit of a rapport with Milner now and you might skew the balance. You know what it's like.'

'An A/V feed will do nicely.'

'This way.'

She led him through the main CID office to a small room with a TV set up on a table, wires from the back of it disappearing into the walls. There were two chairs.

'Switch it on in a couple of minutes.'

She left and he sat down and called Daniels to tell her where to find him, then switched on the TV. It came to life, giving a split-screen view of an interview room consisting of one table with four chairs, two either side of it, and a tape machine bolted to the wall and table. Sparse.

The cameras gave a view from two positions. One would be over the heads and shoulders of the interviewing officers, the other focused on where the interviewee would be sitting.

Henry glanced around as Daniels entered, looking flushed and excited. 'What's happening?' she asked.

'They're going to interview Milner. I thought I'd look in on it as it's the one we're reviewing.'

'Has he admitted anything so far?'

Henry shook his head.

'You think he did it?'

'Never say never, but no. What have you got?'

Daniels exhaled. 'You're not gonna like this.'

'Hang fire,' Henry said as, at that moment, the interview-room door opened and four people entered: the two detectives, Runcie and Saul; the prisoner, Milner, now attired in a forensic suit; and a woman Henry assumed was either the duty solicitor or Milner's own chosen brief.

The two detectives sat on one side of the table, Milner and the woman on the other. Following the usual preliminaries – unpacking of sealed tapes, insertion into the tape recorder, introductions, time, day, date and location, during which Henry learned the woman was Milner's own solicitor – Runcie cautioned Milner and the interview commenced.

Runcie said, 'Firstly, I want to tell you I am now arresting you on suspicion of committing armed robbery.'

Henry focused on Milner's face. He thought he saw the colour drain out of him on those words, but when Runcie continued to say that the robbery had been committed last year in Portsea when a security guard had been shot in the leg, Henry saw Milner's expression change and his whole body visibly relaxed. In that moment, Henry knew Milner was not guilty of that particular crime. He had been reading body language for a long time, and Milner's whole frame suddenly oozed relief and self-confidence.

'That's the robbery linked to the bullets found in Salter, isn't it?' Daniels said.

Henry nodded. He glanced at Daniels, who was watching the interview closely.

She eyed Henry and said, 'He didn't do it. His body language screams it.'

'Well spotted.'

'OK,' Runcie said in the interview room. 'Do you have anything to say about that?' She laid a file on the table between them.

Milner shook his head.

'For the benefit of the tape, Mr Milner has just shaken his head,' Runcie said.

Henry muttered, 'This is going to be a long one,' and Daniels snickered.

'As you are aware, following your arrest earlier, officers

searched your premises,' Runcie stated, getting zero response from Milner. 'And, hidden underneath the shed in your back garden, a member of the search team found this.' She reached down by her side and pulled up a clear plastic evidence bag. It contained the Russian Makarov semi-automatic pistol. She placed it gently on the table between herself and Milner, who was directly opposite. 'Just in case you are wondering, it has been made safe by one of our firearms officers.'

'Would you like me to pick it up so my fingerprints are on it?' Milner asked. 'Because they aren't.'

'It has yet to be examined for prints. Same with these.'

She picked up another evidence bag from down by her side. It contained two ammunition magazines for the Makarov. 'One of these is fully loaded; the other, which was in the pistol, contained six rounds. It has a capacity for ten,' she said significantly. 'So, four missing.'

Henry said, 'Tom Salter had four bullets pumped into him.'

'It's fitting together very nicely,' Daniels said cynically.

'Innit just?'

On screen, Milner shrugged. 'What's that supposed to mean?' he said.

'Just bear it in mind and I'll come back to that point.'

'Er, no,' Milner's brief cut in. 'You made the point. I believe you should explain its meaning because, clearly, the statement does have some significance. I don't want any games here, Detective.'

Henry imagined Runcie's eyes burning laser holes into the solicitor's skull.

'Very well. Tom Salter was killed by four bullets. The magazine in the gun, this one' – she tapped it – 'had six bullets in it when it has a capacity of ten.'

Milner shook his head.

'Which proves nothing,' the solicitor pointed out.

'Maybe not yet,' Runcie conceded, 'but what I want to do in this interview is give your client the opportunity to tell me all about this gun. At the moment, it has not been analysed, but I thought it would be prudent for me to paint the picture as I see it and give Mr Milner the chance to respond truthfully.'

Milner glanced sideways at his brief. She gave a small gesture, then to Runcie, she said, 'Better paint your picture then.'

Daniels said to Henry, 'Do you think she's the one who phoned Alison about us?'

'Her or someone connected to her.'

'What are you going to do about it?'

'Save it for the time being.'

'Towards the end of last year, a security guard was shot once during an armed robbery,' Runcie said. 'No one has yet been arrested for this offence and the weapon used hasn't been found. However, the bullet was analysed – a nine-millimetre round. Did you use this gun and commit that robbery, Mr Milner?'

'No,' he said confidently.

'OK. Tom Salter was murdered six months ago. The bullets used to kill him came from the same gun used to shoot the guard. Did you murder Tom Salter?'

'No.' Just as confident.

Daniels said, 'No, he didn't,' to Henry.

'So you don't actually know yet if that gun is the one used to shoot the guard and later to kill Mr Salter?' the solicitor said. 'Because it hasn't been to ballistics yet.'

'Not yet,' Runcie said.

'So why, exactly, are we having this conversation?'

'Because I want to give Mr Milner the chance to come clean and make it easy on us all. He is in very deep as regards to his possession of a Section One firearm as it stands anyway, and I'll bet, once it has been examined, I will be proved right.'

Milner said, 'Bollocks.'

'Tell me about the gun, then,' Runcie insisted.

'The gun has sod all to do with me. My guess is you're desperate and you've planted it.'

'A serious allegation.'

'Yep.'

Henry said, 'And I too have a funny feeling that the gun will be linked to those two jobs. What do you say, Diane?'

'Call me a cynic, but yeah.'

Henry said, 'You're a cynic.'

They listened to the interview as it continued. Runcie and Saul outlined the offences in more detail – times, dates, MOs – but Milner remained passive and confident in his responses.

He'd obviously been briefed not to lose his cool, even when
the detectives piled on the pressure.

From Henry's point of view, Milner's big problem was the
discovery of the gun under the shed. He had no rational explan-
ation for it, other than to claim it had been planted there. This
was his weak spot. Unless he could come up with something
convincing, he was in big trouble, and from Henry's reading of
his body language as the interview continued, Milner began to
realize this, becoming increasingly agitated and aggressive, which
wasn't doing him any favours, especially when he raised a fist
in anger and received a stern warning from his solicitor – and
from Runcie, who had been verbally prodding and prodding him
into reacting.

Finally, the interview was terminated.

'How reliable is he?' Henry asked of Daniels.

'Town drunk reliable.'

'Two-pence pieces? Covering the peepholes?' he asked
incredulously.

'That's what he said.'

'Far-fetched.' Henry cast his mind back to his walk through
the old cell complex at Portsea nick, that veritable warren of
corridors and dead ends. Visualizing the peepholes, he guessed
they were just a bit bigger than a two-pence piece and maybe
that size of coin would just about block any view through them.
'But possible. You didn't manage to speak to any of the others?'

'Not so far. I can do if you want.'

Time had gone on. It was well into the afternoon and Henry
and Daniels had driven back to the hotel, claimed a table in the
bar and ordered afternoon tea. It seemed a long time since
breakfast.

When it arrived, scones with cream and strawberry jam and
tiny sandwiches, Henry did the honours, then sipped his Earl
Grey tea and ate while thoughtfully watching the outside world
on the quayside.

As nice as the present situation was – the view, the food, the
company – he had a horrible feeling in his gut again. Daniels
kept quiet.

Eventually he said, 'Fuck.'

'I was reaching the same conclusion.'

'Part of me has been ducking and diving away from it,' Henry disclosed. 'I don't like to think that cops can be bad – certainly not in this way. I don't really want to go down any road I might regret, at least not until I'm certain we're on the right route, Diane.'

'I know what you mean.'

Daniels' unsaid 'but' hovered there.

Henry smeared clotted cream on the bottom half of a scone and added a dollop of thick jam. He was about to open his mouth wide when his phone rang.

'Henry, where the fuck are you?'

'Taking tiffin – afternoon tea,' he answered, happy to wind up his chief constable who was on the line.

'Life of Riley . . . Is Daniels with you?'

Henry said she was.

'Good. I need to see both of you.'

'We are in Portsea, that's on the Central Yorkshire coast.'

'And so am I – just visiting my new, if temporary, force. Give me your location, please, and order me what you're having.'

Somehow FB managed to find a parking space for his large Jaguar on the quayside. Henry watched him trundle across the road and enter the hotel. His requested afternoon tea was waiting for him. He was thirsty and famished and tucked in with relish and no formalities, only pausing to take a breath when a full scone and half a cup of tea had been devoured.

'I never realized how far it was. Taken me four hours, not including a stop on the way,' he said. Then, 'Brief me.'

Henry and Daniels did so succinctly, and FB's face turned from simply serious to horrified.

When they'd finished, he said, 'Conclusions?'

'As you told me, both Detective Superintendent Culver and Mr Burnham were deeply suspicious of the lack of progress in the two murders and that it could be a symptom of something more serious, though I wish you'd told me that a bit sooner. Anyway, neither man knew what was going on and neither do we, yet. A cover-up, corruption on a big scale or small scale. Could be personal stuff, affairs of the heart, debts, gambling, connections to criminals – but if Culver's or Burnham's deaths are connected to all this, someone is pretty desperate, especially if you include all the shit that's happened to us.'

'Move on it, Henry,' FB commanded.

Henry shook his head.

'Why the fuck not?'

''Cos I don't know what the fuck I'm dealing with.' Henry knew he was one of the few officers of lower rank who could get away with responding like that to FB. Their joint history over almost thirty years gave him that right. But he also knew not to overstep the mark.

'Never stopped you before,' FB pointed out.

Daniels laughed. FB glared at her, and she immediately reverted to her professional face.

'I want ducks in a row,' Henry said. 'Words on paper, facts recorded, evidence gathered, stuff like that. When I catch my fish I don't want it wriggling off the hook.'

'You mix metaphors badly.' FB shook his head. He looked at Daniels. 'Are you OK after the assault?'

'Fine, boss, thanks.'

'Good. As regards the stop I made on the way over, I did something for you as requested.' He had come in with his attaché case, which he placed on his lap – it seemed very heavy – flipped the catches and opened it. He handed Daniels a DVD. 'That's what you wanted, given to me by a very sheepish guy called Newsham, who had been informed by officers from Central Yorkshire Police, whose names he cannot recall – conveniently – not to hand anything over to either of you because you are both under investigation for corruption.'

'They moved quickly,' Daniels commented.

FB nodded. 'I assume it's footage of your tyres being slashed. I haven't looked at it.'

'I hope so.'

'I'll get my laptop,' Daniels said, and hurried away to her room.

'This force is one big mess,' FB said to Henry. 'I'm off to their headquarters at Lowgate next. I have a series of meetings with various key people to see what I can do to save this sorry excuse of a force. I already hear the neighbouring ones are lining

up for a piece of the pie if it ends up being divvied up or amalgamated.' He bit another chunk of his scone, getting jam and
cream in his moustache.

Much to Daniels' surprise, FB had gone by the time she returned
with her laptop.

'Something I said?' she asked, sat down and powered up.

'No, he's always that rude.'

She inserted the disc FB had given her and the screen came
to life. She made room on the table for the laptop between the
cups and plates and angled it so Henry could see, though they
had to come together shoulder to shoulder and both were aware
of this almost intimate proximity.

She pressed play and they found themselves watching split-
screen images of the car park at the service station.

They watched a green Peugeot 406 pull in and park, and then
themselves get out and walk into the service building.

The sequence was cut, then a Vauxhall Insignia drove in and
parked next to a large motorhome. It had two people on board.

Henry sat upright and Daniels felt his tension.

'What is it?'

'I know that car – pretty sure I do.' *A Vauxhall Insignia parking
at the front of The Tawny Owl as he sat perusing the murder
books.*

On screen, the passenger door opened and a man got out and
made his way, at a crouch, along a row of parked cars, keeping
low until he reached Daniels' Peugeot, where he squatted down
beside it. He wasn't there long, then he was scurrying back to
the Vauxhall and climbing into it. Moments later, it drove away.

'How do you know?' Daniels asked.

Then it clicked in Henry's brain – one of those 'somethings'
that had been evading him.

'The guys in that car came to The Tawny Owl.'

'You what?'

'I was sitting outside, watched them pull up and come in. They
ate there, for God's sake, claimed they were agricultural reps.
Obviously complete bullshit. Didn't know cow shit from horse
shit. Didn't have business cards. Didn't even want to know about
selling anything. You know what I thought when I first laid eyes

on them – a tall white guy and a shorter, stockier black guy? Cops! And when they walked towards me I was having my first read of the murder books. I closed them but I'm pretty sure the tall, lanky white guy was close enough to read the cover – see the Central Yorkshire crest at the very least.'

'Is that important?'

'No one knew that Burnham had copied the books and no one knew he'd given them to me.'

'Like I said, is that important?'

Henry looked at Daniels, their faces only inches apart. 'On my first meeting with Runcie here in the bar, she knew I'd seen the murder books. She shouldn't have known. Those guys could have told her – must have. They're the only ones who saw me with the books.'

'You think they're detectives?'

Henry turned away, feeling desolate and tired. 'Yes, I do, and I also think they pushed me down the steps, even though I thought they'd gone. I also think the guy who assaulted you this morning is that guy there.' He pointed accusingly at the laptop screen.

'You can say black guy, you know.'

'Black guy,' Henry said. 'Plus something Rik Dean told me this morning: a white man and a black man seen in a car close to the house in Bacup where Burnham was murdered.'

'What's the next step, then?'

Henry looked at her bleakly. 'Take control of everything, then start arresting people and fuck the consequences.'

'I like the sound of that,' she said as Henry's mobile started to ring, as did Daniels'.

Being thin on the ground, they had to go their separate ways with a view to reconvening in a couple of hours, all being well.

Henry walked back to the police station.

Daniels drove out towards a house she had visited earlier.

The CID offices were virtually empty, as was the Serious Crime Team office, a situation Henry understood. These were the quiet hours, between five p.m. and seven p.m., when most self-respecting jacks would be out having their tea somewhere.

Henry wandered through the almost-deserted offices, trying to

look disinterested to the couple of detectives who were at their
desks, typing away. He almost put his hands in his pockets and
whistled.

'Help you, boss?' one asked.

'Just waiting for DCI Runcie to return.'

'OK, no probs.'

'You wouldn't know where she is, would you?'

'No, but I could call her if you wanted.'

'It's OK. I'll wait.'

He continued his mooch, pretending to read the various posters
and other notices on the walls, pausing to glance at family photos
on desks and the occasional group photos either on walls or in
frames on desks. He found Saul's desk, on which was a photo
of the man himself and maybe his wife. Henry looked at it. Next
to that was an old class photo from some detective course or
other. He picked this up and saw that Saul was on the end of the
front row. It was an advanced detective course run at a regional
training centre near Harrogate – the course Henry remembered
giving a lecture at.

In the far corner of the room, Henry saw two desks pushed
together, each with a plaque on giving the name of the incumbent:
DS Silverthwaite on one, DC Hawkswood on the other. Unlike
the other desks, these were meticulously tidy and impersonal –
no photos of anything or anyone.

He frowned. He had met very few tidy detectives in his time.
Certainly not this tidy, and very few, other than those in the
throes of divorce, who didn't have personal photos on their
desktops.

Silverthwaite and Hawkswood.

He logged the names.

Then he made a show of checking his watch and pretending
to make a decision. He walked out of the office, mee-mawing to
the detective he had spoken to that he would be back.

He went down to the custody suite, juggling the loose change
in his pocket. He had at least one two-pence piece in there.

It was quiet in here also – again, teatime, when the guests
were fed.

He was pleased to see that the custody sergeant was the same
one from earlier. She looked up from the desk and her face fell.

From the custody records he'd copied, he remembered her name was PS Anna Calder.

'Sarge.' He greeted her affably.

'Boss. Hello.' Her voice was guarded.

'I want to see Milner, please.'

'Uh, he's having his tea.'

'What's he having?'

'Burger on a bun, chips, mug of tea.'

'In that case, he can come and eat it in the interview room – one without an A/V feed, please. In fact, I'll tell you what, I'll go and get him.' He opened his palm for the cell keys.

'I'm not sure I can let you.'

Henry leaned over the desk, just enough to be on the brink of intimidation. 'Yes, you can. Put an entry into the record to that effect and I'll gladly sign it. Something like, "Detective Superintendent Christie, Lancs Police, requests to speak to the detainee on matters not connected to the present enquiry." Something along those lines. Keys.' He waggled his fingers. Reluctantly, she eased the keyring off her belt and gave the keys to him. 'Cell four, I believe?'

'Yes, boss.'

If she'd had an Adam's apple, Henry was sure he would have seen it rise and fall.

Wearing a thin smile, he left the custody office and entered the cell corridors, firstly going to the wing of cells in which Martin Sowerbutts had been detained.

He walked slowly past each cell and stopped at an empty one, the door open, ready for the next occupant.

The cell doors were heavily built and very old fashioned. Even new ones had to be heavy to withstand the constant battering they got from aggrieved inmates, but in this wing of the complex they were Victorian-heavy with a sliding hatch just below eye level and the peephole just above this, a circle of toughened glass set in the thickness of the door. Very basic stuff. Inmates often stuck toilet roll over them to prevent gaolers looking in.

And sometimes detectives put two-pence pieces in them to stop inmates looking out.

Henry got the two-pence coin out of his pocket and held it with his thumb over the glass. It fitted nicely, almost covering the whole area of glass and making it impossible for anyone in the cell to see out. Simple and cost-effective.

He smiled at his own little joke.

Then he moved down the corridor to cell number six, currently empty, which Sowerbutts had been in. He stood on the threshold. There was nothing to see: it was basic and clean. There was a bench bed and steel toilet.

He spent a few moments in contemplation, then turned away and headed towards Milner's cell, which was in another wing.

Behind the custody desk, PS Anna Carter watched all of Henry's movements on the CCTV screen.

Although she was not certain, she was pretty sure that her legs had just turned to mush.

SEVENTEEN

Daniels knocked on the door instead of using the bell. She – like most cops – preferred to knock. Just one of those mini-psychological things, as knocks could be varied from timid to 'answer the fucking door or I'll kick it down'.

This was her mid-range 'I'm back' knock.

She stood back slightly and scanned the front of the house while waiting for an answer, then cast her eyes around this well-heeled cul-de-sac.

From inside, she heard someone approaching, saw a shape through the frosted glass, then heard a bark and the rush of a dog again. Its nose to the glass.

'This better be good,' Daniels said to herself as Melissa Phillips yanked the beast away and opened the door a few inches. From the first glance of her face, Daniels could see she had been crying.

Milner balanced a plastic plate on his lap, his mug of tea on the bench next to him. He'd half-devoured the burger and was putting some chips into his mouth when the cell door opened to reveal Henry Christie beckoning him with a jerk of the head.

'Yeah, right, it's teatime. I know my rights,' Milner said.

'We need to talk.'

'I don't even know who the hell you are. I'm presuming some detective or other, so unless my brief is back, which I doubt, no talkee.'

'OK, have it your way.' Henry stepped back. 'It's just that I'm the guy who might just save you from going to prison for the rest of your shitty life. Your move, mate.'

The dog was manoeuvred into the kitchen and locked away.

In the lounge, Daniels waited for Melissa to return, which she did.

Daniels had not taken a seat.

Instead, she hovered by the window, feeling slightly annoyed for some reason, thinking this could just be a waste of time.

'What's this about?' she asked Melissa.

'I wasn't entirely honest with you before.'

'I'd never have guessed.'

Melissa ignored the sarcastic jibe. 'I want to tell the truth.'

Daniels heard movement in the hallway. 'Which is?'

'You said you thought Tom Salter was probably seeing someone.'

Daniels nodded.

'Well, not me. I'm not, never have been or wanted to be his bit on the side,' she said. Daniels waited, then Melissa called out, 'Miriam! Come in now, please.'

The living-room door opened slowly and a woman a little younger entered, a little prettier, a little slimmer, yet very similar to Melissa, who said, 'This is my sister. She needs to talk to you.'

Miriam wasn't the only person to enter the room. Behind her came a devastatingly beautiful young girl, maybe fifteen years old, Daniels guessed, with high cheekbones and searing brown eyes that astounded the detective.

'Who's this?' Daniels asked.

Melissa said, 'This is Amira and she's an illegal immigrant. Tom Salter believed he saved her life but, in so doing, lost his.'

There was no doubt in Henry Christie's mind that Jamie Milner could be a very dangerous individual, capable of inflicting pain on anyone. He was a fit-looking young man, obviously worked out in a gym and could probably have strangled Henry in about thirty seconds.

Henry had done a quick check on Milner's previous convictions – all mainly from his youth, all involving separating people forcibly from their money; more recently, he had a conviction for an armed robbery where a shotgun was discharged, injuring a security guard, though not seriously. He was also suspected of involvement in robberies up and down the country and was on the National Crime Agency's radar, but nothing could be proved against him. He was definitely a professional crim.

Henry was unfazed and unintimidated by him.

He enjoyed looking across interview-room tables at bad people.

Defiantly and with a smug grin on his face, Milner folded a couple of chips into his mouth.

'Tell me about the gun,' Henry said.

'What gun?'

'The one the police found under your shed.'

'I thought I didn't need a brief?'

'You don't. Entirely off the record, this one.' He pointed to the tape machine, which was empty, then up to the walls, on which there were no cameras. 'Nothing said here can be used as evidence against you.'

Milner did not look impressed. He snorted in disbelief.

'I'm here to help you, but I can only do so if you are open and honest with me, two concepts which I realize are probably alien to you.'

Milner swigged a mouthful of sweet tea. 'Who the fuck are you?'

Henry explained patiently, then said, 'The gun.'

'Not mine. Never seen it before in my life. You know about me – you know I'm a sawn-off kinda guy.'

'It wouldn't be a surprise to discover you used a pistol, though.'

'Maybe not.'

'Did you kill Tom Salter?'

Milner sighed tetchily. 'I rob vans moving cash about.'

'That's not what I asked.'

'No, I didn't. I don't just kill people. In fact, I've never killed anyone, and I don't intend to start.'

'The detectives here seem to think you did.'

'And by pure coincidence, they find what I bet turns out to be the murder weapon under my shed. Under my shed, for fuck's sake!'

'I've found guns hidden in worse places. Most villains haven't got a lot of imagination. I once found a revolver in a biscuit tin. You are a proper villain, aren't you? But I'll lay odds you don't have much imagination.'

'Two things.' Milner leaned over his plate. 'One, yeah, I'm a villain. Two, I don't shit on my own doorstep.'

'You would say that. You need to do better, otherwise you'll end up being convicted of a murder, and frankly you're not helping yourself here. You need to think very carefully about where you were on the night of this killing and come up with a real alibi, otherwise you'll go down for life.'

They moved to the dining room at the back of the house, overlooking a well-tended garden with a sweeping lawn, down to what Daniels thought was a tacky water feature.

At the table, Daniels said, 'What do you have to tell me?'

The young girl sat there primly, her slim fingers interlocked on her lap. She wore a simple dress, showing her long legs.

Melissa, the older sister, looked sternly at Miriam. 'Tell her,' she ordered. 'We need to get this behind us.'

Miriam's eyes were wet and bloodshot from crying. The conflict and fear inside her were visible externally too. She was screwed up as tight as a dishcloth being wrung out.

Daniels saw the pain. 'Tell me,' she said softly, then prompted, 'were you seeing Tom Salter?'

Numbly, Miriam nodded.

'I'll take my chances,' Milner said stubbornly. 'That fuckin' gun's not mine, I have no idea who, what's he called, Tom Salter, is or was. I've never met the guy and I certainly didn't plug him with bullets. You won't find any evidence of me ever having handled that gun, not in a million years.'

'I admire your confidence.'

'I don't admire you trying to sneak a confession out of me.' His eyes roved the room. 'Not being recorded? Bull!'

Henry hadn't expected this to be straightforward. Dealing with a professional villain's inherent mistrust of the cops was always difficult.

'I did watch you being interviewed earlier,' Henry said. 'When DCI Runcie started talking, your body language told me a few things.'

'You going to psychoanalyse me now?'

'Maybe. I saw you go from being worried – when she put the allegation to you – to being confident because you knew that when she went into detail she was barking up the wrong tree.'

'Very perceptive for a cop.'

'But just knowing you didn't do it is one thing; proving you didn't is entirely another matter. Me seeing your body language doesn't prove a thing. The only thing that proves anything is hard evidence, Jamie. You haven't got any in your favour at this moment and I very much doubt you ever will.'

'Girlfriend, alibi,' he said.

'They'll speak to her before you do and run rings round her.'

Milner's eyes narrowed. 'Just what is your game?'

'I'm not playing a game. I don't play games where murder and murderers are concerned. I'm just telling you that if you don't come up with something very quickly there's a chance you won't even make bail. They might be so sure that gun *is* the murder weapon that you'll get charged and put before court in the morning, and never see the true light of day other than above a prison exercise yard for what, minimum fifteen years. Maybe twenty. You could be seen as a menace to society.'

'He was going to leave his wife. The marriage was over,' Miriam said through her tears, and Daniels wondered how many million times that line had been spun. However, she nodded sympathetic- ally, encouraging Miriam to continue.

The young girl, Amira, sat immoveable, hands still clasped.

'We'd spent most of that day together.' She glanced at Daniels. 'Slept together. Spent time, y'know?'

'OK.'

'Eventually he picked up his phones and left for a meeting and I never saw him again.'

Melissa had made a mug of tea for each of them. Miriam picked up hers with dithering hands and took a sip.

'Who was he meeting?'

Placing the mug down, Miriam then dragged her fingers across her face, stretching her pretty features. She looked beyond exhausted, Daniels guessed by the burden she had been carrying around in her head for the last six months. Daniels glanced at the young girl, wondering how she fitted into this picture.

'The people who killed him.'

'Who are these people?'

'I don't know. I just know they are dangerous and I think cops are involved. He even mentioned the New York underworld.'

'Had Tom crossed them or something?'

'Not really. I don't think so. He'd got involved . . . been involved for a while, but then he wanted out, couldn't handle it.'

'Handle what?'

'The violence, but mainly the suffering caused.' Miriam looked at the girl. 'She's the one who changed him, just like that. He wasn't really a bad man, just a bit of a rogue, got into money problems and problems with the cops and chose the wrong people to get involved with.'

'I ask you again: who were they? I need names, Miriam.'

'I don't know. He never told me, just said they were connected . . . whatever that means.'

'OK, so you were with him all day and then he went out to meet these people. Presumably his office was the meeting venue?'

'As far as I know.'

'So he met his killers in his office. It wasn't just burglars or someone like that who stumbled across him?'

She shook her head.

Daniels looked at the young girl again. 'And how is Amira involved in all this?'

Miriam swallowed and closed her eyes desperately. 'She's one of the girls Tom brought into this country using his haulage firm.'

Daniels tensed up. 'He was a people trafficker?'

Miriam nodded. 'He needed the money. He knew it was wrong – that's why he had to give it up. When he saw Amira he knew he couldn't do it any more. He saved her and allowed all the others he'd brought over on the run to go. It lost the people he worked for a lot of money. I think that was why he was killed.

I took Amira under my wing and looked after her. She has no papers, nothing.' She paused. 'There was other stuff, too . . . Big scams going on, and someone was murdered, a man in a car, stabbed to death.'

Milner walked ahead of Henry along the cell corridor. The prisoner had said hardly anything since Henry had speculated on the length of a jail sentence. Now Henry was putting him back in his cell, unable to decide if he was Tom Salter's killer or not. Maybe he was. Maybe he was just doing what many crims did: lie and deny. Maybe he had not thought deeply enough about where to hide the gun. Just another dim felon, not quite as smart as he thought.

Milner's cell door was open. 'In you go,' Henry said.

The prisoner stopped abruptly and turned to Henry, who thought, *I hope he doesn't hit me. I can do without another tussle.*

Milner said, 'Are you on the level?'

'What do you mean?'

'You honest?'

Henry considered a quip. Instead he said seriously, 'Yes, I am.'

'You think I'll go to prison for this?'

'Every chance. I suppose it could be reduced to manslaughter, but even so, that comes with a mandatory life sentence.'

'I didn't do it. I didn't fucking do it. I am a villain – I get my kicks and cash from it, but I didn't do it.'

Henry regarded him and shrugged.

'I was somewhere else on that day.'

'Can you prove that?'

'Only if I admit to it.'

'Admit to what?'

'Check your crime reports – New Cross, London, near a Travelodge. I was robbing a cash delivery van outside a Barclays Bank. Me an' another guy. I won't tell you who.'

'Go on.'

'I fired me shotgun just to scare the crap outta the guards. Didn't hit anyone. Got away with the best part of a hundred grand.' He stopped. 'It were the morning the guy Salter got shot, so I couldn't physically have been there and you can go into my phone records, I suppose. They'll put me in the Smoke the day before.'

'Go on. So far you've proved nothing.'

'I can tell you where the sawn-off's hidden, and me gear and me mask – in a hole under the shed, so you guys even missed that.'

PS Calder was at the desk in the custody office when Henry emerged from the cells. She watched him warily.

'Milner's back in his cell,' he informed her. 'Let me put an entry on the record.'

Calder spun the open file around and Henry, trying to keep his hand from dithering with excitement, wrote up his entry concerning Milner, keeping it vague but truthful. Then he looked steadily at Calder. 'The prisoner, Sowerbutts? When he was released from custody, he was OK, yeah?'

'I think I've already told you that, boss.'

'He was in cell six, wing two, wasn't he?'

She nodded.

'How many prisoners have been in that cell since?'

'Er, don't know. None, I don't think. It's kind of an overflow wing. We don't generally use it unless we get really busy and full. It's the furthest away from here.'

'How inconvenient,' Henry said, meaning, *How convenient.* Then he gave a curt nod and went back into the cell complex, down into wing two, cell six, unoccupied still from his last look round. He stood on the threshold now with fresh eyes, his nostrils dilating as he thought through his next moves. In respect of Sowerbutts, the first thing to do was close the cell door and declare the cell as a crime scene, not to be interfered with. There would be nothing lost in doing this if, as he suspected, Sowerbutts left the cell possibly having been assaulted in it, even though it had been mopped clean. There would still be plenty of blood traces to find by any competent CSI or forensic investigator. He pushed the door closed, except that it would not shut because the lock had been left in the 'locked' position, with the bolt sticking out. He got this. Unoccupied cells were often left this way so that there was less chance of a member of staff being accidentally locked inside.

He needed the key which he had returned to Calder.

He went back to the custody office, but Calder was nowhere to be seen.

She had gone down to visit a prisoner down the main cell corridor, which is where Henry bumped into her. He told her to follow him to wing two.

She did, with a perplexed, worried expression on her face.

At the entrance to cell six, he turned to her. 'I want this cell locked and kept locked,' he told her.

'Why's that, boss?'

'Because it's now a crime scene.'

'Eh?' She had the cell keys in her hand.

'No one goes in it without my say-so. The next person in it will be a CSI who will be accompanied by me, Sarge. Understand? Say, "Yes, boss."'

'Yes, boss.'

She inserted the key and drew back the bolt.

Henry's jaw rotated as he kept thinking about his moves. He leaned in and took one last glance around the cell. He was just about to step away as the door began to close.

He glanced at Calder. She now had a look of grim determination on her face and, before Henry could react – he knew what was coming and, even in that flash of a moment, kicked himself – she pushed him hard into the cell. He stumbled in, off balance, and she slammed the door and suddenly Henry was the one in custody.

On the wall outside she disabled the emergency call button and drew out a coin from her pocket. It was a two-pence piece with a tiny blob of Blu-Tack on one side, which she pressed into the peephole with her thumb.

She walked swiftly away, hearing the pounding of Henry's fists and feet on the cell door, and the muted sound of his shouts.

Daniels listened to the story told by Miriam of an affair and the man she loved embroiled in a situation from which he was futilely trying to extract himself. Of scams involving hugely expensive heavy plant such as excavators, crushers and screeners, of running illegal immigrants through Portsea docks and of the toll of it all weighing heavily on Tom Salter.

'I don't know the ins and outs of it,' she insisted (even though Daniels suspected she knew much more than she was divulging and would need a real serious interview). 'I just know bits of it – snippets – and can only piece them together.'

'I get it,' Daniels said. 'Look, me, you and this young lady need to spend quite some time together.' She smiled at Amira, who, in halting English, had told her some of the horrors she had endured in a bid for supposed freedom in the UK. She'd been raped and beaten – and it seemed that Tom Salter had seen all this by just looking into her eyes, and he'd stepped in and saved her from the rest of her life, for which she would be forever grateful. 'We need to get somewhere safe and secure and really talk about things. I will need statements from you both.'

'I understand,' Miriam said.

Daniels was already thinking that these two females should be taken over to Lancashire and housed at the constabulary training centre, where they would be safe. 'I need to call my boss first.' She stood up and went to the front door into the garden. Her hand was shaking as she speed-dialled Henry's number and waited for the connection. Frustratingly, it went straight to voicemail. She shook her phone crossly, tried again and got the same result.

'Bugger.'

Back in the house, the three women were sitting subdued around the dining-room table.

'I can't get through to him,' Daniels explained. She was about to tell them to hold tight while she went to get Henry – until something dawned on her in a flash. She stopped talking and looked at Miriam.

'You said something to me earlier, about when you last saw Tom that day, when he left you.'

Miriam waited.

'Unless I misheard, you told me he took his *phones* with him. Phones, not phone. Did he have more than one mobile phone?'

'Yes, he always had two – one work, one personal – which I don't think his wife knew about.'

'So when he contacted you he used his personal one?'

'Always.'

'Contract or pay as you go?'

'I . . . I don't know.'

'But he definitely set off with two phones in his possession?' Daniels asked to confirm, and Miriam nodded. Daniels knew that only one phone had been listed in Salter's possessions, so the other was missing. The questions for Daniels at that point were is it missing or has it been destroyed and was it critical to the investigation – or was it just a red herring? Would it reveal any clues as to who Salter had been in contact with that day? They were all important things for her to get answers for. She asked Miriam to give her the number of the missing phone.

'Right. Please stay here, will you?' she asked of the three women. They said they would. 'There's a few things I need to do, one of which is get my boss up here . . . and I'll be back as soon as I can.' She left, hurrying back to her car. In it, she made another call to Henry, which also went straight to voicemail.

This time she left a message. 'Boss, it's Diane. Look, I've discovered that Salter had two phones – one business, one private. As far as I can tell, it's the business one listed in his property . . . anyway, I'm just going on a hunch first. I'm going to see if I can get into his office and see if the missing phone's in there, maybe fallen down a crack or something. Wouldn't surprise me if these local tossers didn't find it. Then I need to speak to you urgently, face-to-face. I've a lot to tell you. Ring me when you get this. Cheers.'

She ended the call and sped away.

EIGHTEEN

Henry stood on the cell bench with his mobile phone in hand, reaching high towards the ceiling, trying to get a signal on the fucking thing.

Not a chance.

He dropped back to the floor and walked to the door, kicking it repeatedly, thumping it with the side of his fist and jabbing the call button but got no response, then he attempted to peer through the peephole. The two-pence piece was still in place and effectively blocked any view.

He swore furiously, then sat back on the bench, hoping to get at least one bar of signal on his phone. It never came.

He sat and waited, knowing they would come.

On the wall, his eye caught some words gouged into the plaster by a previous occupant: *All coppers are basturds*.

'Couldn't agree more,' he muttered.

The best hotel in Portsea was the Metropole, a huge, five-star monstrosity on a headland overlooking the North Sea. It had been recently refurbished for countless millions by a well-known chain and had only just reopened its doors to guests. There were three dining rooms. The one simply named *A-la-C* had already started to build a reputation for excellent, if simple, dining.

DCI Jane Runcie sat in the bar next to *A-la-C* sipping a vodka Martini which tasted of ice and spices. She sat atop a barstool and wore a split skirt displaying her shapely legs all the way up to the enticing top and also, just as tantalizing, was her blouse, which displayed her just-right boobs, hitched up for best effect.

Although she had rushed to get ready, she looked sheer class and the epitome of cool, even if below the surface veneer of nice tits and fanny, her mind was a churning clutter.

The thing was – she was certain – that shit-faced cunt of a detective superintendent called Henry Christie did not yet know a fucking thing about a fucking thing, but she could tell he was on the cusp of discovery, which is why she felt she'd had to act so quickly in the Salter murder investigation, because that clearly was not going to go away any time soon.

Thank fuck, she thought – she always 'thought' in foul expletives – she'd had the foresight to snaffle that Makarov.

It had proved to be a godsend; the thing she hoped would save the day and head that fucker off at the pass, as it were.

Many months earlier, following national initiatives, there had been a firearms amnesty across the county and the no-questions-asked bin at Portsea nick had been inundated with guns of all makes and sizes. No questions did not actually mean not having each weapon analysed to check if it had been involved in serious offences.

Runcie had been in charge of the administration of the firearms amnesty – even making a plea on local TV – and it hadn't been difficult for her to palm the Makarov out of the system without anyone knowing.

Access to an illegal firearm, she'd speculated, could be useful at some juncture, just one of those things on the backburner for later use if necessary. Corrupt cops needed to keep their options open.

So when the decision had been made above her head to kill Salter, that was when the gun – which had been handed in fully loaded and with a full spare magazine – came into its own.

Obviously she had been in a position to take charge of the murder investigation due to a lack of superintendent SIOs and had promised Tullane she could control the fallout. When the bullets that had been shot into Salter had been analysed, she'd been as surprised as anyone that they matched a bullet taken from the leg of a wounded security guard injured during an armed robbery from way back, and for which no one had been arrested.

She had thought everything was under control. That also included the murder of Mark James Wright, whose correct suspicions that he was being scammed had got him knifed to death before he got the chance to blow the whistle (another murder she'd been put in charge of). She'd thought she was outwardly showing she was doing everything to solve these jobs, though pleading that, even sometimes, one's best is not good enough. It helped that her force was falling apart at the seams in many other ways, so it was easy to deflect interest away from a couple of murder investigations to the other stuff that was going on – like funding being reduced and morale being at an all-time low.

That was until the arrival of John Burnham, the new chief constable, who wanted renewed efforts to be made into solving unsolved murders, of which there were six in the force, a very big number compared to the force's size. Four had nothing to do with Runcie. They'd occurred in other divisions. Two, of course, had.

Burnham sent Jack Culver to check up and see why no results were forthcoming.

He got too close, too quickly, to the truth.

The problem then was that Runcie did not know how much Culver had revealed to Burnham.

It escalated horribly, and Runcie knew it had to be nipped in the bud by dealing with both Culver and Burnham, under the assumption that whatever Culver knew had only got as far as Burnham.

Unfortunately she hadn't been quick enough to get to Burnham before he got across to Lancashire and engaged the services of Henry Christie.

What she had wanted to do with Christie – thinking on her feet – was to demonstrate that all was well in both investigations. They were proceeding well, even if results were not forthcoming.

Christie's problem – having survived a fall down some cellar steps – was that he was simply a nosy fuck-twat and he'd arrived at the force at an inopportune moment because of Runcie's current dealings with sex offender Sowerbutts. Runcie almost had a heart attack when he turned up at the scene of Sowerbutts' spectacular cliff suicide and then insisted on attending the PM. Hopefully that had all been covered up nicely.

Planting the gun under Milner's shed was done on the hoof, swiftly followed by his arrest on suspicion of murder, prompted by an anonymous call to *Crimestoppers*, which she had made.

Milner had been as good a choice as anyone.

Known to be violent, known to use firearms, known to rob people. He was a brilliant suspect and Runcie had been quietly chuffed by her choice, but was then blindsided by Christie wanting to observe the interviews, which therefore had to be played by the book.

Her face twitched at the thought.

However, she was again sure she'd pulled the whole thing off and that her acting had been of an Oscar-winning standard.

Tullane entered the bar, ending her musings.

As ever, he looked immaculate. Beautiful suit, well-trimmed hair and goatee beard, just under fifty years old and six feet tall. He was walking ahead of Silverthwaite, who had picked him up from Manchester airport, driven him back and settled him in the Metropole – under an assumed identity.

Runcie slid from the stool and slinked towards him. She knew he would have to be kept very sweet that night, as ever, and they would end up back in his room later, where she would give him the fuck of his life, as she had done many times before.

'Mr Tullane,' she cooed quietly, stretching out her hand.

'Ms Runcie.' He kissed the back of it and they turned back to the bar.

None of them had noticed the tall, good-looking man sitting in a dark alcove in the corner of the bar, sipping iced water, nibbling nuts and constantly reading the menu, but whose clear blue eyes were watching every move being made.

Runcie's phone was on the bar, vibrating as a call came in. She glanced at Tullane. 'Do you mind?'

'Go 'head.'

Runcie crushed the phone to her ear and stalked across the bar to within earshot of the man tipping the water.

'What the hell do you want?' she whispered, then listened. 'Fuck, fuck . . . you've done what? Fuck me!' Her eyes briefly caught those of the unknown man and she whirled away, dropping her voice even further. 'Keep him . . . I'll send Silverthwaite and Hawkswood over. Yeah, yeah, you did right. Don't panic.'

The good-looking man observed Runcie's demeanour change dramatically from chic cool to cold dread. As she ended the call, she visibly got a grip of herself, ran her hands down her thighs and shuddered. Her face changed from a snarl to an alluring smile. Once more, she caught the eye of the man in the alcove.

'Fuck you looking at, shit-head?' she demanded of him. He raised his hands defensively. She jerked him the finger, said, 'Swivel,' then walked back to Tullane at the bar.

Tullane asked, 'Problem?'

'Nothing I can't handle.'

Henry Christie shivered. It was chilly in the cell and, as he sat there, he had time to explore how his body was feeling. From the bullet wound to the knocks and bruises sustained in the fall, to the bang from the assault on the riverside. On the whole, it all felt fairly grotty. Assessment over.

He turned his mind to his present predicament and how he had managed to end up locked in a cell.

What should have been a routine job to provide a bit of a helping hand to a struggling police force had turned out to be something very different. He still hadn't joined all the dots; if, in fact, there were connections at all.

Two murders, both unsolved, seemingly bearing no relation to each other, except the police investigation into them both was shit-poor.

Or perhaps the phrase should have been deliberately poor.

Clearly the local cops were unsettled by his and Daniels' appearance on the scene.

Unsettled enough to try and ensure they never made it to Portsea in the first place by pushing him down a set of steps? By slashing tyres? By ambushing Daniels?

By killing their chief constable?

And the black man and white man in the Vauxhall.

Who were they? Were they the false 'reps' who'd turned up at The Tawny Owl? Had to be, had to be.

Shit. Fancy being pushed into a cell.

He heard footsteps approaching, voices down the cell corridor.

A key being inserted into the door.

Henry stood up slowly, knowing the answers to all of his questions were on the other side.

The man in the alcove who had watched Tullane walk into the bar and meet the woman with a bad attitude knew who Tullane was.

He had no idea who the woman was, nor the man who'd walked into the bar behind Tullane, though he did catch the woman's name – Ms Runcie – as spoken by Tullane. The man with Tullane had the air of a senior cop and, if that assumption was right, was the woman also a cop? And, if so, why was Tullane meeting her?

That wasn't the only question on the man's mind.

To all intents and purposes, Tullane had arrived in this country alone, but the man knew this was not the case.

Because while waiting for Tullane's appearance through the arrival gates at Manchester airport, another man had walked out well ahead of all the passengers on that flight carrying only hand luggage, and the man, sitting in the Costa café opposite the gates, had recognized him. His instinct told him something was going to happen.

He sipped his coffee and watched the first man through take up a position by one of the pillars so he could observe all the other arrivals coming through the gate.

The man drinking coffee did not know this guy personally, but had seen his photograph on many occasions and knew he was a killer. There was a smile on his face and excitement coursing through his body. Back at the sharp end, he thought.

'Shall we dine?' Tullane asked. He gave a slight, graceful bow and gestured for Runcie to lead him through to the restaurant. Once seated, they ordered wine and food and, after these preliminaries and when the waiter was no longer in earshot, Tullane said, 'Speak to me.'

'Everything's good,' she promised.

'That's not what I heard.'

'What have you heard?'

'That you've lost control of things. That what you promised could be controlled hasn't been. That your days are numbered,' he concluded bleakly.

Runcie raised her wine glass to her lips, desperate to stop her hands shaking.

'Who've you heard this from?'

'Sources, but none of your business. So, what I need now, Ms Runcie, is reassurance. Reassurance that you can tighten everything up and find another reliable transporter.'

'I can do all of those things. In fact,' she smiled in anticipation, 'I will demonstrate the level of my control later on this evening.' She tilted her glass towards him, then took a sip.

The good-looking man entered the restaurant and sat alone at a table.

The cell door swung open and, in spite of the predicament, Henry almost had to laugh.

Instead, he said, 'I could have sworn you were agricultural reps,' to the pair of men who had tried that subterfuge on their visit to The Tawny Owl. 'But no, let me guess.' He pointed to the taller of the two men staring menacingly on the threshold. 'You're Silverthwaite, and you' – he pointed to the smaller, stocky one – 'have got to be Hawkswood, DS and DC respectively.'

He'd memorized the names from his mooch around the CID office and knew he had a fifty/fifty chance of getting the name-game right. Although the two men tried to cover it, his knowledge put anxious expressions on their face, and he knew he'd got the names the right way round.

'You're a smart arse,' Silverthwaite said.

'Which one of you pushed me down the steps?'

Hawkswood grinned and said, 'That'd be me.' He stuck out his tongue at Henry, who could clearly see the deep bite marks across it, still seeping blood. It looked very painful and Henry vividly remembered Daniels' thrust of the heel of her hand up into the chin of her attacker on the track by the river. Henry went cold and became even more furious, if that was possible. 'And you attacked a lone woman. Hey, you're two brave guys.'

Henry's eyes dropped and caught sight of the extendable batons each man held down by his side.

'You don't know the half of it,' the Lanky One sneered.

'Good at slashing car tyres too.' Henry looked at Hawkswood. 'Yeah, I managed to get that video . . . I assume you're the dim muscle in this partnership?'

'Like I said, you don't know the half of it,' Silverthwaite reiterated, trying to get ahead of the game.

'I think I do,' Henry corrected him. 'Well, now I do. Which of you whacked your chief constable?' he punted, recalling what Rik Dean had told him about a white man and a black man having been seen in a car close to Burnham's mother's house. 'What was it? A wrecking bar?'

Silverthwaite, obviously the senior of the two and the leader, let his mouth sag. 'Maybe you do know too much.'

'The net, as they say, is tightening, you pair of dim twats.'

'Where is Daniels?' Hawkswood demanded.

'Fucked if I'd tell you even if I knew . . . Look, guys, it's time to start acting like big boys now. Let me out. Let's get this all sorted before it goes too far.' Henry knew it had gone too far already. Even so, he walked confidently towards them.

Hawkswood moved first. He contorted menacingly past Silverthwaite, gave his baton a flick with his wrist, extending it with a metallic snap, and in the same movement it arced through the air and struck Henry on the left bicep – hard. The pain of the blow resonated down to his fingertips and also across his chest up to his right shoulder. He gasped, clutched his arm and staggered sideways against the cell wall, cowering as the next blow came, hitting him in exactly the same spot, sending equally painful tremors across his body. He made to turn away and raised his left forearm to protect himself, but Hawkswood was fast and proficient and pounded the baton against Henry's arm. Henry dropped to his knees and tried to go into a protective ball.

Hawkswood dragged him to his feet.

Henry swayed unsteadily, his whole body encased in sheer agony from the blows.

And he was afraid.

Hawkswood stuck out his ragged, bloody tongue again and spat blood on to Henry's chest.

Then he dropped the baton with a clatter, curled his right hand into a very big fist and smashed it into Henry's right shoulder, again and again, until Henry was back down on his knees, cowering and whimpering.

'That'll do.' Silverthwaite placed a hand on Hawkswood's shoulder, holding him back. 'Let's get him out of here first.'

Silverthwaite flat-footed Henry with contempt over on to the floor while Hawkswood flipped him on to his front and bent his arms around his back. Henry cried out. Then he was handcuffed and the position of his arms up his back tore at his wounded shoulder agonizingly.

Hawkswood smeared a ready-cut length of duct tape over Henry's mouth.

'Put a spit hood on him, too,' Silverthwaite said.

Next thing, Henry felt a thin mesh hood being placed over his head.

He knew how controversial spit hoods were and, as far as he knew, not a single force in the UK had ever used them, although some were considering trialling them. They prevented prisoners from spitting in the faces of arresting officers but they were subject to outcries from human rights pressure groups.

There were different types of masks. Usually a thin, transparent mesh, but the one put over Henry's head was also of the type used to protect the identity of the prisoner and the front section of it was totally blacked out, although Henry could just about see out through the mesh.

He heard Silverthwaite shout, 'Get the CCTV off,' and assumed he was telling the custody sergeant what to do.

Hawkswood dropped with one knee on Henry's back, driving it into his spine just between the shoulder blades. It forced all the breath out of Henry's lungs and put so much weight and pressure on his heart he thought it would burst, but not in a good way. Then Hawkswood stood up, brought Henry with him and, jammed between the two cops, they kept his head low and rushed him off balance up the cell and out through the custody office. Out back their Vauxhall Insignia was waiting, reversed up to the door, boot already open.

They tipped Henry into it and slammed the lid.

It was an intense conversation.

Even though he could not hear their hushed, urgent words, the man who had followed Tullane from Manchester airport could see the as-yet unidentified woman was doing her best to convince Tullane of something, though his responsive body language remained unimpressed and distant.

She seemed to be losing the argument.

'Everything has to be discreet, under the radar,' Tullane said to Runcie. 'My bosses insist.'

'I thought you were the boss.'

'We all have bosses. I'm the area manager, shall we say? I was happy to send a man to sort out the festering problem that was Salter for you. After that, it should have been plain sailing.'

'It was. Is.'

'You made promises about a replacement for him. None seems to have materialized. That means we struggle in both directions. Our trade has fallen to virtually zero.'

'I have a new transporter. It took time, yeah, but he's in place now. Also a new business is up and running and we expect deliveries next week . . . three crushers, three screeners, just short of a million pounds. They'll be onsite next week and in Holland two days later. Fixed.'

Tullane nodded. At last, there was the flicker of a smile.

*   *   *

Purposely, they drove roughly, throwing the car around bends, fast over speed bumps, and Henry could only brace himself but was unable to prevent himself from being tossed around the boot space, banging his head continually. Even so, he tried to ease the spit hood from his head, but the elastic kept it in place.

After more bends and turns, the car slowed. He heard the murmur of conversation between Silverthwaite and Hawkswood, probably discussing Henry's fate.

Henry lambasted himself for not realizing what a field of shit he'd stepped into. And then, as things had dawned on him, he asked himself why he hadn't acted straight away. He'd had the chance – especially after discovering Sowerbutts was dead before plummeting off a cliff. His reservations, even, about the lack of scene preservation on the field, how the mobile crane had just been allowed to churn it up before CSIs had worked it. How he had wanted to get his ducks in a row. That had seemed such a good, sensible option . . . and may have come to fruition if he hadn't allowed himself to be pushed into a cell. Not that he could have expected that. Police stations were his domain, places he controlled, felt comfortable in. But not Portsea.

Another hump jolted him, sending sparks of pain across his upper torso.

At least Daniels was still out there and, from what he knew of her, she wouldn't take any shit.

Now the car stopped.

Henry waited.

Nothing happened for a few moments, but then the boot opened and the two detectives towered over him.

The spit hood was whipped off his head. The half-light did not hurt Henry's eyes and they adjusted easily.

He knew he had been dragged out of the car into a building of some sort and, as he glanced around, he saw he was in a small, commercial garage premises with a concrete floor, an old-style vehicle inspection pit to his right and a lean-to office by the wall.

A Transit van was parked nose-up to the far wall. He thought it could have been the one from which he'd seen Daniels' attacker get out of. Hawkswood.

The two detectives had dumped him on a plastic-seated,

metal-framed chair. His ankles had been bound to the thin, tubular legs and duct tape had been run around his chest and the back of the chair, binding him to it. His hands were still cuffed behind him and the position was painful and uncomfortable – as it was supposed to be. He was facing into the building and the two detectives were standing in front of him.

Inwardly, he swore. He could not speak because the tape still covered his mouth.

They were now both wearing forensic protection suits with skull caps and slip-over covers for their shoes. Face masks hung below their chins, not yet in place.

All this, Henry knew, was not a good sign.

Silverthwaite, the older of the two, was gasping for breath following the exertion of manhandling a squirming Henry Christie from the car. Hawkswood showed no sign of the effort.

The latter stepped forward and ripped the tape from Henry's mouth. That hurt, and he gritted his teeth.

'Not going to end well, this, Henry,' Silverthwaite gasped.

'You got that right.'

'For you, I mean.'

'So what are you going to do? Kill me? How exactly is that going to be explained?'

'We'll think of something. I'm sure we can come up with some kinda gangland execution type-A thing . . . Won't be any connection with us nice guys who welcomed you to our force.'

'You guys and your boss are well and truly fucked.'

Henry was going to launch a verbal tirade, but it was cut short by Hawkswood slapping him hard across the face with his open hand, momentarily knocking Henry's jaw out of line. A slap may sound pretty feeble, but Henry had seen jaws broken by well-aimed ones. He rolled his jaw and spat out something: blood and phlegm.

Then he looked insolently at Hawkswood, who was obviously the more volatile and aggressive of the two.

'Now you've got my DNA on you,' Henry said.

Hawkswood's eyes showed a dither of uncertainty, then he became confident again. 'I can wash,' he said.

'Whatever.' Henry spat a second time, but it drizzled down his chin on to his chest. He did not suck it back.

Hawkswood bent over and picked up something from the floor which made Henry freeze in terror – not only because of what he had picked up, but because of what was next to it. He recognized John Burnham's attaché case, the initials *JB* engraved in the leather. Burnham had had it with him at Henry's house in Blackpool.

The item that Hawkswood had picked up also terrified him and he watched it, riveted, as the man held it in his right hand and bounced it threateningly on the palm of his left.

'Know what this is?' Hawkswood asked.

'A stick of Blackpool rock?'

'Eh?' Silverthwaite interjected. 'You know we were in fucking Blackpool?'

'I didn't, but I do now,' Henry said, remembering the car parked down the avenue, two men on board, and attaching no significance to it as FB and Burnham drove away from his house after offering him this simple job.

'No matter,' Hawkswood said, still bouncing the item in his hand. It was a T-type wrecking bar. 'So what is this?'

'Something similar to the instrument that killed your chief constable. It can't be the actual one because that was left in his head. Killing your own chief – pretty fucking desperate.'

'Not half as desperate as killing a visiting superintendent and his sidekick,' Hawkswood said with promise.

'Which brings me back to the question: where is she?' Silverthwaite asked.

At which moment, Henry's mobile phone, still in his jacket pocket, beeped to indicate a message had arrived.

'Let's have that,' Silverthwaite said. He stepped in front of Henry and rummaged in his pockets. His face came close to Henry's, almost eyeball to eyeball as he searched for the phone.

Henry could not resist.

He quickly jerked his head back and slammed it forwards into Silverthwaite's left eye socket. It wasn't great as headbutts go. It hurt him and sent Silverthwaite spinning away, clutching his head, dropping Henry's phone.

'Bastard, bastard,' he groaned, picked himself up and came back at Henry, fists flying. Hawkswood stood aside, smiling, and let him do it.

The assault probably only lasted ten seconds, but when

Silverthwaite backed off, having delivered punch after punch, Henry's face was a battered mess, bleeding and cut, his left eye swelling instantly and closing. He wondered if his previously broken cheekbone had been cracked again. It felt like it.

He spat out again. And again the combination of blood and phlegm trickled thickly down his chin. He raised his head, forced himself to smile and said, 'DNA again.'

Silverthwaite glowered at him, his chest rising and falling.

Hawkswood bent to pick up Henry's phone, which was still in one piece. He tucked the wrecking bar under his arm and looked at the phone, which he was able to access because Henry had never bothered to put a passcode on it.

He saw Hawkswood's mouth twitch – the beginnings of a smirk. 'What have we here? Let's have a listen.'

'You have one new voicemail message,' the metallic female voice said. 'To listen to your messages, press one.' Hawkswood did so. 'First new message . . .'

Henry went cold as he heard Daniels' voice.

'Boss, it's Diane. Look, I've discovered that Salter had two phones, one business, one private. As far as I can tell, it's the business one in his property. Anyway, I'm just going on a hunch first. I'm going to see if I can get into his office and see if the missing phone's in there, maybe fallen down a crack or something. Wouldn't surprise me if these local tossers didn't find it. Then I need to speak to you urgently, face-to-face. I've a lot to tell you. Ring me when you get this. Cheers.'

'End of messages,' the metallic lady said.

Hawkswood pulled out his bloodied rump steak of a tongue and said, 'She's mine.'

NINETEEN

Daniels stood with her nose pressed up to the closed and locked steel palisade gates and raised her eyes to look uncertainly at the triple pointed tips and across at the flat-wrap razor wire adorning the fencing around the industrial unit and large yard that formed Tom Salter's business premises. The protection made the scaling not easy or safe, and the thought of implanting herself on the trident-like tips made her shiver.

She rattled the gates. They were securely locked.

Then had a thought.

She walked to her Peugeot, got in and drove it up to the gate, so that its radiator grille was almost touching. Going to the boot, she rummaged in it, flinging various items aside until she uncovered the old picnic blanket that her mother had made probably twenty-five years before. It had always been in the back of her dad's cars just in case. They had been a picnicking kind of family back then. She dragged it out and said, 'Sorry, Mum,' before clambering on to the bonnet and saying 'Sorry, Dad,' sending the blanket spinning high with a swing of her shoulders like casting a fishing net. It landed across the spiked tips of the gate.

She clamped her mini Maglite torch between her teeth and gingerly hauled herself up and over the gate, still able to feel the spear-like points through the thick blanket, and dropped cat-like into the yard beyond. There were plenty of things she could use to put up against the gate to climb back from this side, such as barrels, boxes and bins.

She walked across to the office building, activating the security lights, only now wondering how she could gain entry. The discarded fire extinguisher in a bucket by the door proved to be the answer to that conundrum.

Having first tried the door handle, not wanting to waste effort by bashing her way through an unlocked door – it was locked – she took the fire extinguisher in both hands and, using the base of it like a door breaker (of the type she'd used herself as a cop busting down doors in raids), she slammed it against the lock. The impact jarred her, but she steadied herself again, repositioned the extinguisher in her hands, then rammed it and felt the door give slightly.

Ten slams later and the door finally crashed open.

She entered and took the stairs up to the first floor, where she remembered from the murder book that Salter's office was located.

Although she switched on the lights, it did feel creepy and

not a little scary entering a room where she knew a man had been shot to death, even if it was months before. Part of her believed just a little bit in the spirit world.

It seemed as though nothing had been moved following the murder, then the crime-scene investigation.

Salter's chair was still there.

Blood splatter was on the wall behind it.

Lots of blood – and not just blood.

Daniels recalled the gory crime-scene photos and felt herself heave slightly.

'Bloody hell,' she whispered, a little awed by the thought, the knowledge of what had taken place here. Her hands went a little dithery and she had to physically and mentally shake off the sensation of dread and begin to root for what she had come to find. If it was there. If nothing else, this was a starting point.

Other than the blood, the office was basic, the fixtures and fittings old and battered with blinds at the window. A coffee filter machine was on a table, the jug full of cold, black coffee now with a mouldy green crust that she could smell. Her top lip curled in disgust.

Then she got to work using the technique she'd been taught on a search training course she'd once attended, which simply applied good logic to the task: walls, ceiling, floor, doors . . . Furniture in that order, missing nothing.

She found nothing.

Two phones, she thought.

One found and recovered, the other not.

Why not?

Why one, not the other? Surely he would keep them together?

The same questions tumbled through her mind.

One phone in police possession. Was the personal one hidden away somewhere? Maybe from his poor wife, but not when he wasn't in her company.

She stood up, inhaled deeply and let her eyes work their way around the office again – a quick skim at first, then slowly traversing everything, up, down, across, until they settled on an adjustable air-vent cover on the external wall. It had a sliding fly-screen grille cover behind the vents and was fixed to the wall with Philips head screws, one in each corner, although the one on the bottom left was missing and one of the mesh fly screens was also missing.

The vent was perhaps seven feet from the floor, just under the level of the ceiling.

Daniels walked towards it and peered up at it on tiptoe.

One screw was definitely missing and the other three in place, which meant nothing. It was a tatty office. But the lack of the fly screen behind one of the vents slightly intrigued her. She could just about reach the cover and get her fingertips under it to pull it away from the wall a little, but although the plastic was fairly flexible, it did not want to move, and force would only snap it.

She backed off, then went through the drawers in Salter's desk again, remembering she'd seen a couple of screwdrivers in them. One was a Philips crosshead type. She dragged a chair over to the wall, climbed up, coming level with the vent and now able to apply eye to hole.

An involuntary grunt of triumph caught in her throat because propped up behind the vent hole with the missing fly screen was a mobile phone. Quickly, she unfastened the screws, eased the vent away from the wall and trapped it between her knees before reaching in for the phone, picking it out carefully between her finger and thumb.

Her eyes narrowed thoughtfully.

What the hell was it doing in an air vent?

It was a Samsung phone, similar to the one she owned, though a slightly older model and encased in a rubberized industrial case for added protection, useful in the type of environment Salter had worked in.

Daniels turned it on, but it was dead, the battery flat.

She lowered herself to the floor, switched off the lights and left the office, closing the front door behind her, very aware she could not lock it properly seeing as she'd bashed it open. She was certain Henry would be happy to turn a joiner out to secure it, based on what she had found, whether it proved to be useful or otherwise. She jogged across to the gate, rolled an industrial wheelie bin under the picnic blanket and climbed cagily back over on to the bonnet, then got behind the wheel, started the old engine and plugged the phone into the mobile charger unit.

She gave it a moment, then sat back and switched the phone on.

The first screen that appeared was the one requiring a four-digit PIN to be entered in order to access the phone.

She groaned in frustration.

Then tapped in one, two, three, four.

And with a squeak of glee, she was in.

She looked at a list of the calls made and received the day Salter died. There were several, none of which meant anything to Daniels. The text inbox and sent messages were both empty.

The last thing she clicked on was the camera icon.

The phone had been well positioned behind the vent, giving its lens an uninterrupted view of the office.

Transfixed, Daniels watched the scene: Tom Salter behind his desk, two people entering the office. DCI Runcie was clearly identifiable. The other person, male, was wearing something that covered his head and body. Runcie went to Salter's desk. The man lounged by the door.

Daniels turned up the volume and heard voices, not clear but audible enough.

She listened, then witnessed a cold-blooded murder.

The recording ran on long after the killing, Tom Salter sitting dead in his chair, unmoving.

Suddenly, Daniels was terrified. Stunned, she placed the phone down in the tray in the centre console of her car just as the driver's-door window was smashed by Hawkswood's baton, sending a million crumbs of glass over her. Before she could even react, he ripped open the door and dragged her out on to the ground.

Silverthwaite drew a chair up to Henry, who could see the man's eye swelling nicely.

'You're a bit old for this shit, aren't you?' Henry said. 'What are you, fifty? You must be close to retirement. You must have your thirty in.'

'That's the kettle calling the pot black.'

'I guess it's a money thing, can't be anything else really.' Henry took a punt. 'This must be a retirement fund. What are you – a gambler, a womanizer, a rent-boy fucker?'

That brought a hard slap.

Henry spat out again, shaking his head. 'You're going to have to wash real well, pal. More DNA.'

'Womanizer,' Silverthwaite said, ignoring him. 'And when I'm done here, know where I'm going? I'll tell you. The Tawny Owl. That landlady looks just my sort of bint. I'm going to enjoy raping her, Henry.'

Although a surge of fury gripped Henry, he said, 'Best of luck with that, mate. She'll rip your bollocks off.'

Silverthwaite arched his eyebrows.

'So which one of you did Mark James Wright? I'm assuming that's all tied in with this mess you'll never, ever get out of.'

'He got wind of a scam – the scam we were pulling with Tom Salter. Wright was going to go to the cops, ironically. We couldn't discourage him so he had to go.' Silverthwaite zipped his forefinger across his throat. 'My mate, DC Hawkswood. Very good with a knife.'

'And a wrecking bar. Made a mess of Burnham.'

'Another one who found out or suspected. It's all too lucrative to let go. Money for nothing, really.'

'You can't just keep killing people who discover what you're up to.'

Silverthwaite looked Henry in the eye and Henry saw pure madness there when he responded, ''Course we can.'

Henry laughed, trying to keep his rising fear in check.

'And why Martin Sowerbutts?'

'Don't know what you mean?'

'Stand by for a shock: I've already had a second post-mortem carried out on him.'

'Liar.'

'Nah. I know he was murdered. My pathologist knows, my chief knows and I know exactly how much your local tame pathologist was paid to falsify the cause of death . . . suck on that. I'd get running if I were you. Got a passport ready? Got your money stashed? My advice: do a runner. Now.' Henry spat blood again. 'I'll give you a twenty-four-hour start if you like, just for sport.'

The door to the unit crashed open and Silverthwaite looked up. Hawkswood shoved Daniels through. She crashed to her knees, then on to all fours. Her face was a bloodsoaked mess, as was Hawkswood's forensic suit. He came around to be side-on to her and delivered a massive kick into her ribs, sending her sprawling and groaning in pain.

'I'm never going to work with you again, Henry Christie.'

Daniels' head sagged, her chin close to her chest, blood streaming from her broken nose. Her arms had been bound behind her, then she'd been placed on a chair next to Henry and duct-taped to it.

Henry's head, too, had dropped. 'Don't blame you.'

'Fuck, Henry . . . fuck!'

Across the unit, Silverthwaite and Hawkswood were in deep, animated conversation.

Daniels went on, keeping her voice low: 'He doesn't know I got into Salter's office.'

'Is that a good thing?'

'I found a phone – Salter's second phone. It's still in my car.'

'Is that good?'

'Salter hid the phone and recorded footage of his own murder.'

'That's good.'

'He must have feared the worst. Runcie was there. Another guy shot him; I don't know who he is. Neither of these two, I don't think. I sent the footage to you and to others. FB, Jerry Tope . . .'

Henry's phone beeped. He looked up. The phone was in Silverthwaite's hand. He looked at what had just landed and Henry could not prevent himself from smiling wickedly as the two men, heads together, watched the video Daniels had sent him from Salter's phone. Their dumbfounded faces were a picture to behold.

Hawkswood rushed over and grabbed Daniels' face, crushing it between his fingers. 'Where's the phone?'

'Not gonna lie – in my car. You can have it.'

'Where the fuck was it hidden?'

'In his office, behind a vent. And, like I said, you can have my phone. I've sent the video to all sorts of people so at the very least, your boss is fucked.'

'And so, by definition, are you,' Henry added.

The good-looking man was called Karl Donaldson. He was eating his starter – an old fashioned but brilliant prawn cocktail,

made with iceberg lettuce, very seventies. Marie Rose sauce
and big fat juicy prawns, all in a cocktail glass. He was also
keeping an eye on the situation with Tullane, the woman and
the guy who looked like an ageing cop, who was sitting alone
at another table.

Donaldson worked for the FBI from the American Embassy
in London, where he was a legal attaché. It was a job he'd been
doing for many years now but he still loved it. He had once been
an operational FBI agent but, when he'd fallen in love with and
subsequently married a policewoman from Lancashire who he'd
met while investigating mob activity in the north-west of England,
he'd landed the London job and never looked back. Now he was
happily married with kids that had grown up too fast, and lived
in a nice commuting village in Hampshire.

In theory, his operational days were behind him.

In practice, he still enjoyed the occasional foray into the cutting
edge and flexing his not inconsiderable muscles.

His job mainly involved intelligence gathering and analysis
and delicate liaisons with police forces and other law enforce-
ment organizations across Europe, mostly in connection with
terrorism.

That did not mean to say that 'normal' criminals were sidelined
– and people like Barney Tullane always remained on the list of
people of interest to the feds.

Donaldson had never personally encountered Tullane but knew
who he was, because Donaldson always spent any spare time he
had, which was very little, leafing through intelligence dossiers
and mugshot books of known villains.

So he knew Tullane was a low-level operator, though with
links to top-flight Mafia bosses in New York and Las Vegas. He
was a scam artist, known for setting up deals through shell
companies, taking money from innocent, though usually greedy
victims and disappearing into the ether. Donaldson recalled that
Tullane had been spotted in Europe a few times and there were
unconfirmed rumours that his bosses were linked to the very
lucrative human-trafficking trade that was like a cancer in Europe,
and that Tullane was a fixer in the chain, though it remained only
speculation.

It was by pure chance that an FBI surveillance team had

tailed another 'person of interest' (read, terrorist) to JFK airport in New York, and one eagle-eyed member of the team had spotted Tullane at the baggage check-in for a Manchester flight. The agent had found the details and passed them on routinely, though quickly, to the FBI office in London who, of course, had no one to meet the flight in Manchester, except that Karl Donaldson was taking a short break visiting his wife's mother, who still lived in Lancashire. Knowing this, and Donaldson's keenness, his secretary contacted him with the information on Tullane's flight.

Donaldson had thanked her and then looked at his wife and mother-in-law. He had hoped to spend a little time on his rare visit north with his old, good friend Henry Christie, but it looked as though it was not to be. Donaldson and Henry had met all those years before when the American had met his wife-to-be. The mother-in-law thing had been taking up all his time and he was desperate to get a break from it. If he could not get to see Henry, then the Tullane visit was a damned good excuse to get that break.

With a sad face, Donaldson broke the news that work wanted him to go to the airport and, if necessary, do a bit of legwork following Tullane.

His wife saw straight through the lie and told him to go, wishing that the FBI had asked her instead, as her mother was just on the verge of intolerability.

Which is how and why he came to be at the airport watching a man with a backpack come out of the Arrivals gate, and because of Donaldson's file and face-reading hobby, he had also recognized that young man as one of Tullane's lieutenants – a dangerous killer called Tommy Dawson who liked shooting holes in people.

Tullane had been met by the guy who looked like a cop, been taken to a car in the short-stay car park and driven away. Donaldson had lost track of Dawson because he decided to stick with Tullane instead, who was the main man. And that journey took him across northern England to the Metropole Hotel in Portsea and the eventual meetup of Tullane and the woman called Runcie.

Even though Donaldson had lost Dawson, he was pretty sure

he would not be too far away, but Donaldson had enough street skills to know that he had not been noticed by Tullane or Dawson.

He finished his prawn cocktail and pretended to check his phone just at the same moment the woman took another call on hers.

She rose out of her chair when the phone vibrated in her handbag. She smiled apologetically at Tullane and said, 'If you'll excuse me.' She left the restaurant and took the call in the bar.

'What's happening?' she demanded.

Henry watched Silverthwaite make the call. He assumed he was speaking to Runcie, but could have been wrong. Silverthwaite moved to the far corner of the unit, keeping his voice low but urgent and Henry, whose ears were still ringing from his battering, could not hear a word of what was being said.

He guessed there was bad news being passed, but it still did not mean that he and Daniels would walk out of this place, wherever the hell it was. Henry had no idea. These people had resorted to the most terrible acts of violence to protect their criminal endeavours. Henry hoped for them they thought it had all been worthwhile.

Yet, other than finding out what had happened to Sowerbutts, Henry himself had not really discovered anything. Runcie could have bluffed her way out of that one, as could the pathologist, by saying he was having a bad day. And maybe, if the custody sergeant hadn't been so eager to lock him in a cell and panic, then maybe Runcie could have blagged her way out of that one too. Maybe.

But Daniels' discovery was dynamite and was the real game changer, even though Henry had yet to see it and might never see it, because he truly thought he was going to end up dead in a field with his brains blown out alongside Daniels.

'You did a good job,' Henry said to her. 'Just want you to know that.'

'Thanks. I still won't work with you again.'

'I know. I get it.'

Silverthwaite's phone call ended. He walked to Henry and Daniels.

'Have you just booked your flight out of here?' Henry asked, and giggled slightly hysterically. No point not laughing now. He heard Daniels chuckle.

Silverthwaite scowled but said nothing. He tapped Hawkswood on the shoulder and beckoned him out of earshot of the two prisoners. They had another huddled conversation.

'They're screwed and they know it,' Henry muttered.

'Oh, good,' she said.

Henry had to turn his head to look at her properly. Her head was still hanging loose to her chest, blood still drizzling from her nose, completely saturating her jacket and blouse. Her breathing was a gurgling noise.

'Hang in there,' he urged her.

'I intend to,' she told him.

He looked across at the two detectives, then sat a little more upright when he saw them both peel off their forensic suits, step out of them, roll them into balls and throw them down.

Without making any eye contact with Henry or Daniels, they walked past them, out through the door of the unit, and were gone.

TWENTY

The issue uppermost in Karl Donaldson's mind as he watched Tullane and the woman, plus the other guy, leave the restaurant was that Tommy Dawson would probably, unknown to the woman and the guy, have Tullane's back. He would be secreted somewhere out there, watching and ready to protect him at a signal from Tullane. It might even have been that Tullane and Dawson were linked via radio mikes, Dawson could hear every word being said and be ready to react in an instant.

Though Donaldson was certain he himself had not been 'made', getting up and following these characters was a dicey game that could easily blow his cover. In some respects, that would not necessarily be a terrible thing. It might prevent Tullane from doing whatever it was he had come to this country for, though that was not Donaldson's preferred option. He wanted to catch Tullane with his fingers in the till.

It might also make Donaldson vulnerable, even though he had no fear of coming up against people like Tullane or Dawson, but even Donaldson could not deflect a bullet as he had once found out, much to his chagrin, when face-to-face with a desperate terrorist in Barcelona some years ago.

And nor was he armed.

He watched the trio pause in the entrance foyer of the hotel.

For his main course, he had ordered a T-bone, and the serrated steak knife had already been placed on the table. He picked it up and slid it, blade upwards, up his jacket sleeve. He stood up and walked out of the restaurant, having noticed that Tullane had peeled off and gone towards the toilets at the back of Reception.

The woman and her companion were having a hurried conversation.

Donaldson walked past them and out of the hotel into the chill night. Being exposed on a headland, the blast of air from the North Sea made him shiver and button up his jacket.

His car, a four-wheel-drive Jeep, was in the far corner of the big car park. Keeping his head down against the wind, he headed towards it but at the same time checked the car park for any sign of Tommy Dawson, who was maybe hunched in a car or hiding in a shadow somewhere.

As Donaldson climbed into his car, he spotted a leather-clad motorcyclist astride a fairly big-looking machine tucked up on the side street at the northern gable end of the hotel. Though in leathers, bulking him up, and wearing a helmet, Donaldson thought it could be Tommy Dawson.

If it was, Donaldson knew he had revealed his hand and could not just sit all innocent in his car and wait for Tullane to come out. He now had to drive away, make a decision about where to park up and hope he hadn't screwed up his chances of finding out what Tullane was up to.

He swore softly, started up and flicked on his lights.

Pulling out of his parking spot, he was relieved to see Tullane and the two others walking down the front steps, getting into a Citroën Picasso parked in the pull-in directly outside the hotel.

The woman got behind the wheel, Tullane slid in alongside her and the other guy got in the back seat.

As the Citroën moved away, the motorbike fired up and the rider dropped his visor down. Donaldson had purposely crawled across the car park and stopped at the exit. The Citroën drove directly past him just as the motorcyclist crept out of the side street and followed the Citroën.

Reluctantly, Donaldson had to turn in the opposite direction, but not before the biker had gone past him and lit up his head-lights. He was certain it was Dawson.

Donaldson turned into the street from which Dawson had just come. It was narrow, with cars parked on either side; however, he mounted the kerb in a gap and swung the big car around in a fast five-point turn, powered back, then went in the direction taken by the Citroën and the motorbike. It made no difference to Donaldson that he knew nothing about the geography of Portsea. From here on in would be guesswork, luck and maybe a little cunning.

Tullane glanced in the passenger-door mirror and was relieved to see the headlights of the motorbike some distance behind.

He was sure Runcie hadn't noticed the follower, but could not be sure about the guy in the back seat whose name was Saul.

'I intend to show you just how in control of this I am,' Runcie was saying earnestly to him while driving.

He was becoming less impressed by the minute, feeling very uncomfortable by the claims that she had a lid on everything.

Maybe the time had come to cut loose. If so, it was a decision he would make that would be understood and accepted by his bosses back home. His finger was on the pulse and he had been responsible for setting up the whole business anyway. Now it seemed that the good times were over. He was the one who had been working among the foreign gang on behalf of his bosses, helping to arrange transport for illegals across from Europe into the UK, usually via shady haulage and shipping companies such as the business run by Tom Salter; part of that was the reverse scam back to Europe, which meant that in a very short space of time they had grossed somewhere in the region of ten million dollars, of which Tullane had skimmed about twenty-five per cent for himself and his bosses. It had been a good two-way trade – never an empty truck.

Runcie and her corrupt crew had become involved when the cops carried out raids in connection with modern slavery, which resulted in her coming into contact with Salter. She had been greedy, easy to bribe, happy to turn a blind eye but also to get involved with the machinery plant side of the business, setting up the non-existent companies and running their short-lived lives with her own equally greedy and corrupt nucleus of detectives and other cops. She was a cold-steel person with no conscience, just an insatiable desire for wealth.

Perfect fodder for people like Tullane.

Cops on the books were always a good thing.

However, things had started to go awry when that eagle-eyed contractor became suspicious, was immune to bribery and threated to find some honest cops.

He'd had to be disposed of. And Runcie had been given the word. A simple job for one of her cronies. The man had been lured to an isolated location and simply stabbed to death. End of problem – especially as Runcie was in charge of the subsequent murder investigation.

The more fundamental problem occurred with Tom Salter when he found his conscience, and that was something that had to be addressed by people further up the chain. Again, it was all good that Runcie ran the murder investigation, ironically having been at the scene of it when it occurred.

But all good things must come to an end. Perhaps it was only a matter of time before Runcie's cop bosses started to interfere and demand answers.

Instead of a tactical withdrawal, Runcie's response had been outrageous in the extreme. Even the Mafia don't go around killing cops unless absolutely necessary; the fallout from such rash actions was never pretty.

Tullane himself wasn't an excessively violent individual. If he had to, yes, but he was a scam artist, always ready to cut and run if things became too heated. He had already got other scams bubbling that would please his bosses, so he wasn't too worried about severing ties with Runcie.

As he was driven along, he squirmed. He had heard enough,

had enough. There was nothing to repair here, which is what he thought he had come to do. It was gone, and he wanted no further part in it.

All he wanted to do was get on a flight home – and already he'd pre-booked two flights out of the UK to America – on separate false passports from two different airports. He would be back on home turf in twelve hours.

First, there was a charade to play out.

He glanced in the mirror. The headlights were still there. Tommy Dawson had his back. Good, because Tullane thought he was about to descend into hell very shortly.

It was the luck element – not judgement – that ensured Donaldson dropped on to the taillight of the motorbike and, two hundred yards ahead of that, the Citroën.

The American eased back, hoping he had not been spotted. One-on-one following and surveillance was impossible to maintain for any length of time, especially if the target was only remotely surveillance-conscious. Donaldson knew that Dawson and Tullane would be. They would both be looking over their shoulders, because that's how they lived their lives.

He tracked the two vehicles through Portsea, from the headland near the hotel through the dockland area, then a large retail park, and beyond that into a huge industrial estate where the traffic fell to almost nil and Donaldson had to pull in and stop or carry on following and completely give the game away.

Runcie drove through a maze of roads on the estate, firstly passing newly built and smart industrial and warehouse units and businesses, further and further in until it became much less salubrious and much more grim, with smaller units, more scrap cars, crushed metal stacked up behind walls and the occasional scrapyard dog with its snout pressed tight up to mesh grilles. She turned into a dead end and parked in a small yard in front of a steel-framed unit with a brickwork and metal-clad exterior with one roller door large enough to admit a good-sized vehicle and a personnel door next to that.

'Bolt hole,' Runcie declared, jarring to a halt. 'Not overlooked, no nosy neighbours and very cheap. Free, actually.'

Tullane nodded. He did not want to know.

'Let me show you.' She switched off the engine and got out, beckoning Tullane to come with her. He climbed out with less enthusiasm just as the motorbike with Dawson on board entered the yard.

Runcie stopped abruptly, as did Saul, who had also got out of the Citroën.

'Who the hell's this?' she demanded.

'Someone you've met before,' Tullane said.

Dawson dismounted and removed his helmet, exposing his face, a gesture not lost on Runcie. She knew who the man was and, in their previous meeting, he had always tried to keep his face from her, as difficult as that was, and the fact that he now did not seem bothered that she and Saul could see him troubled her.

She made a grunting gasp of fear.

But maybe she could make this all work when she displayed to Tullane that there were no problems here, that she was totally in charge – and, of course – that he could fuck her anywhere, anytime, anyhow. That, surely, was also a good incentive for him.

Inside the unit, she envisaged a particular scene in her head.

Her two lackeys – the now comparatively wealthy detective constables Silverthwaite and Hawkswood, who she thought of as numpties but useful, not too bright, easily led and influenced – stood looking reasonably tough, guarding Henry Christie and Diane Daniels, two people far from thick.

Runcie had hoped to be able to control the visiting detectives, but that had quickly gone to rat-shit, starting with Christie's appearance at the clifftop suicide and subsequent post-mortem. Had Sowerbutts not been in the picture, Christie would not have had anything to go on. Instead, they had delved, stuck their noses in, and Runcie and her corrupt little team were on the back foot.

She knew she had lost control but refused to admit it, and the next few minutes would be crucial.

In her head, the word 'cunt' repeated itself continually as she walked into the unit ahead of Saul and her visitors – plus also a vision of a woollen garment unravelling thread by thread. This had to be where it all stopped and, if it meant more dead cops, then so be it.

She was confident she could cover it up.

That was until the moment she pushed through the door.

Christie and Daniels were there in the middle of the floor, their backs to the door, still taped to the chairs.

Silverthwaite and Hawkswood were nowhere to be seen.

Donaldson had lost them somewhere on the industrial estate – 'good and proper', as his friend Henry Christie might have commented. As in, 'You've lost 'em good and proper.' Donaldson smiled at the thought of the man who, though unlikely, had become one of his best friends.

Not wanting to reveal himself, Donaldson had pulled up at the entrance to the estate and thought through the scenario. He could either settle down and wait here, in the hope that they would reappear at some stage, though there was no guarantee they would even come back via this route, or go on the hunt, because this place looked as if there would be many exits and entrances – more than one way in and out.

Even if he was lucky enough to see them emerge, he would still have missed what was going down and he did not have the power to stop them. To do that, he would have to enlist the services of the local cops and, by the time he managed that little rigmarole, it would all be over. There would be nothing to find, he was sure.

What he had to do was plunge in and see what he came out with between his teeth.

He switched off the Jeep's lights and crawled on to the industrial estate, going for a slow, steady cruise in the dark.

Runcie had her mobile phone to her ear, calling Silverthwaite. There was no reply. She called Hawkswood.

To her left, Tullane was standing with the young man she knew she had once picked up from Anglesey many months before, who had without hesitation killed Tom Salter. The two were talking in low tones.

Saul, meanwhile, was standing in front of Christie and Daniels with his arms folded across his chest, looking down at the two detectives with contempt.

Runcie noticed that neither Tullane nor the killer revealed themselves to Christie and Daniels.

The phone rang out, then went to voicemail. Hawkswood was not answering either.

It was only then that Runcie saw the two crumpled-up forensic suits on the floor and realized what she was looking at.

She ended the call and slid away her phone in her clutch bag, then stalked across the floor and stood next to Saul.

Henry Christie raised his battered face and scowled at her. Daniels' chin remained sagging on her chest.

'You look pretty,' Henry croaked hoarsely. Even in his state, he could appreciate the irony of her standing there in her best outfit.

Saul reacted and smashed Henry across the face, flicking his head sideways. Henry knew that more teeth had come loose, but he almost felt indifferent to the blow because he was in so much pain anyway. He did his best to smile, but his head wobbled and, as much as he tried, he could not do it. He was feeling more than disconnected now.

He glanced at Daniels. He thought she was unconscious and he was worried about her.

'I'm not going to arse about talking to you, Henry. This is over, now, you are over . . .' Runcie began.

'Think you'll find you're the one that's over,' he corrected her.

'Oh, get real . . .'

'Check the video on my phone,' he suggested. 'Pretty pictures. You in Tom Salter's office with some guy shooting him. Good old Tom Salter; he knew how dangerous you were and recorded it all on his phone.'

'Yeah, he tried to,' Runcie sneered, 'but I got his phone off him and deleted it.'

'He had two phones,' Daniels said without lifting her head up.

Henry did smile now – with relief.

'One was hidden in the wall, filming you,' Daniels said, this time managing to raise her chin and look at Runcie, victory in her battered eyes.

'And Lanky Man and Tight Fit have done a runner,' Henry added.

'Eh?'

'Your two running mates – you know, those agricultural reps? They've gone, Jane, and, if you've any sense, you'll do the same. Run. Run, now . . . because I'm coming after you. Hell, am I coming after you.' Henry looked at Saul. 'You too, but I know I'll catch you first. You don't look right fit.'

That brought another blow from Saul, knocking Henry's head in the opposite direction. This time his vision and hearing swam and he felt like he was in the bottom of a fish tank.

Runcie looked behind Henry and Daniels.

'We need to talk,' Henry heard someone say. He had not realized that other people were in the unit. He'd thought it was just Runcie and Saul.

Runcie gave Saul a gesture – stay here – then walked out of Henry's line of sight. He twisted his head slightly, trying to listen, but could hear nothing other than the drumming of his own blood through his head.

Tullane said, 'These guys are more cops?' in disbelief to Runcie. She did not answer.

'It has to stop, now,' he warned her.

'It will, with these two. Once they're gone, it's over.'

Tullane shook his head. 'You're right, it is over.' He nodded quickly to Dawson, who was standing just behind them and, at the same time, Tullane grabbed Runcie.

With the same speed and lack of hesitation he had shown when killing Tom Salter, Dawson stepped forwards, pulling out the small revolver he had tucked in the waistband of his motorbike leather. He brought it up and stood behind and between Henry and Daniels.

He fired four rounds of the six that the gun held into Saul's head and chest. The man crumpled as his face imploded.

Henry watched Saul collapse, unable to comprehend what had just happened for a moment. The sound of gunfire at the side of his head disorientated him even more.

Dawson stepped back and Tullane hurled Runcie at him. He caught her easily, spun her into him, one hand across her mouth, and he dragged her around so he was in front of Henry and Daniels, where he forced Runcie down on to her knees and held her easily, even as she struggled.

Had he not been strapped to the chair, Henry would have leapt with shock when he felt a hand grip his shoulder.

Tullane was standing behind him, a hand on Henry and one on Daniels.

He said, 'This is over now, and you need to know that this will be your fate should you ever come after me.'

He nodded at Dawson.

Now, instead of a gun, there was a knife in his hand.

Again, without hesitation, Dawson jerked Runcie's head back and stuck the knife into her neck with a hard, twisting motion, the blade severing her carotid artery instantly, sending a spume of blood sideways like water from a hosepipe as Dawson carried on remorselessly, a hacking and sawing motion, cutting her wind-pipe. She made a terrible gurgling sound and her eyes seemed to plead with Henry as her mouth opened and blood gushed out, but then Dawson withdrew the knife and, with a gentle push, Runcie toppled over.

Donaldson knew he had lost them for good and he thumped the steering wheel in frustration as he crawled slowly through the side roads of this immense industrial park.

He was annoyed, but also philosophical about it, and thought that perhaps the best course of action would now be to make his way back to the Metropole Hotel and resume his dinner, maybe reorder his T-bone and wait to see if Tullane returned. There was every chance the man would do just that once his business here was concluded.

If he didn't, at least Donaldson would have some valuable intelligence to submit.

His lights were still off, but with this change of mind, he turned on the main beam and jammed his foot on to the gas pedal.

Tullane and Dawson left the unit swiftly but not in panic. They were experienced in situations like these.

They went straight to Dawson's motorbike, which had been stolen by pre-order and picked up in Manchester, along with the firearm he had just used on Saul and the knife on Runcie. Dawson refitted his helmet and straddled the bike as he rocked it off its stand. There was a spare helmet for Tullane in the pannier, which Dawson handed to him as he fired up the powerful engine. Tullane mounted the bike behind him as he fiddled with the helmet.

Dawson paused, but Tullane tapped him on the shoulder to

go, even though he hadn't fitted the helmet. He was fiddling with the strap as Dawson swung the bike around and applied power with a huge roar, engaged first gear and released the clutch.

Donaldson did not have a chance, even though he would bet money on the speed of his reactions in most circumstances. One moment he was travelling along at twenty mph, passing the opening to the yard of an industrial unit. Next there was a huge flash to his left, the sound of a screaming engine and the bike carrying Dawson and Tullane emerged from that yard, Dawson twisting the throttle as Tullane was just about to fit the helmet.

Under normal circumstances, the bike (which was a Suzuki) could have reached sixty mph in about three seconds.

It had been travelling, and accelerating, for one-point-five seconds when it smashed into the passenger door of Donaldson's Jeep.

In the way of these things, physics took over.

A speeding object hitting what, in effect, was a brick wall.

Dawson was flung over the roof of the Jeep, flying like a drunken acrobat, twirling several times and landing head first in the road. Tullane, who had not yet fitted his helmet at that point, did not take the same trajectory. He surged forward, straight over the handlebars, and his head smashed through the passenger window.

Just for that briefest of moments, Donaldson could not compute what had happened. He'd been sideswiped, that he knew, but other than that it took a few seconds for him to put it all together.

Then he looked to his left and saw the crumpled door and Tullane's head and shoulders sticking through the smashed window. He reached across and felt for a pulse in the man's neck. There was none.

Next, he glanced right and saw the sprawled-out figure of Tommy Dawson on the opposite side of the road, his head skewed at an unnatural angle, unmoving.

Donaldson had to barge his shoulder against his door to open it as the impact had twisted the whole of the Jeep's body out of shape. He climbed out and stood there a moment, just checking himself and brushing off the tiny chunks of broken glass that he'd been showered with when Tullane's head had smashed the window.

He knew he was unhurt, just slightly shaken.

He crossed to Dawson, squatted next to him and felt for a neck pulse under the helmet. There was none.

Donaldson stood up, looked at his precious car and wondered just how difficult and evasive the insurance company was going to be about this. Extracting a forty-grand payout would not be easy, he thought.

He walked around the car, looking at the bike and Tullane's body lying across the top of it, then walked into the yard of the unit, past the parked Citroën and went inside, wondering what shit he was going to find in there.

TWENTY-ONE

One month later, the unravelling had still only really just begun.

On Fanshaw-Bayley's instructions, the whole investigation had been taken over by Lancashire Constabulary and Rik Dean was put in charge of something with the potential to last for a very long time. Rik moved an FMIT team across the Pennines en masse, including Jerry Tope as the chief intelligence analyst, and took over the offices of the Serious Crime Team at Portsea police station, very much to the chagrin of the local CID, and there was a lot of ill-feeling in the air as well as, Rik thought, relief. Although no one had yet admitted it, many knew about Runcie and her team's corrupt practices, if not the detail and scale of them.

It also took the best part of that month to track down Silverthwaite and Hawkswood.

Both had gone to ground, but it was only a matter of time before they had to run. Two teams of determined Lancashire detectives were constantly on their trail, closing in every day.

Silverthwaite was picked up boarding a cross-channel ferry at Dover, using a false passport and carrying just short of 30,000 euros. Hawkswood was heading in the opposite direction and was arrested in Heysham, Lancashire, about to get on a ferry to Belfast. He, too, had a large stash of money with him.

They were lodged in cells in Blackburn, as it was thought wise not to bring them back to Portsea where they might still have influence.

Both were very hard to crack initially, but persistent and skilled questioning soon had them both offering to tell their sides of a very sorry story. The same was true of the custody sergeant, Anna Calder, who, in her attempts to wriggle off the hook, told a grim tale of bullying, intimidation and a fear of Runcie, who had coerced her to falsify custody records and act totally out of character – none of which washed with the interviewing officers.

During that period, Henry and Daniels recovered from their ordeals but saw little of each other. Both were off sick, and Daniels sought the protection and warmth of her family. She talked occasionally to Henry by phone and met him for a coffee a couple of times.

Henry could see she had been traumatized by the nightmare, and could understand it. What both of them had gone through in a very short space of time had been devastating. She was having counselling that the force provided, but Henry could see that progress was slow.

On one of the coffee meets – at Costa Coffee on Forton services on the M6 south of Lancaster – Henry broached the subject of a return to work and what she might like to do.

'So, have you thought about it?'

'I have,' she said tersely.

'And . . .?'

'I know I'm not ready yet,' she admitted. 'I want to come back and I will come back, but just at the moment I feel I might let someone down at a critical moment.'

'That's honest, but you're probably wrong,' Henry said.

She shrugged.

'You're a bloody good cop.'

'Thank you for saying that, and I'm touched. It's just . . . I don't know . . . Hawkswood beating me up the second time. God, he was mental, and I thought he was going to kill me, I really did.' She took two hands to lift her coffee cup to her mouth. 'He was insane.'

In her mind, she saw it all happening again – being dragged out of her car outside Tom Salter's yard. Then the terrible beating she had endured at Hawkswood's hands.

Henry watched her carefully, knowing this was what she was seeing.

'Is there some way of dealing with it that my counsellor hasn't revealed?' she asked.

'No,' he answered truthfully. 'It'll be there all your life. I've stuff . . . here . . .' He touched his head. 'Mostly it's tucked away but there are some occasions – usually in the middle of the night – when the demons come . . .'

'Isn't that a line from a film?' she asked.

'Probably. Look, Diane, you deal with things in your own way eventually. You determine your own strategies and it does take time.'

'And then the way that Runcie and Saul were killed in front of us.' She sighed with a deep judder.

'Well, at least we weren't killed, which is a plus. And there was a bit of instant justice applied there, too.'

'Yeah, I guess so.'

They drank more coffee, deep in their own thoughts.

'I can't tell anyone how to deal with it, but for me work is always a good option. Like I said, you are a good cop, I mean a great cop, and the public needs cops like you. I mean, the way you got that Miriam woman to open up about Tom Salter . . . that was great, and what you uncovered – that second phone – was crucial, damning, acting on a hunch . . . I like that.'

He smiled and, for the first time, she did too.

'You really think I'm OK?'

'You want me to keep massaging your ego?'

'Yes, please.'

'It would be a pleasure. Where exactly is it?' Henry wriggled his fingers suggestively and they laughed again. He became serious and asked, 'If you'd like me to get you a place on FMIT, that is within my power.'

She considered the offer, then shook her head. 'Nah. Know what? If it's in your power, what I'd like to do is get back on Child Protection.'

'That's not an easy option,' he warned her.

'I know, but I think it's where I can do my best work, maybe come back to the serious crime stuff a bit further down the line. I think I want to know I'm going to be in one place and be helping kids and mums – and dads, of course, and families – plus . . .' she held up her left hand and pointed to the engagement ring, which she had previously not really explained well, '. . . this is all back on, and it'll help if I do not have to whizz all over the county or country all the time.'

'It's in my power,' Henry said.

Henry spent a lot of time crossing over to Central Yorkshire and back as he improved health-wise, mainly just to assist Rik Dean, who really didn't need all that much help. He did what he thought he would have been doing on his first trip to that force, sitting down and reading how an investigation was being conducted and offering what he thought were suggestions for improvements, if any.

If he was honest, he had little to say because Rik really did have control of the whole thing, and he humoured Henry more than anything.

He saw very little of FB, who was grappling with the more strategic complexities of trying to manage a failing force, but as much as FB was doing to help it turn the corner, the news and rumour coming out of headquarters wasn't good. It did seem like it was a done deal that Central Yorkshire would be amalgamated wholesale into one of its neighbouring forces, and maybe that was for the best. It needed new blood and a new direction.

On one of those days when Henry felt like he was getting under Rik Dean's feet and had probably exhausted his tips for the day, he decided on a stroll around Portsea. On his way back to the police station, he thought he would call it a day, get back to The Tawny Owl and leave Rik alone from now on.

As he approached the old police station, intending to enter via the enquiry desk, he saw a man leaning on the wall outside, who watched Henry as he went in through the door. Henry caught his eye.

The foyer was quiet and Henry walked up to the desk. He had not yet and never would be given a swipe card to enable him to access the building, so he still had to wait for doors to be opened for him.

The lady behind the desk recognized him and quickly waved him over to her.

'Boss, have you just walked past a man outside, a bit of a scruffy, middle-aged bloke, jeans and a jacket?' she asked.

'Yep, I did,' Henry said. 'He's still out there.'

'I know it's a big ask,' the PEA said, 'but is there any chance you could have a word with him? He was in here a few moments ago and said he wanted to talk to a detective. He was all jittery and nervous and, when I picked the phone up to call someone in CID, he left. I've seen him pacing about outside since, though, and I just wonder . . . I know you're busy and you're a superintendent and all that.'

'Yeah, 'course,' Henry said. 'Did he give a name?'

'No, sorry. But thanks so much . . . he did look really troubled.'

Henry nodded and went back outside.

The man was still there leaning against the wall, now smoking a roll-up. Henry saw his hands were shaking as he put the cigarette to his lips. He clocked Henry approaching and seemed to shrink in himself, lose any confidence he might have had, then turn and start to walk away.

Henry speeded up a little. 'Excuse me,' he called. 'Did you want to speak to a detective?' He dug out his warrant card. The man stopped and turned. His eyes reminded Henry of a hunted animal. He showed him his warrant card and introduced himself. 'Can I help you in some way?'

There was an interview room off the entrance foyer – not one geared up for cops to speak to people under caution, but for members of the public calling in who had delicate things to discuss.

Henry managed to persuade the man to come with him back into the nick and he ushered him into this room, indicating to the PEA that a cuppa would be useful.

'Take a seat,' Henry offered. There was a table and four chairs. 'There's a brew coming, if that's OK.'

The man had extinguished his cigarette and sat on the chair, leaning forwards with his elbows on his knees. Henry saw his hands were shaking badly and that he constantly touched his face nervously.

'I don't know your name,' Henry said.

'Donald . . . Don . . . Pierce.'

'OK, Don, what can I do for you? I can see you seem to have something on your mind. Is it something I can help you with?'

The man called Don hung his head but did not reply.

Henry half thought about being in his car, driving home and seeing Alison.

That was until the man said, 'I've come about Martin Sowerbutts,' and suddenly Henry was very interested indeed.

Five minutes later, the man was in custody. Twenty minutes after that he was being led into an interview room by Henry, together with Rik Dean and a duty solicitor.

Henry went through the preliminaries – caution, tapes, introductions – then said to Donald Pierce, 'Now then, can you tell me again what you told me in the interview room at the front desk?'

Pierce stared at the table top for a very long time, then said, 'It's wrong, it's all wrong.'

'What is, Don?' Henry asked.

'Sowerbutts. Martin Sowerbutts.'

The two detectives were sitting on the opposite side of the table, waiting patiently. The whirring of the tapes could be heard in the silence.

Pierce looked at them. 'I read it in the paper . . . how Sowerbutts killed and raped them kids. It's all wrong.'

'What exactly do you mean?' Henry asked.

'I know for a fact he didn't do it.' Pierce closed his eyes. 'Thing is, you see, I can take you to the bodies . . . four more bodies – four bodies of kids that you don't even fucking know about. Other kids. You know about some, but not all of 'em.' He opened his eyes and Henry saw them change. This man was no longer hunted or haunted – he was the hunter and the ghost. He felt a chill.

'Tell me,' Henry said.

'I don't even know who fuckin' Sowerbutts is, but he didn't kill them kids, at least not the kids you lot think he killed, because I did. I killed them. I abducted them. I raped them. And then I strangled them to death. I dumped some bodies but I've kept others – for various reasons. And now I want to tell you all about it. But that poor fucker – he didn't do it. I did. You got the wrong man.'